HYMNS AND BARRIERS

Phil Morgans

Print ISBN 978-1-8382805-5-0

Published by

Llyfrau Cambria Books, Wales, United Kingdom.

Cambria Books is a division of

Cambria Publishing.

Discover our other books at: www.cambriabooks.co.uk

To Carol, my wife,
thank you for your love and support.

CONTENTS

JOHN

1

The daily walk home was worse in winter, the dark, the cold, the rain. The lightness of the reflection of the moon could be seen in the puddles along the side of the road. It was only October but John knew what to expect in the next few months. After finishing work and cleaning up it meant leaving the shop after 6.20. At least there was a bit of a moon as the black-out was still in operation, though not as tight as in the first years of the war. There had only been one sighting of an enemy aircraft during the whole of the war, as it searched to drop its bombs on the steelworks in the next valley. Be a bit of a waste of a bomb if one landed here, John thought, chuckling to himself. If a visitor arrived after the bomb dropped they'd have to point out which bit had been damaged. John trudged on, every day the same, except Thursdays and Sundays. Thursdays were pretty good, half-day closing which gave him a bit of time to spend doing whatever he wanted to, though he couldn't think what, and Sundays provided a little bit of free time between going to chapel and Sunday school three times. Suppose that replaced one type of drudgery with another on a Sunday, but it kept Mam happy.

John had worked in the ironmongers shop for fifteen months now. He enjoyed the banter between the solely male staff that worked in the shop, but he found the days long. With the passing of time, he couldn't match the enthusiasm of that first week on the job. He had left school for the last time on the Friday and started working in the shop on the following Monday. The anticipation of money in his pocket, life as a grown-up and the thoughts of not being bullied by the teachers, who he was sure considered the pupils in their charge to be on an army parade ground, all fostered an enthusiasm for work. No longer would he have to go upstairs and pretend to do his homework, which he rarely completed. John had a comfortable life at home and in the rare moments when he was being honest with himself he appreciated that he had not used his abilities and not applied himself in the way God had intended. Fifteen months after leaving school he couldn't contemplate working in the ironmongers shop forever. His efforts there were supervised by Lionel, a kind, helpful man, in his early fifties, who had started working in the shop at fourteen, and saw John as his protégé. John walked on past the Workingmen's Institute which always sparked a period of reflection because every time he passed it as a young lad his dad would say, always remember, son, the things in there were paid for by the local miners, and their blood and sweat. John was thankful that he worked in an ironmongers shop and not down one of the local mines.

There was another factor playing on John's mind as he made his way home, the country had been at war for five years, Mam found it difficult to put food on the table, though she was resourceful. A saving grace, Dad was able to find work and had been in the steelworks in the next valley for over four years, unlike the previous ten years when work was impossible to find during 'the Depression', and John and his younger brother, David, by five years, had a tough time growing up, as did many families who struggled for money in this South Wales valley town. If John cast his mind back ten years previously he could remember walking over to the personnel office in the steelworks where Dad now worked. It was a walk of hope. John was just seven years of age but he skipped along the mountain track alongside his dad who chatted cheerfully. He had heard they were taking workers on. John sat on a large oak bench in the waiting area while his dad was speaking to a man in an office he could see through a glass panel. He sat quietly as his Dad trusted him to, until a kind lady brought him a glass of water and a biscuit. He could hear the quiet mumble of a conversation, taking place in the office where his dad was being interviewed. Dad never raised his voice, a quiet man, a well-respected man, who had grown up in a family of thirteen children, always taught to be grateful for any offering, however small. After perhaps twenty minutes Dad came towards the door, turned, shook the other gentleman's hand, thanked him and held his hand out for John to grasp. However young John was he sensed that Dad didn't want to speak. The long journey home was in silence. Only once did John look up at his father to catch him wiping a tear away and trying to smile at him. He said quietly to John "another day son, another day."

At home, John always had to appear grateful for what he had, including his job.

Other thoughts crowded into his mind. In the following February he would be eighteen and he would get his call-up papers. He followed the war news avidly, partly because he realised he would soon be a part of it. The war was going well. Allied troops had been fighting in France since June and were making progress. Likewise, the army in Italy seemed to be pushing the Germans back though you heard less of that 'theatre.' The Americans were capturing island after island as they pushed towards the Japanese mainland and the Russians were getting nearer and nearer to Berlin.

How much war would be left by February, was a thought that was constantly with him. Sometimes he hoped a good deal so he could return a hero. He would be able to wear his new uniform with a string of medals on his chest to meet Elizabeth, a girl he had met and spoken to while at his 'Short-hand and Typing' evening class on a Thursday night. He was looking forward to getting a uniform. He had seen men home on leave wearing their uniforms, often outside one of the local pubs. He wondered at first why they wore these uniforms everywhere. Did their other clothes no longer fit them? Now he was older he realised why they strutted about in their uniforms, often stopping to chat to local girls. When he joined up he would do the same and would walk out with Elizabeth, or whoever on his arm and people would look up to him as he passed.

At other times he wished the war would finish soon. He had heard conversations in hushed tones as he went to help Mam with her shopping, where the women while chatting would mention a casualty, someone shot, blown up or sunk. The worse times were after he had been to the cinema to see the latest war films where you could see in films and newsreels what was happening or as near as damn it. That would put the fear of God in him with the thought of death or severe injury, that could be him in six months time.

As he came to the junction of Queen Street and Commercial Street, he could see his mate, Dennis, just in front of him. Dennis had been in his class in school but was four months younger. He was in the swimming club with John but that had finished at the end of August as it was an outdoor swimming pool and the club would only meet from May until August, and when the weather was bad even those four months seemed too long. Both John and Dennis were tall and thin as were many during this time of rationing, but whereas John was good looking in a sort of boyish sense Dennis was more rugged and looked tougher and older for his age. Dennis managed to get a job in a newsagents shop and John thought he had certainly tidied himself up compared to how he dressed when he was in school. Dennis had told him, Mr Coles, the newsagent, was strict and this suggested he had told Dennis he had to look smart while he was in the shop. On occasions, Dennis would be given the spare copies of newspapers to take home. He would also read the papers during the quiet times in the shop making him the 'fount of all war knowledge.' John would often refer to him as 'Monty' as he seemed to know so much about the progress of the war.

"How's the shovels and spades?" Dennis said stopping and turning around.

"I find myself talking to them from time to time, I'm so bored," John replied.

"I can't stop to chat, mam's got a pie on for a quarter to seven," Dennis stated, "Thursday tomorrow, do you fancy going down the park for a kick about in the afternoon?"

"Yes fine, about three o'clock after I've washed mam's windows," replied John, to a fast disappearing Dennis.

John shouted "ta ra," to a figure now lost in the dark.

2

John entered the park through a large set of gates left open by the park keeper during the day. The park was like another world, large areas of grass people could picnic or sunbathe in when the weather was warm, beautifully kept flower beds, countless species of trees, many of them from exotic countries, and a bandstand used by the remaining members of the local brass band who had not been called-up. The band would hold concerts on a Saturday evening and Sunday afternoon. There were tennis courts, a bowling green and an outdoor swimming pool. The park had been the garden of a large manor house owned by an 'ironmaster', the owner of an ironworks, now closed down. When the family moved away the house and gardens had been bequeathed to the local community. The park was a clear contrast to the landscape outside its walls, where the town was mostly drab and in need of a lick of paint.

John lived about a quarter of a mile from the park and he would often come into it, find a bench and sit. He would watch the squirrels playing on the grass or imagine what the park was like when the ironmasters owned it sixty years before. He thought it must have been one of the biggest gardens in Wales with the ladies walking elegantly with their parasols in Spring, stopping to admire the daffodils or throwing small pieces of bread to the swans in the ponds they had created.

"You're a real daydreamer," his Mam would tell him, as he failed to answer her question for the second time because he had drifted into another world while walking through the park with his parents on a Summer's evening. He came here less often since he had been working but promised himself that he would come more often to plan out his future.

John walked down a sloping path to the ponds where swans and ducks nested. He could see Dennis, sat on one of the benches overlooking the ponds, a paper bag in one hand and a football alongside him.

As John came up closer Dennis got up and proceeded to hide the bag in the bushes.

"Kickabout first," he said.

Both boys crossed to the nearby area of grass. They put their coats down as goalposts. Dennis went in goal and John dribbled the ragged leather ball along the ground towards him. It was easier to go in goal than to kick the ball, as it was a heavy thing with bits of leather hanging off it that stung your toes and instep when you kicked it. It was impossible to head because it was too heavy to lift off the ground when you kicked it and if you could get it off the ground you would avoid heading it as it would give you a severe headache and might even be doing you permanent damage. The activity proved to be less than satisfying with only two of them to play, and they both got fed up quickly and went back to the bench. Dennis retrieved the paper bag from the bushes and took out two bottles of brown ale.

"Where'd you get those from?" asked John.

"Roger got them for me, though it cost me," replied Dennis. Roger was his older brother by five years.

"Picked them up in the Cambrian last Saturday, hidden them from Mum since then."

"How we gonna open 'em?" asked John

"Give it here," replied Dennis, taking the bottle and prizing the cap off with his teeth.

John winced, "You'll break your teeth like that."

"What and spoil my good looks."

They settled down and took a few swigs from the bottles.

"When you seeing that girl from your evening class, Lizzy, is it?" asked Dennis.

"It's Elizabeth, to you," replied John.

"Fuck me, posh is she?" Dennis smirked.

John tried not to swear, as he was afraid it would become a habit and if it slipped out in front of his mother she would kill him. He was repairing the outside toilet door a few months back when his hand slipped and he caught his thumb with the hammer. His "fucking hell" didn't find favour as his mum gave him a very sharp smack across the back of his head and this was followed by a threat to tell his father and the deacons in the chapel. The hidden threat of shame and possible eternal damnation always worked. If Dad found out he wouldn't touch him as he had never hit John or brother David, but the feeling of letting Dad down would be enough.

"I haven't asked her out yet," said John quietly

"She seems alright to me. Well, from a distance, as I've not seen her close up. Andy said she's quiet and it's a shame she's from the bottom end of town but let's be honest it's the best you are going to do," laughed Dennis, ducking away from the inevitable swipe from John.

Dennis was just about to throw his empty bottle at the swans when John grabbed it.

"Don't do that, they didn't do you any harm," said John.

John walked off, putting the empty bottles in the bin as they walked back up the path to the park gates.

"What are you doing that evening class for anyway?" asked Dennis, "you'll be in the army in a few months killing Germans. What are you going to do, throw a typewriter at 'em?"

John replied "the war's not going to go on forever and I don't want to be working in an ironmongers forever. We all need to think about the future, otherwise, you get stuck in some dead-end job."

"Ooh hark at 'im, you'll be after Ernie Bevin's job next. Anyway, I'm sorted. My uncle's got a business hiring out limousines for weddings and funerals in Newport, says as soon as I pass my test I can get a job driving for him, posh uniform too," said Dennis grabbing the lapels of his worn cardigan. John thought that he had never seen Dennis in anything else. Dennis once told him the cardigan was a family heirloom and that the elbows had been patched by somebody famous in his family in the distant past. Dennis not having a clue about history or dates said he had heard it was somebody who wore it to the Crusades. John, with a bit more common sense and understanding, just laughed at some of the stupid things Dennis said.

"Wow, not Monty but Monty's chauffeur," John answered in a mocking tone.

"Ah, you wait till I'm picking up Rosemary Roberts in my limousine," said Dennis.

John broke down with an over-the-top belly laugh, "you've got no chance with Rosemary Roberts, she was the cleverest girl in the class, so she'll be looking for a solicitor or a rich businessman, not the likes of you."

Dennis cuffed him across the back of the head and ran off in front, through the park gates and along the street, stopping at John's front door where John's mother was wiping the window with a cloth.

"Afternoon Mrs Evans," said Dennis, "thought John had washed your windows?"

"So did I, Dennis, so did I," replied Mrs Evans, "if he fights like he washes windows when he joins the forces, we'll all be speaking German in a few months."

Dennis, smirking behind her back said, "well I'll be off, see you on the weekend, if you're not too busy with your girlfriend, John."

"Oh, first I've heard about this," said Mrs Evans.

"He's winding you up Mam," said John, glaring at his mate.

John and his mother went inside the house, No 2, Union Street, through the front door, which opened straight out onto the street.

The house was a classic 'two up, two down', working man's terraced house. Treafon was a small mining town. The mines and the steelworks in the next valley provided ninety per cent of the jobs in the town. Consequently, there were thousands of small terraced houses occupied by poorly paid workers.

The front door led onto a small living room, which had one or two small pictures on the wall and a set of shelves with a few ornaments. There were two easy chairs and two stools with cushions on and these had been placed around a small fireplace. In the corner was a small table with a very large wireless on it and everything smelt of furniture polish. A door at the back of the room led to a kitchen. This had a small oven with two gas rings on top. A wooden table big enough to seat four people was pushed against the wall. A large armchair was placed in the corner, this was his dad's chair and he would sit there and doze quietly after a day's work and his bath and meal. On the back wall was a large 'Welsh dresser', which carried the 'best' china. John could only ever remember it being used on Christmas days and twice when his Aunty Rachel had visited. John vividly remembered seeing the dresser for the first time when they moved into the house when he was about seven years of age. He had helped his mam and dad carry a lot of the furniture and other things, including their clothes. His dad pushed a barrow, which he had borrowed, with a flat wooden platform piled up with their possessions along the journey of about half a mile. When he went into this house for the first time he stopped and stared at this enormous dresser, thinking, where did that come from, and thank God we didn't have to move that. Truth was that the previous tenants had found it too big to move and had simply left it there to John's mother's eternal gratitude. John thought, how did anyone ever get that through the door. To the back of the kitchen was a small sink and alongside it the back door. Outside there was a very small yard with a tin bath hanging on the wall, an outside toilet at the top of a set of steps and a coal hole which could be filled from the street outside and the coal collected by the householder through a small wooden door. John's mam had planted a few primroses and daffodils in pots and jam jars on the wall between their house and next door. Though these were dead at the moment she hoped they would blossom again next Spring. Upstairs there were two bedrooms, the front bedroom occupied by John's parents with a double bed with a cast iron frame and a large wooden wardrobe, and on the one wall a door leading to the back bedroom where there were two single beds for John and David, a bedside table alongside each bed, a small wardrobe with drawers at the bottom and a small bookcase with John's and David's books, a tiny collection of David's cricket books, a sport he loved, one or two copies of Dicken's classics, a Bible given to John for his fifteenth birthday and signed by his Mam, Dad and David and two novels John had received as Christmas presents. The house was a duplicate in almost every way of the thousands of houses spread throughout the South Wales coalfield.

Going through to the kitchen John's mother asked, "What's he talking about, the weekend, you're in work all day Saturday and chapel on Sunday?"

"Don't know Mam, you know Dennis," replied John.

"What's this about a girl?" asked John's mother.

"I said Mam, he's taking the mickey," repeated John as he disappeared towards the front door.

3

John followed his usual Thursday routine, a sandwich and a cup of tea at about five-thirty, as he was able to have his main meal at lunchtime just after the shop closed. Dad came home at about four-thirty and bathed in the tin bath in front of the fire in the kitchen. His food had been cooked at lunchtime when John had his food with his mother. David had lunch in school and ate with his dad at five-thirty. David's and his father's meals had been warmed up for them.

"Suppose you've had your food?" dad said to make a point, "Davy and I just get leftovers." This was said with a smile, but John was never quite sure whether his dad meant it.

David piped up "Mammy's boy, that's what he is."

"Yea, yea," John replied giving David a shove in the back as he went upstairs to change.

John was thinking about evening class and Elizabeth. He shaved, using the water in the china bowl he kept on his bedside table, not that there was much to remove but it gave him the chance to splash on a little bit of aftershave he had received as last year's Christmas present from Aunty Rachel. He spread a layer of Brylcreem on his hair, as this was popular at the time. He rummaged through his wardrobe and drawers and came up with the best shirt, jumper, and trousers he could find. He could hear the strains of Bing Crosby and the Andrews Sisters singing 'Don't fence me in', and as he got changed he thought, that's appropriate.

Thirty minutes later he shouted "Ta ra," to everyone as he had difficulty closing the front door with his notebook and pencil case under his arm.

It took John a further half an hour to walk to the 'Tech', where the evening classes were held. The 'Tech' was an old Victorian building, which had been converted into workshops and classrooms to help improve and develop the technical skills of the local population in an effort to make them more employable during the depression of the thirties. It was a large building with a wrought iron fence around it and large gates, which opened out onto the street. The main doors were shut and about half a dozen people, mainly young like John, or quite a bit older, around perhaps fifty years of age were milling around or were sitting on the wall at the side of the Technical School, smoking or just chatting. He could see Elizabeth with the same two friends she was usually with. One of them was quite quiet like Elizabeth, the other one louder and more out-going. John rose his hand about waist height and she acknowledged him by raising her hand. John stood against the wall waiting for the doors to open. After a short while, the caretaker opened the doors and the students slowly trooped in. The woman taking the class, Mrs Watkins, in her late fifties or early sixties stood behind the desk at the front of the class. She asked the students to sit in pairs, one on either side of the desk facing each other. John paired up with Cyril, a surly, older man with a limp. Mrs Watkins then went around the class with sheets of paper with a printed text on it. She then asked one member of the pair to read the text slowly and quietly and the other member of the pair to write down the text in shorthand. Cyril quickly grabbed the sheet with the text and John picked up his writing pad that he had placed on the floor. John found that if he looked just past Cyril's head he could see Elizabeth, two rows back. Cyril began to read the text and John continued to smile at Elizabeth every few minutes. All of a sudden Cyril raised his voice quite deliberately loudly, "Are you listening to me or pulling stupid bloody faces?"

The whole class could hear and some began to giggle quietly. John could feel his face begin to redden. John then began to give the task a little more concentration. The pair then repeated the task with John reading the text and Cyril copying it down in shorthand. They were then asked to put their names on the sheets and hand them in. They then got to break-time and as it was raining outside they went out to a back corridor and porch. Some, including Elizabeth's forthright friend lit up cigarettes while others chatted. John didn't smoke, partly because he didn't particularly like it and partly because he couldn't afford cigarettes anyway. John noticed a gap against the wall next to Cyril and one next to Elizabeth. He opted to stand next to Elizabeth.

She turned to him and said, "I found that really difficult, I don't think I'm ever going to get the hang of it."

John replied, "Me neither."

Elizabeth asked, "will it help you in your work?"

"In an ironmongers shop, I don't think so. Lionel in the shop thinks shorthand courses help you manage a short shovel," John laughed at his own joke while Elizabeth smiled.

Elizabeth replied, "Me neither, I work in Hancock's sweetshop, no shorthand needed there."

John said, "that's amazing, that's only just down the street from my shop, we're practically neighbours."

They went on to chat about friends. Elizabeth said she came to the class with two friends, Jennifer and Marjorie. John said, "let me guess, Marjorie is the …,' he thought for a second and finished the sentence 'nice girl that's a bit louder than the other one."

Elizabeth smiled and said, "that's one way of putting it, but she is very kind and generous."

John said, "sorry, I didn't mean anything by it."

They went on to talk about films they had seen and just as John was trying to pluck up enough courage to ask her to go to the cinema with him Mrs Watkins called them back into the class.

Elizabeth turned quickly to go in and John had missed his chance. At the end of the evening, Elizabeth left with her friends and John shuffled quickly away but could never quite catch up to them. He followed them to the top of town but he knew he wouldn't strike up a conversation with all three of them and they lived in a different part of town and took a left turn where he took a right.

During the following week, he forced himself to take a walk past the sweetshop several times and eventually surprised himself by going in. Elizabeth smiled and said "hello," but he was served by the other assistant and had to think quickly what he would say he wanted.

He then bought four ounces of pear drops, not forgetting to hand over his ration card. Two days later he went back again but Elizabeth was not there, and so he was served by the same assistant as previously. On the Thursday lunchtime, he asked Lionel if he could leave five minutes early to get to the cobblers' shop. When Lionel said he could, he quickly sprinted out through the door to catch the sweetshop before it closed. As he went through the door the young assistant who had served him twice before shouted across to Elizabeth, "Your boyfriends back, the one who's suddenly become a sweet addict."

John coloured up and asked Elizabeth for four ounces of mint humbugs and once again handed over his ration card and asked would she be at evening class that night. She said she would.

John replied "Great, I need to ask you something."'He turned to leave the shop sticking his tongue out at the other assistant as he left.

She laughed and as he went out, shouted after him "can I be a bridesmaid?"

At evening class that night they were given their papers back from the previous week. John's was covered in red corrections and as Mrs Watkins handed it back to him she said, "Boy scouts meet on a Thursday night, you know. That is if you are looking for something to do." John pulled a face.

They were asked to go into the next room, sit at a typewriter and copy out the text from a piece of paper alongside it. They were given thirty minutes to complete the task.

In the break, they went to sit outside on the wall and Elizabeth sat next to John and said, 'you wanted to ask me something?'

John could feel himself getting redder and was about to make up some stupid question, something different from what he had planned all day to ask, but then he found some courage and quickly blurted out "there's a new John Mills film in the 'lymp', I'm going on Saturday night, would you like to come with me?" This was followed by a huge exhalation of breath.

Elizabeth smiling replied, "Yes, that would be great, what time?"

John quickly said, "seven o'clock, outside."

Elizabeth got up to go back to her friends shouting over her shoulder "see you then."

The rest of the night was a complete blur and John even found himself going down the wrong street on his way home and not realising why he was there.

4

Saturday evening came with much apprehension on John's part. He wondered if Elizabeth would turn up, but at seven o'clock outside the Olympia cinema, known to the locals as the 'lymp', there she was. John paid and in they went. John took seats about halfway down the cinema, as the back seats had a bit of a reputation and John didn't want Elizabeth to think he had an ulterior motive. He liked Elizabeth and had made his mind up that he saw a future in this relationship. They sat and watched the first feature and the newsreels in silence and it was only halfway through the main feature that John pushed his hand across to try to hold Elizabeth's hand. She didn't push him away and they continued to hold hands until the end of the film. After this victory, John felt that was far enough for a first date. He found after the evening ended he could not remember anything about it as he was continually thinking about what he should be doing and what he would be doing. He promised himself that he would come back and watch the film in the week, as this was a film he really wanted to see.

John asked to walk Elizabeth home and though she told him it was too far out of his way, he insisted. They chatted on the way to Elizabeth's home about family and what they hoped to do with their lives. Elizabeth asked John whether he was likely to be called-up in the near future and which of the forces he hoped to join. The evening ended with a brief kiss at the front gate outside Elizabeth's house and a promise to see each other on the following Saturday.

As John was leaving work on Tuesday evening he found Dennis waiting for him outside the shop. Dennis said, "How about going to the dogs next Saturday afternoon?"

John thought for a moment and said he would be busy Saturday evening. Dennis turned to him "Oo, seeing your bit of stuff eh?"

John replied, "taking Elizabeth out, yes."

"Well, the dogs are at 2 o'clock so unless she's about ten and you plan to take her to the Saturday matinee you'll be fine," Dennis said, with a stupid grin on his face "so if you happen to be available it's two o'clock at the fence," and with that, he ran off.

High above the town on the valley side was a flat area of ground, fenced off and behind it was a greyhound track. It cost three pence to go in if there were races on, A high price to pay, so the boys decided to sneak in through a broken part of the fence. There were four of them, John, Dennis, Peter, who was the clever one in school and had a plan to train as a doctor. His father was an under-manager in the local Co-op and consequently Peter was better dressed than the others. His chances of medical training would have to wait until after the war, and Rob, who lived with his dad who would regularly get drunk and beat him and consequently Rob was very much of a nervous disposition and would often have to be coaxed to do anything remotely adventurous. Rob, like Dennis, always looked pale and under-nourished and like Dennis always wore the same patched clothes, which were usually 'hand-me-downs' from other sympathetic people.

John was the last to arrive outside the fence and initially couldn't speak after climbing the steep incline leading up to the greyhound track. The other three laughed at the comments Dennis made about John's level of fitness.

After they got through the fence they went to sit on an old railway sleeper away from the other spectators, perhaps fifty people mostly crowded at the other end.

Some of the men-only crowd were milling around and two men sat at an old desk and seemed to be counting money.

"If anyone wants to put a bet on let me know," said Dennis "Roger's over there and he'll do it for me."

Peter mimicking one of the Hollywood gangster films he had seen, piped up "Yea, five hundred knicker on the grey with five legs."

"You been drinking?" John asked, and they all laughed.

After a few minutes of silence, Rob asked when their birthdays were. They had all been in the same class at school and so all would be called-up before the Summer. It was clear it was John who would be the first to go and the conversation immediately brought the fear factor back into his thoughts. Rob then nervously said, "Well at least it gets me away from dad, it'll be a sergeant major thumping me not my dear old dad."

Dennis said, "The war might be over by the time we come to go."

Peter said, "Don't you believe it, if we win the war which looks increasingly likely we'll have thousands of prisoners to look after for quite a while. They're not going to release thousands of Germans to reorganise and start another war. They did that once before. There'll be countries to re-build, food to import. They'll need an army, air force and navy to help organise that and I can see lots of trouble abroad, India will want her independence and perhaps some of the African countries. It's all going to need people to help with that. I think they'll keep the armed forces for many years if anything to stop it happening again."

Dennis turned to Peter "who's going to want to go in the army, air force or navy after all this killing?"

Peter replied "you may not have any choice like now you get your papers, you go. What's to stop the government carrying that on until everything is stable again, perhaps for ten years or more."

John said, "you are bloody cheery, I'd better put my plans to become the town's first millionaire on hold."

"Married with a stack of kids you'll be with sweet Elizabeth. Pass that violin will you Rob?" said Dennis.

John picked up a clod of earth and threw it at Dennis. The boys noticed a tall thick-set man in an overcoat coming towards them, who said "Didn't see you boys paying at the gate, can you show me your tickets?"

The boys looked at each other before Dennis said, "we only came in to see what was going on, we'll be off now if that's ok?"

The man replied, "see that you do"

As the boys left, Dennis said to John "that bloke is a police sergeant down at the station."

John replied, "perhaps he's working undercover."

Dennis said, "I don't think so, I'm pretty sure I saw him put a bet on with those blokes at the table."

The boys went back out of the greyhound track through the hole in the fence and sat for a while on the grass bank overlooking the town.

Rob said, "we can't sit here, the grass is wet and my old man'll paste me for getting my trousers wet."

"Sit down for God's sake," said Dennis.

"I don't mind telling you I'm shitting myself at the thought of joining up," said John,

"Me too," said Rob.

"Cannon fodder we'll be," said Dennis, "pushed into the front line against some big SS bastard who'll be fighting for his life as he's retreated 200 miles back towards Germany and doesn't want to go any further."

"Best not to think too much about it," said Peter, "we won't have any choice in the matter, we'll be ordered to do things and we'll have to do them or get arrested, put up against a wall and shot."

"Do they still do that?" asked Rob.

"If they don't, you'll be shamed forever and never allowed back in this town," stated Dennis.

"Think I'll try and get into army intelligence," John answered.

"Not really equipped for that are you," said Dennis as the others fell about laughing. All of which was a bit over the top and an attempt to mask the nervousness and the genuine worries and concerns that each of them had.

Three of the boys ran back down the slope to the town while John sat for a few moments longer, contemplating the next few months. He looked down at the town, shrouded in smoke and dust from the coal mines and the coal tips which surrounded it. It had a strange beauty and he could remember having a warm feeling when he came home after a holiday with his gran in Pembrokeshire, two years before. Everybody kept saying you'll love Pembrokeshire, you'll be able to go walking along the coast and see seabirds you don't see in Treafon. The sea air will be good for you. John loved the tiny ferry they had to go on to get to his gran's to save the long journey all the way around the estuary. He had found that exciting, but after a few days he began to miss the town he had grown up in, his friends and the noises he had become used to, the clanking of the railways as they made their way ponderously through the town, the banging and crashing of the work carried on in the gasworks and the brickworks and the sight of the miners with their black faces coming back through town from the railway station, at the end of their shifts, ready for their baths in front of the kitchen fire. Towards the end of the week, he got excited about the return journey and had a dispute with David because he told him he was looking forward to going home. He had been to the bigger towns and cities in South Wales, which were outside the coal mining area and didn't have the ever pervading smoke and dust and the slight redness, which marked the buildings when the wind blew particles from the steelworks. All the rows of terraced houses were tinged with dirt, more so as time went on, as the men had little time or money to paint them with the usual white masonry paint. John remembered a visit from Aunty Rachel who had married a fairly wealthy man and moved to Nottingham. John had never been there but she would constantly tell him how wonderful life was in Nottingham and how John should work hard in school to get a good education and a good job and escape Treafon. Aunty Rachel's visits, thankfully infrequent, would result in tension between his mam and dad. His dad would say "there she goes again, filling the boy's head with a load of nonsense. Easy for her to say, she didn't work very hard in school, just managed to marry money." Mam would defend her sister but only to go through the motions and not enough to cause a row. She would simply find something to do until dad had calmed down.

John thought, many people would hate to live here but it had an unusual fascination. The people were so friendly. They had little, but most would give their last to their fellow human beings and John was sure that didn't happen everywhere.

Well, he thought, I might find out what it is like somewhere else compared to Treafon after this war and praise God I will be able to return.

The following Thursday at evening class John decided to sit on the wall at the break and watch Elizabeth and her two friends. He thought she looked lovely, shoulder-length dark hair, waved in the modern way women now did, slim, perhaps on the thin side but that was how everybody looked with rationing. John remembered squeezing through the fence at the dog track and thought I had no trouble doing that being a skinny bugger. She wore a simple cotton dress with an overcoat with a narrow faux fur collar, no stockings as you couldn't get them for love or money, so his mam said, and shoes with a slight heel, a bit battered but presentable. John thought she bore a resemblance to a photograph he had seen in his mam's catalogue, of a girl modelling an over-coat. The image which stayed with him through that day and for many months and years to come was the vision of Elizabeth's face. She had quite a round face and with her hair swept back it opened her face up. Most significant of all was her smile, which could best be described as radiant. She had a row of white teeth and when she smiled the corners of her eyes crinkled into small creases. When John saw her laugh, even from a distance he wanted to laugh with her and hoped he would many times. He didn't have a chance to speak to her for long but she did say, "don't forget Saturday, same time, same place," as she was about to leave.

5

The next few months were some of the most confused John had ever experienced. He got into a pattern of meeting Elizabeth once and sometimes twice a week. He ignored Dennis' constant questions about how far their relationship had developed. Every time John saw him the conversation began with "Have you done this, or have you done that?" In evening classes, he often paired up with Elizabeth for certain tasks and at work was constantly reprimanded by Lionel for daydreaming when customers needed to be served. Just before Christmas Elizabeth invited him down to Sunday tea. He promised his mother he would be back to go to evening service in chapel.

John had been quietly reprimanded by his mother who said, "I know you are seeing this girl and she sounds lovely but you have missed chapel now on several occasions and I don't think our Lord would be very pleased if when you turned up at the pearly gates you said, 'sorry lord I missed chapel on quite a lot of times because I found something more important to do."

John took the criticism on the chin, as it was easier to shut up and allow his mam to berate him than to argue back, though he thought his mother was getting everything out of proportion.

He put on his best suit and walked down to the bottom end of town. He knew that area of town well as his grandmother lived nearby. Elizabeth lived opposite the gas-holder, a significant landmark in the town. He knocked on the door and was ushered in by Elizabeth. He was introduced to her father who she had earlier referred to as 'a gruff old bird.' Mr Williams, Elizabeth's father said little for a while as he listened to the news on the BBC Home Service.

He had been a soldier in the First World War until he returned home with a 'blighty', a wound in the leg sufficiently bad to warrant him unfit to return to active service and he spent the rest of the war in a series of hospitals and then as an assistant cook in a training camp. He had spent nearly three years in the trenches and was keen to describe his experiences in detail to John, who listened patiently. Elizabeth's mother had died some four years ago of tuberculosis when Elizabeth was thirteen and she had left school immediately to look after her father.

After Mr Williams had finished listening to the news on the wireless he turned his attention to the couple. The afternoon dragged a little as it was dominated by Elizabeth's father's memories of his army life. The last thing John wanted to hear about were the horrors of war and he gave little opportunity for Elizabeth or John to speak. As John was leaving Elizabeth's father shouted out "bet you can't wait to join up," and after a seconds thought he stated, "Oh, if I was twenty years younger."

John quietly said to Elizabeth, "you could then go instead of me."

John got back to the house just as his mother, father and brother were leaving for chapel. The chapel was at the end of the street.

"Hope you haven't got messed up?" his mother said, as she brushed John's jacket "what's this on your tie?" his mother remarked looking down at a greasy spot.

"It's probably a bit of egg," John replied

"Well go and wipe it off with warm water," his mother instructed, "here's warm water in the kettle, it hasn't long boiled."

John went to clean up his tie and then left the house to catch them up. They went into chapel and took their places in the same pew they did every week. Aunty Maggie, John's mother's sister, came down to speak to them but quickly went back to her seat as the organist started to play.

The service lasted an hour with the alternating sermon, hymns and prayers. The preacher was a visiting preacher and was of an evangelical disposition, and he made John giggle as he threw his arms around pointing at various people stating that they could expect eternal damnation if they didn't seek God's forgiveness, and mend their ways. It amused John as one of the people the preacher kept pointing at was Mr Symes, who John knew could often be seen sitting on the pavement outside the Red Lion pub on a Saturday night because he was too drunk to stand. John assumed he spent most of Sunday morning recovering only to emerge for Sunday evening service.

On Boxing Day Elizabeth visited John's family and in a much more relaxed atmosphere, she chatted with his parents about life during wartime and whether Elizabeth attended chapel. Everyone breathed a sigh of relief when Elizabeth said she attended chapel near her house at the other end of town, and she went up a few notches when they discovered that it was the same chapel that John's father's sister attended.

John was feeling relaxed in his relationship with Elizabeth. She was good company and there was no pressure on either of them. Apart from the odd kiss, nothing much else happened between them and John seemed happy with that as he became more and more pre-occupied with his impending call-up. He decided at the end of January he would travel to Cardiff and visit the recruitment office of the Royal Navy, not because he particularly wanted to join the navy but because he thought he would be choosing a service rather than one choosing him. He had also given it a little thought and reckoned he would have a better chance of surviving the war in the navy than the army. When he got to the recruitment office, having taken a Saturday off work and travelled down by bus, taking him nearly two hours to get to Cardiff, as it stopped in every town and village, he was told that they were not taking any further recruits. In a sudden flash of inspiration, he asked where the Merchant Navy offices were. He made his way down to Cardiff docks thinking perhaps that this walk might have been more dangerous than any wartime experience. When he got there he was told that they, like the Royal Navy were not recruiting immediately, but that they might be in six months time. He knew his call-up papers would come before that, offering him no choice.

John's eighteenth birthday came at the end of February. He had a very pleasant birthday tea in the chapel vestry with presents, cards and greetings from friends and family. His mother gave him a hat, scarf and gloves, his dad and brother went halves in a hardcover book, a novel which had just been published by a well known Welsh author and Elizabeth handed him a present wrapped in fancy paper and ribbons.

He joked "is this a box of sweets?" When he opened it, it was a brand new Box Brownie camera and he was genuinely 'over the moon' with it.

He came down to earth a week later when his mother handed him a brown paper envelope addressed to him. Without opening it he placed it on the table and stared at it. His mother said, "well, aren't you going to open it?" He quickly picked it up and sprinted up to his bedroom. He sat on his bed and he freely admitted that he wouldn't have been able to describe his emotions, as they were so confused. He felt a mixture of total fear and anticipation, unprepared as he was for what might happen. He also felt to a very small degree, excitement. Eventually, he picked up the letter and opened it. It was a little bit like opening your school report, except that his school report could never kill him, though his mother would use that phrase from time to time in referring to his school reports. The consequences of opening this letter might kill him, which gave him a dizzy, sick feeling.

He tried to read the letter but noticed only a few phrases, 'Dear Mr Evans', 'army', 'report to' and 'Derby.' This gave him the gist of what was about to happen to him. He took the letter back downstairs and faced his mother and brother who looked at him in silence. He reported to them that he was to begin basic training in Derby on the fifteenth of March, two weeks away. He asked his brother to pop into the ironmongers on his way to school and tell them he wouldn't be in today, as he was feeling sick. The thought flashed through his mind that the statement about sickness wasn't that far from the truth at that moment.

He then went across town to Elizabeth's sweet shop, being very careful to avoid the ironmongers. He asked Elizabeth's colleague whom he now knew as Audrey if he could speak to Elizabeth for two minutes and could Audrey look after the shop. Elizabeth and John went through to the back of the shop where he told her what would be happening in two weeks time. Elizabeth accepted the news quietly, as it didn't really sink in that John wouldn't be around after that for a while.

He went into the ironmongers the next day and explained that he had been called-up and agreed with them he would work the next week and take the following week off to visit friends and relatives before leaving for basic training.

The next two weeks were a whirl of activity. He visited cousins, his grandmother and friends, including Dennis, who remained unusually quiet. John thought that Dennis realised that in a few weeks time he would probably be in the same position. Finally, two days before he was due to leave there was another smaller family party in the chapel vestry to wish John good luck. Elizabeth's father came along and met John's parents for the first time. John took his new Box Brownie and took a whole roll of film of friends and relatives, including several photographs of Elizabeth sitting and standing in different positions, until she couldn't stand posing any further, and walked off. That evening David and his father left John and his mother in the kitchen on their own and quietly closed the door to the living room to give them some privacy. Mrs Evans stemmed back the tears she could feel coming and turned to John.

"You must be true and honest to yourself John. You've not been away on your own for any length of time and you must not succumb to temptation," she said quietly.

John said, "This sounds more like one of Mr Davies' sermons Mam."

"No, I mean it John, other men that will be with you will try to persuade you to do things you don't want to do and you might do them to be popular, but John, it is more important that you are strong and true to yourself."

"Mam I'm sure I'll be fine, there'll be lots of other blokes there who'll be from the same sort of background as me and they'll be the friends I'll make," John said a little sheepishly.

Suddenly his mother started to cry and John didn't know how to respond. He'd rarely seen his mother upset and so he just sat quietly and waited for her to compose herself.

She dabbed at her eyes with a handkerchief and turned to give John a quick hug, then pushed him away "Well be off with you now and get to bed, you've got a busy day tomorrow."

John spent his last morning at home and then in the afternoon walking in the park with Elizabeth. She got very emotional and several times had to walk away from him to dab at the tears in her eyes. He walked her home and following a brief embrace and a kiss on the doorstep he left to go home, despondent that he would not now see her before he left for the army. How many million times had this happened to how many million men? It made no difference to his mood, as he kept thinking about how many never came back.

6

John leaned out over the rail of the ship at the clear sparkling blue of the Eastern Mediterranean Sea. The sun beat down even though it was mid-November and John thought about those back home who would be huddled around the fire by now. It seemed a little poignant as 'I'll Walk Alone', by Dinah Shore was quietly playing over the loudspeakers of the ship. John thought 'I've done a lot of that on this ship, so far, and smiled to himself.

The voyage had not all been like this, the days after leaving port had been cold and stormy. John had been allocated a position in the galley and given the times at which he could take his meals. He had an empty space next to him for the first week of the voyage and John thought nothing of it until suddenly at the end of that week another soldier appeared, explaining to John that he had been seasick for the whole of that time, taking only drinks of water and a few slices of bread he could persuade the members of the galley crew to give him.

The voyage so far had given him no new experiences. The weather was like the few very hot days John had experienced back home and all he had seen was the ship. They were sailing half way around the world but it gave John no new sights as yet. He realised those would come.

The war had caused many boys to grow up fast. He thought that he had left home a child and while he was aware he was still very inexperienced he did feel that he had begun to grow up and that he certainly had more confidence. He had learned to be more independent and to make decisions which he would then have to stand by. He remembered arriving at the camp to begin basic training, very frightened and alone. He thought that if anyone had raised their voice to him as he arrived at the main gate of the camp he would have run away. The growth in confidence had given him a feeling of near invincibility. He knew this was stupid and that he had no idea what lay in front of him, but he couldn't perceive of anything that would any longer frighten him though he accepted that might change. The growth in confidence seemed to be associated with an inner calmness. His immediate response to aggression from those ranks above him or those of the same rank who sought to bait him was to remain quiet. The aggressor often found that unsettling and it was something that he had added to his armour along with his bayonet and rifle.

John had left home in mid-March and was instructed to go to a district of Derby called Markeaton, which turned out to be a large area of parkland turned into an army camp. He had reported to the camp on time and in the first few days, he had been given a full medical and was passed A1. Equipped with a full kit and fatigues, he had been given a very severe haircut and he had been asked to fill in many forms, often with the same information. He had been given vaccinations and by the end of April, he had received training in how to handle a rifle and a light machine gun. He had spent hours on the parade ground with his company sergeant bellowing at the group in general, whether they made mistakes or not, and he began to realise that what the sergeant major shouted either at him or the group was not to be taken personally. He had been asked to donate blood and by the end of May, he had experienced a gas chamber test, been given training in how to throw grenades and how to use a mortar. He had been told that all of these skills would be returned to at a more advanced level before the end of basic training.

A significant event in early May was the end of the war in Europe. This was received by almost all of his fellow soldiers with a huge degree of relief, as they would no longer be expected to be leaving for active service in France or Germany. This news was celebrated by all with a piss-up in one of the pubs in Derby on VE day where the only thing John could remember was spending what was left of the night in a doorway before meeting up with the rest of the lads to make their way back to camp the following morning. John was still feeling rough as the sergeant put them through their paces on the parade ground two days later. John had made a few friends, though the corporals and sergeants warned against becoming too 'pally' as they would probably all end up in different places and never see their new found friends again.

John was given nine days leave in early June, and made his way back home. After being greeted by a tearful mother and a curious father and brother who peppered him with questions over a cup of tea and a piece of cake John excused himself to go out to the back of the house to have a cigarette.

His mam followed him out with "I hope that's the only bad habit you've picked up," followed by a scowl.

John quickly disarmed her by saying, "the daffs are looking nice."

She looked back at John and said, "don't you go stubbing out your fag ends in those vases, my lad."

He answered "no mam."

John didn't want to upset her but felt that after a long journey home he needed to relax with a cigarette, a habit followed by virtually every member of his company. After what he deemed to be a reasonable time he excused himself to go down to the sweetshop in town. As he walked in, in full uniform, Elizabeth ran from behind the counter and threw her arms around him.

Audrey remained behind the counter saying "well if it isn't General Patton?"

They spent much of John's leave together when Elizabeth was not working, and weekends were a real bonus when they would walk in the hills around the town, but there were more tears when John left to go back.

John wrote to Elizabeth during his time away and between them they planned to take a holiday during his next leave by going to Bournemouth to stay with Elizabeth's sister, Joan, who was in domestic service in the town. Strangely enough, Elizabeth had spent little time with Joan as there were seventeen years between them and Joan had left to go into domestic service when Elizabeth was a small baby. Elizabeth's elder brother, Wesley was only six years older, and was now in the RAF and was much closer to Elizabeth as they had spent more time together growing up.

The couple made their way to Bournemouth and arrived at Joan and Bill's flat. It was a bit cramped in the small flat and Joan's husband, Bill who had just been de-mobbed from the Navy, seemed a bit put out that he had to share the flat with these two incumbents, but the week went well and John thought the highlight of the week was the fact that both he and Elizabeth lost their virginity while Elizabeth's sister and husband were at work. They had arrived on the Saturday afternoon and John was bedded down on the sofa while Elizabeth had a camp bed in Joan and Bill's bedroom. Both lay quietly awake while Joan and Bill got ready to go to work on the Monday morning. Bill had managed to get a job with the local council, clearing bomb sites ready for re-building. Elizabeth quickly got up to make a cup of tea but John grabbed her and pulled her on top of Joan and Bill's bed. They kissed each other and despite Elizabeth being a reluctant participant at first, quoting the fact that they were both from chapel backgrounds, and what would their parents think, she eventually got caught up in the emotion and John's insistence and relented and slowly they shed the few bed-clothes they were wearing. Both were a little hesitant and fully realised what they were doing. While Elizabeth seemed prepared to stop, John was more insistent.

He had thought about this time for many hours while they travelled down and had made his mind up it was going to happen while they were away. John had been well prepared and left the bedroom to collect the 'French Letters' as they were called, that he had purchased from the local barber.

On entering the barber's shop John had asked: "can I buy something to stop babies?"

"So you want something for the weekend, sir, something to bring a little joy and happiness," the barber replied passing John the small packets.

John made sure the shop was empty when he went in, and passed over his money and left embarrassed, passing a customer on his way out.

They were both gentle and passionate with each other and though it was not quite the earth-shattering moment they were led to believe, they lay back on their respective sides of the bed in silence for a few moments and then almost as if it had been rehearsed they both burst out laughing.

Elizabeth quickly said, "so that was it?" and in a mocking tone, turned to John and said, in a silly voice "was it good for you?"

John replied, also in a mock serious voice "I've had better, but, well you take what you can get."

He ducked the swipe from Elizabeth and they both ended up in each other's arms.

It suddenly dawned on Elizabeth that it was John's first time as well. It was something that they'd not really talked about, but up until then, she had assumed that she was not the first. The realisation gave her a warm glow and she felt even closer to him.

This then became the normal pattern for them both for the remainder of the time they were in Bournemouth. They would wait patiently for Joan and Bill to go to work and would then make love on their bed in the early morning, always making sure to put a towel on the bed first in case they stained the quilt, and to carefully make the bed after.

They both felt that this brought them together and though they had a knowing look from Joan when she got home from work, they both tried to look innocent. John and Elizabeth treated Joan and Bill to a meal in a Lyons café in the centre of Bournemouth on the day before they left, with Joan and Bill promising to come home to see dad as soon as they got time off, and they had saved enough to afford the journey to South Wales. Though no definite plans were made John and Elizabeth talked about their futures during the bus and train journey back home. They had enjoyed their time in Bournemouth, the weather had been good, they had walked on the promenade, sunbathed in the gardens and had explored and discovered a good deal about each other's minds and bodies.

There had been great excitement during July with the General Election. John was convinced Winston Churchill would be victorious after seeming to win the war for Britain and the Commonwealth, but the Labour Party had won a landslide and in the Labour heartland of Treafon there had been great celebrations. John's dad was absolutely ecstatic. John had never seen him so pleased. He rarely said much but the election victory rendered him totally speechless. He kept punching the air and every time John spoke to him about the politics of the last month all he could do was shake his head in total incredulity.

John went back to camp at the end of July having explained that it would be highly unlikely he would get any more leave before the end of basic training.

One small piece of information for John to note came towards the end of August when the Japanese surrendered to the Allies and a day in August was identified as VJ day. John thought this probably had more significance for the Americans and didn't really spare a thought for the British troops fighting in India and Burma. They had been given the designation 'the Forgotten Army.' In John's case, this was completely true. Little did he appreciate the significance for him personally at this point in time. A few of the blokes decided to go for a beer as they had brothers or other relatives fighting in the Far East and this would probably mean they would be able to return home, but it didn't seem to warrant the celebrations that were held for VE day.

All the lads had dropped into a steady routine and there was little friction between them despite the nervousness as they got through September and would soon find out where they would be posted. The 'Markeaton Lancers' as they designated themselves had many photographs taken of groups and individuals and swapping of addresses as they got nearer to the end of September. Sergeant Reynolds, their mentor, told them that lists of postings would go up on 2nd October, they would probably get leave and then would move on to their first official army posting.

Everyone got a little more nervous as the day got nearer. Private Campbell, a Scot kept lookout at the barrack room door and spotted the captain going into the Admin block with a sheaf of papers. Just after the captain had left and disappeared around the corner there was a mad scramble from the hut and several other huts to get to the papers that had been posted up. John pushed his way to the front and after a time was close enough to read the list, running his eye down to 'E', Evans J, Private – India Command.'

He left the hut stunned. He quietly said under his breath "shit, shit, shit." Swearing had been another habit he had picked up while at the camp. His response was due to the fact that all trainees while discussing what would likely happen to them next wanted to avoid going anywhere near the Far East where the war had only finished in August with the surrender of the Japanese. The papers were still reporting pockets of fighting from groups that had refused to surrender and there were many minor wars where local groups were taking advantage of the vacuum left at the end of the war to try to take control of countries and regions for themselves.

Ray Stockham, who was billeted in the same hut as John came up behind him, "where you off to mate?"

"Back to the hut," John replied.

Ray laughed "I didn't mean now, I meant after this."

"Oh, India by the looks of it," John replied still feeling a little shell shocked, "where are you off to Ray?" he asked.

"Germany, apparently," answered Ray who walked away looking quite pleased with himself, shouting over his shoulder "it'll be a bit nearer for me to come home on leave. By the time you get home, it'll be time to go back. It's a long way to India."

"Thanks for those few kind words," John said under his breath.

John went back to his hut to enquire whether anybody else had been posted to India. There was no reply. He then went into the two huts either side of his own and following his question he was greeted with the same silence. He could find no one who had been posted to India. Someone said, "I think there's a bloke over in Hut 15 who's been posted to India, or did he say China, I can't remember." John couldn't think why anyone would be posted to China, and he couldn't be bothered to go and look for some bloke he'd never met.

During his last few weeks in Markeaton he was given vaccinations for India, more than anyone else he knew, except those posted to areas of Africa or a few who had been posted to the West Indies. He met a few blokes who were posted to Jamaica to guard training airfields and he thought that sounded pretty good, a few who were posted to Kenya where insurrection was expected, and who looked as sick as he did after a whole range of vaccinations. Two of the men in his own hut were posted to Canada to guard prisoners of war, allegedly, and after some considerable time he tracked down two others who were to be posted to India, Private Freddy Graham and Private James Sullivan. He spent some time with these two as he thought he might be seeing more of them in the future.

He then left the camp with all his kit, many rolls of film to be developed and a very well used address book. They went into Derby on the last Friday night and all made promises to meet up again though they all knew that would be highly unlikely.

John began his embarkation leave in mid October. He would be home for thirteen days and would then have to make his way to Southampton to leave for India at the end of the month.

He saw as much of Elizabeth as he could and though they could not pursue any further sexual activities due to being watched by various members of the family virtually all the time and the fact that the weather was dreadful and far too wet and cold to be attempting anything outdoors. They had to be content with kissing and cuddling, as the end of the month loomed large. John got absolutely legless with Dennis on the weekend before he had to return to the army, who was also home from basic training at a camp near Weymouth. John had to face the wrath of Elizabeth who was not best pleased that John had chosen to go out with Dennis instead of her on his last Friday at home. John spent that night in Dennis' house as his mother didn't seem to mind but John had to face many questions the following day from his mother when he returned home looking more than a little dishevelled.

She looked disgusted at John and turning said, "you won't be joining us in chapel on Sunday, nor in the future, until you have lost these dreadful habits you seem to have picked up." John's dad raised his eyes to the heavens but said nothing. John made up with Elizabeth on the Saturday night though all he really wanted to do was go home to go to bed. He said his goodbyes on the Sunday night with promises "to write loads."

By Monday morning when John was due to leave, his mam's attitude had thawed a little and she gave him a big hug and a kiss and said, "for heaven's sake look after yourself and come home safe, and make sure we get plenty of letters from you, certainly more than we got from you in Derby."

John picked up his kit bag and smiled "promise Mam," and walked off towards the bus station, blowing kisses as he went.

All these thoughts were going through his mind as he leaned on the rail of the boat. He had taken photographs of the boat and photos of the coastline of Gibraltar, Malta and Morocco when they passed. By the end of the next day, they would be in the Suez Canal. He wrote the names of all the places they passed in a small notebook, as he was afraid he would forget them in time. It was essential he remembered them if he was going to relate stories of his travels to Elizabeth or to his mates in the local pub. The truth was most of these places were a thin pencil line on the horizon and could have been Porthcawl or Aberystwyth for all he knew. He smiled to himself as he thought of showing off his photos in the pub, now this line is Morocco and this line is Malta and as you can see this line is Gibraltar. Dennis piping up "they all look the fucking same." He kept thinking, who would have thought I would travel this far before my nineteenth birthday, but he hadn't seen anything yet except the ship and a lot of horizons.

He remembered a funny story Peter related to him. His dad had met someone distantly related to him who had joined the navy at the beginning of the war. Peter's dad said, "Join the navy and see the world Eh?" The bloke looked at Peter's dad and said, "no mate, I'm in submarines, you've probably seen more of the world than me."

John realised how lonely he felt on board the ship, despite there being hundreds of men onboard., He spent some time with a few of the blokes who had trained at Markeaton but he didn't really know them and so he was left alone with his own thoughts and his experiences in silence. A shame, he thought, as part of the fun was to share these experiences with friends and family, He would have loads to tell them when he got back home but there was a good degree of apprehension about what he would find when he landed in India. The ship docked in Port Said for a short time and those aboard were allowed shore leave. John left the ship full of anticipation. He wandered the streets following a group of soldiers about the same age as himself. They all seemed a little uncertain of themselves but shielded their nervousness by being boisterous. Eventually, John got fed up with walking in circles around the port and steeled himself to go off on his own. He simply peeled off the back of the group and wandered down a small alley. The thing that struck him most clearly was the whiteness of everything. The contrast with the rows of dirty terraced houses in Treafon and even some of the towns in England was stark. All the buildings seemed to be white and the reflection of the strong sunlight hurt his eyes. Another feature that lodged in his brain was the very obvious poverty of the people. There was poverty in South Wales, but here many children had no shoes, most of those under about five years of age were almost completely naked. Grey washing hanging on lines on the top floors of buildings, which looked unfinished, or hung between buildings, and was ragged and dirty. He had to constantly fend off people begging, making the huge mistake of giving money to the first beggars that accosted him and finding that others seemed to appear from nowhere. He escaped into a shop where the shopkeeper shooed them away and tut-tutted at him for his lack of local knowledge. Port Said was his first experience of another culture, coming across people that he could not communicate with, as they spoke another language, a different level of law and order, a world where he was not in control. He thought, there will be much of this in the next few years, best to keep silent, look and learn before I speak and show my ignorance, and perhaps above all look confident, even if I'm not.

7

John docked in Bombay in the first week of December 1945. All the troops on board were instructed to collect their kit and leave by the gangplanks, which had been situated alongside the ship. John looked down upon a scene which seemed to be absolutely chaotic. Many Indian males were running in all directions, some with their turbans tied on top of their heads with a range of cases and bags on top. Some of them in long lines, but all of them seemed to be shouting, either replies or orders. Desks were arranged at the bottom of the gangplanks and each soldier would offer his army documents to the non-commissioned officers sat at the desk. They would then be allocated a truck number and on the return of their documents would proceed to their truck. No one had a clue where they were going but trusted army organisation and efficiency to take them to the right place. John had struggled to get his kit bag to the truck due to the intense heat. It seemed a different sort of heat to that experienced in Britain during the few hot Summer's days they had. He thought that he might have acclimatised to the heat during the voyage through the Mediterranean Sea and in the few days they spent in Port Said waiting their turn to pass through the Suez Canal, but on the ship there was always a constant breeze. This heat was relentless, and he couldn't wait to get under the canvas that was drawn over the back of the trucks. He didn't recognise any of the other troops in the back of the truck, who spent the first hour or so singing and telling jokes. As the truck trundled on over roads full of potholes the men became weary and nodded off to sleep, and mercifully from John's point of view stopped singing the few songs they knew the words to, over and over. After about two and a half hours they stopped and were given bowls of a thin tasteless soup and mugs of water. Some of the men went round to the front of the trucks to speak to the drivers. When they got back in they said the trucks had come from Deolali Camp, or 'Doolally Camp' as they referred to it, and they were returning there.

They arrived at the camp a few hours later and were allocated camp beds in rows of small tents. The heat seemed to penetrate the tents and remain there, making them increasingly hot as the day went on. You would see men coming out of the tents and taking gasps of air before they returned inside. They were told to use the mosquito nets at night to avoid malaria, and to be aware of wild animals who might get into the camp at night, particularly snakes and spiders.

The day after John arrived he went for a walk around the camp. He walked in one direction for twenty minutes and he could still not see the edge of the camp, just hundreds and probably thousands of tents. The camp was vast with thousands of men mostly just wandering around or sitting outside their tents waiting for orders.

John spent a month at the camp, mixing with soldiers, sailors and airmen who had just arrived in India like himself, as well as troops who were returning after fighting in some parts of the Far East. You could easily tell the difference between them. The new arrivals seemed like excited children compared to the hard-bitten troops who were returning home. They would resort to teasing each other and at times fights would break out between nervous individuals and those seemingly at the end of their tether. The camp had a cinema, which often showed the same film night after night, resulting in men shouting lewd abuse right throughout the film. It was like a return to 'silent movies' as the audience would have to guess what was being said on the screen because you couldn't hear a word the actors said. There was a restaurant which served food to those who had money to pay, above their normal rations, but its quality was little better unless you liked curry, which many hated as they had eaten curry every day of their stay in the camp and were now thoroughly sick of the taste of it. Most men simply sat about waiting to hear when they might be moved on. Every day there was a procession to the notice boards to seek out new information. After about three weeks at the camp, John noticed a list of men on the noticeboard with his name included. The men on the list were commanded to see a Captain Lockhart as soon as possible.

John sought out the temporary office where Captain Lockhart

was based and joined a queue outside the hut. After about forty minutes of waiting John entered the office in the company of a sergeant major, he promptly saluted and was ordered to stand at ease.

Captain Lockhart asked John's full name rank and serial number and then shuffled through a sheaf of papers on his desk. Having found what he required he held up two pieces of paper and proceeded to read from the first one "well, congratulations Private Evans it seems that it has been confirmed that you are to be promoted to Sergeant and transferred, if that is the correct term, to RASC. Well done, and that will obviously be a rise in pay as well. Do you have your service book with you, as I will need to sign it to show I have passed the information on to you and I will require your signature on my piece of paper to show you have received the information. We will sort out your stripes before you are moved on, any questions priv…, I mean sergeant."

John was momentarily dumbstruck but eventually stuttered "eh, no sir, thank you, sir."

Captain Lockhart then turned to the second piece of paper and read out "Sergeant Evans is forthwith to be transferred from India Command to Burma Command, and his ship SS Donegal will leave Madras for Rangoon on 17th January and he is to transfer to BBRC."

John knew that RASC stood for, Royal Army Service Corps but he had no idea what BBRC stood for. He said, "excuse me sir but what is BBRC?"

Captain Lockhart replied, "British Base Reinforcement Camp, it's where you'll wait to be allocated your post in Burma." After a moment where both men waited for the other to speak Captain Lockhart said, as if he were brushing a speck off his jacket "if that'll be all?"

John replied, "yes sir," turned about and marched out.

He stood outside the hut a little bemused and thought, well after three weeks I know where I'm going and I seem to have been promoted. It seemed to John that army life was just a succession of camps. He had now been in the army for ten months and the camp in Burma would be his third camp and he still hadn't got to his final posting. He shook his head and walked back to his tent. He suddenly remembered the captain said he was to sail from Madras. He thought, where the fuck's Madras and how do I get there? He thought, I can't go back and ask and I'm certainly not queuing again if I do the captain will think I'm a real clown. He walked back to the doorway and noticed a sergeant lounging in the doorway, he asked him where Madras was and how could he get there, in turn getting a smart-arse reply in a strong cockney accent, "you take a number 10 bus from the Fulham Road and change to a number 42 at Paddington Station."

"Very fucking funny mate, you should be on the stage," sneered John.

"Very fucking funny sergeant, if you don't mind," sneered the sergeant. John was tempted to challenge the sergeant, as he was now a sergeant himself, but thought better of it.

He walked away determined to go back and ask the next day.

John left it two more days before he went back to the Admin block, Captain Lockhart was nowhere to be found so he queued to speak to a young lieutenant who disappeared for a few minutes and on returning said that on the 3rd January a list of men would go up on notice board 17 listing a time and place they were to assemble to be taken by truck to the station to catch a train to Madras, more than that he couldn't say.

Christmas in camp was a fairly raucous affair. Some troops in tents further down the row John was in had managed to get hold of, or make, a sort of moonshine whisky and they could be found passed out all over the area, some on benches, some had fallen onto tents and been thrown onto the sides of the roadways by the tent owners, while two men had managed to buy camels from some locals and were racing them before they were captured and arrested by a group of military police. John smiled as he heard 'Let it snow, let it snow, let it snow', played over the loudspeakers of the camp, as it was forty degrees. He thought someone's got a sense of humour. New Year's

Eve was a more maudlin affair, as most men were thoroughly sick of the camp by then and ready to move on, or mutiny. The list went up on 3rd January as the lieutenant had stated and John found himself on the parade ground with fifty or so other men with all their kit ready to board a series of trucks.

On arrival at the station, they boarded a train, which, they were informed by the older veteran soldiers among them, would take at least three days to get to Madras. One soldier shouted in a clear Birmingham accent, "I can get back home to the fucking smoke faster than that." They were more than a little astounded when they entered the train to find they'd be sitting on wooden boards for the journey. The trooper behind John stated, "I'll have splinters in me arse for months after this."

8

John began to feel lonely on the monotonous rail journey and while the other men chatted to each other, often about mundane things and at times inane things John was content to keep his own company. He thought I put a lot of effort into making friends in Markeaton Camp and they all disappeared in different directions, I made some friends on the boat coming out and where are they now? I made more friends in Deolali Camp and none of those are with me now. "What is the point?"He repeated it and then realised he had said it out loud. The men around him suddenly stopped their conversations and John thought, I'd better be careful doing that they'll think I'm bonkers. John contented himself with looking at the landscape as it passed slowly by. He hadn't seen much of India while in Deolali Camp and so this journey provided the first opportunity to see the countryside. John's abiding impression was of the dryness of the land. Any movement produced a cloud of dust. It was a baked land, and featureless. The train went slowly enough for the passengers, if they so wished, to get a good view of Indian life alongside the railway. He saw men building with clay bricks and women carrying hods of bricks on their heads to help the menfolk. He saw young boys of no more than four or five herding sheep and some even herding cattle. Sometimes the train would stop for no reason and the men would be told it was because there was a cow on the line and the locals seemed very reluctant to move it. They had climbed for a while after leaving Bombay but now they were on a plain. The train passed mud huts with thatched roofs. The men tended to wear turbans or cloths around their heads with some wearing what looked like pyjama trousers. It was the women that were surprising and worthy of note. They wore saris, wrapped around them in the most vibrant colours. They were obviously poor judging by the tiny huts they came out of but the colours they wore were striking, brightening up a generally featureless landscape. It reminded John of books he had read with pictures of birds. Some species of male birds had quite drab plumage but the females were brightly coloured in order to attract a male. When they pulled into a station the train seemed to be surrounded by sellers of all manner of things. One soldier on the bench behind John bought a few packs of cigarettes but as the train pulled off he realised the cigarette papers inside the packets contained grass. He tried to leave the train but contented himself with shouting abuse from the train window as the Indian seller waved politely to him, knowing he was safe. The whole carriage erupted shouting in unison, "he had you." The soldier sat down cursing "the black bastard, I'll have him on the way back."

John wondered what world order had prescribed that he be born in South Wales and not perhaps here in India where he might now be herding cattle or building a mud hut for his family. When John could not answer these questions he tried to force himself to think of something else or he would take a worn paperback out of his kit bag to try to distract himself.

As the journey continued sometimes they were fed on the train out of ladles dipped into large cauldrons and sometimes the train would stop for water or coal and they would have an hour or two to have a smoke and some food. After two days they stopped at Bangalore and were told they could go into town for the day, but they had to be back to leave at seven o'clock that evening. Some of the men went looking for a bar while John palled up with two other men Rob Charnock, a fair haired sergeant from Leicester about the same height as John with an open cheerful face and Steve Robinson, also a sergeant, from Kent, who was slightly taller than John and appeared to be of a more serious disposition. They decided to wander around town. John found them good company. They browsed in a market in the centre of town, bought some food, threw some coins to children who followed them begging but then realised that this attracted a crowd ten times the size of the first group of children and they had to escape down a back alley. They eventually found a small café with a table and chairs outside which sold Indian beer, which wasn't up to British standards, but was wet. They chatted about army life, their backgrounds and their views on India. They played a makeshift game of cricket in the local park with a group of young boys who were far too good for them and eventually made their way back to the station. They sat on the train waiting for it to leave when a truck and a jeep pulled up. Four men were pulled out of the back of the truck by half a dozen burly military policemen and thrown onto the train. Two ended up on the floor of John's carriage and looked unconscious and quite badly bruised around the face. Several hours later after the train had left the station they woke up and lifted themselves onto the benches and could be heard moaning quietly for the next few hours. On arrival at Madras, they all left the train and once again boarded trucks to take them to the docks. Here they boarded an old tramp steamer, which would take them across the Bay of Bengal to Rangoon and the end of their journey. Only five days on the water, they were told. After a fairly uneventful five days, John arrived at the dockside in Rangoon, his home for the next three years.

9

After a short wait on the dockside, the troops were ordered into trucks once again and taken through the centre of Rangoon. The soldiers travelled in silence in the back of an open truck. They could see the destruction left from the war, ruined buildings and craters. It was impossible for the truck drivers to stay on one side of the road as buildings had collapsed into the road and the rubble had not been cleared. One of the soldiers shouted that he was sure he had seen a Japanese soldier in uniform on the street with what looked like a truncheon. One of the others replied that he had heard that because of a drastic shortage of men they had to release some of the Japanese prisoners for police work in the streets, directing traffic and dealing with problems with the local population. It was all a bit difficult to take in. The trucks took a sharp right turn and headed out of the city. After about ten minutes the trucks pulled into a tented camp and the troops climbed out. They were each allocated places in four-man tents, usually with men who were already settled into the camp instead of with mates they had befriended on the journey there. The army obviously thought that they would benefit from the experiences of those already in the camp.

John threw down his kit bag and sat on a camp bed identified by the other three incumbents. He introduced himself and they did likewise but that seemed to be the sole conversation he was to get from a pretty sullen bunch. Two of them left the tent together and he asked the remaining sergeant, Sergeant Marsh, how long he had been there. He replied that he had been shipped over from India at the end of the war and arrived here at the end of September. He said not to take too much notice of the three of them, as they were more than a little fed up, as they all expected to be on their way home after nearly two years service in the Far East. However, they had been told that a troopship was arriving in the following week and they expected to be on it. During the afternoon a sergeant major came around and told

John to report to the camp parade ground by six o'clock the following morning.

On reaching the parade ground the new arrivals were drawn up in order and were marched up and down to 'shake the fucking dust out of their arses' as the sergeant major so eloquently put it. Within a few minutes, a captain arrived and announced that he was Captain Smith-Hodges and that he would be their officer-in-charge until they left the camp, whenever that was. They were instructed to dress for PT that afternoon at two-thirty and that they must be available for 'fatigues' the following morning at six o'clock outside the camp stores. The PT was gruelling, a series of exercises for the first hour, followed by a five-mile run in intense heat which left them a bath of sweat. None of them felt like socialising and after their evening meal they made their way to their tents and bed. When they woke the following morning they noticed that the whole camp was up and about and making their way to what looked like a pile of railway sleepers at one end of the parade ground. The new arrivals all trooped over to the stores, dressed in what looked like rags but were known as 'fatigues.' At the stores, they were each given what looked like a small metal hand pump. They were told this held DDT. One soldier pushed the arm of the pump down and a cloud of evil-smelling smoke came out of the end of it, causing the soldier to drop the pump and run away, rubbing his eyes, much to the delight of the troops waiting behind the railway sleepers.

The sergeant-major bellowed to the troops to drop the camp beds, move them out of the tents along with the kit bags inside, remove the tent pegs and drag the tents to the side of the field. None of the new arrivals had been instructed to fill their kit bags with their possessions and so these were merely thrown to one side, whereas the more experienced troops who knew what was about to happen had filled their kit bags. The camp beds were moved and the tent pegs taken out. The sergeant-major checked the wind direction by throwing a clump of grass in the air, and then turned and set light to a wad of paper he had in his hand. He touched this to the dry brown grass at the end of the field and in no time the flames started to spread across the field. Some of the newly arrived troops found themselves in the path of the flames and were seen quickly running to the other side of the field. One soldier who was a little slower gave out a scream and slid out of the pathway of a very large hooded brown snake slithering away into the jungle away from the flames. One soldier returning to the group near to the railway sleepers shouted, "its like fucking Noah's Ark." The newly arrived troops were speechless watching a whole range of animal life scurrying away. John sidled towards the troops behind the railway sleepers who were falling about laughing. He asked, "how often does this happen?"

One of the soldiers replied "every three weeks or if we get a new batch of troops in." John could hear another sergeant who was stood behind the sleepers shout out "don't bother getting the Crazy Gang out here to entertain us, just do this every day." The troops in their fatigues were then instructed to cover their mouths and spray everything with DDT.

The following day the new arrivals in camp were ordered to one of the huts at the edge of the compound and were given lectures on life in Burma. The key things seemed to be; leave the local women alone unless you wanted to take a present back to blighty with you, always go into town in twos and threes as some men had been attacked and robbed by criminals or dacoits as they were called locally, look after all your kit at all times, as stuff would get pinched and sold to the locals, always be alert for wild animals and insects including snakes, spiders, crocodiles and even tigers and if you lost your rifle you were in 'deep shit' as it would probably be used to shoot one of your mates.

The men were given little free time in the next few weeks and one day when John returned to his tent he found only his kit remained. The others, 'the Happy Bunch' as he had christened them had been shipped out. John immediately went round to Rob Charnock and Steve Robinson's tents and told them to move over to his tent. They had also befriended Sergeant Dave 'Chico' Marling. John immediately felt more relaxed and happier than he had since leaving home, as he was able to chat and spend time with men he identified as friends.

After they had been at the camp for about two weeks they were allowed a day's leave to go into town. All three scrounged a lift on a truck going into Rangoon. They wandered around for a while, taking time over a relaxed cigarette and a beer, then they went into one of the markets and teased Steve Robinson who had haggled over the purchase of a wooden carved elephant lamp.

Chico said, "what the fuck have you bought that for? Have you got electricity on your side of the tent and you haven't told us?" The others fell about laughing and Steve tried to justify his purchase.

Rob said, "you do realise you are going to have to carry that about with you for the whole time you are out here, which might be a very long time."

They then walked into the centre of the city where they could see the huge structure of the Shwedagon Pagoda in front of them. The whole of the pagoda was covered in gold leaf, which shimmered in the bright sunlight. John was dumbstruck and stood in the middle of the road staring at it and was almost run over by a rickshaw pulled by a short muscular Burmese man, with both cart puller and passenger shouting what seemed like abuse at him. He was in total awe of this structure and was determined he would return with his Box Brownie to photograph it from every angle.

As he stood on the side of the road he was joined by a man, smartly dressed in a light grey suit and wearing what looked like a pair of expensive sunglasses. He said, "amazing isn't it, you must be seeing it for the first time, it takes a bit of getting used to. Here, borrow my sunglasses for a second. You'll be able to look at it without the reflection hurting your eyes. There are small sections of the gold leaf missing from the back where Japanese soldiers apparently tried to peel off the gold. People say the soldiers were reported and immediately arrested and publicly executed as they had desecrated a holy Buddhist shrine."

John thought for a moment and replied, "how can there be so

much gold leaf on a religious shrine when the people are so poor?"

The man replied, "it's obviously important to them and they feel the sacrifice of this wealth to their god is worth it."

John said, "our chapel back home has got a very small gold cross below the altar, a silver service of cups and dishes for communion and a stack of worthless pictures of past preachers and deacons in false gold frames, all of which has a total value of about ten quid, it doesn't make sense."

John returned the sunglasses and thanked the man. He said, "I'm a liaison official with the American government, from Chicago, Illinois and we've got the equivalent of the Shwedagon Pagoda in Chicago, New York and San Francisco, we have buildings like this dripping in wealth to our god, the dollar." He laughed and walked away. It took time for his words to sink in but John turned to watch him pass down the street and smiled at the retreating man in a suit.

For the first time in a while, John began to appreciate that he was now in the midst of a totally different culture. He thought, I left Wales, was stuck on a ship for weeks and saw nothing of the rest of the world except for a short stop at Port Said, and then I was dropped here in another world. Unless I'd experienced this I would never have been able to imagine what other cultures were like. He thought, I've never even heard of the Shwedagon Pagoda, but I've never seen anything like it.

As the evening was rapidly arriving and the men knew that darkness would come quickly they started to make their way to where they had arranged a pick-up point with the driver that had brought them in. They climbed into the back of the truck and Rob shouted out to the driver "what's that smell?", as he sat down. The driver stayed silent and a few seconds later all four of them lifted their hands from the floor of the truck, their hands covered in something evil-smelling. The driver shouted back through an open window, "Oh yea, I had to pick up a consignment of chickens for the canteen." So, on their return, a quick trip to the shower block and laundry was required for all four before they could return to their tents, all four meandering through the dark camp, naked, carrying their bundles of clothes.

The four friends passed their first three months in Burma by settling into a regular routine, adjusting to camp life, being shipped out of camp from time to time to assist in organising the movement of food and other goods at the docks and railways, helping clear the nearby airport, the odd trip up-country to escort prisoners back to Rangoon, some Japanese and some Allied miscreants who had committed a crime in the north of the country but needed to return to Rangoon for court-martial.

Finally, in March a group of twelve of the sergeants who had all arrived in Burma at the same time were brought together by their commanding officer, Captain Smith-Hodges and told that they were to be posted to HQ Burma Command in Mingaladon, north of Rangoon. Here, they would become administrators helping to organise the transference of the country to local rule. They were told that the British army was in the process of gradually relinquishing command to the Burmese and that the vast majority of troops, certainly those who had been in Burma since the end of the war, would be shipped home. Others, including those who had arrived since December, would remain in Burma as a reserve force to hand over control in an organised fashion to the locals. This might prove to be a difficult task in such a short time and their work would involve long hours and a degree of dedication to the task. The upside was that they would have access to the facilities already in the country, and used by allied troops since the end of the war, and most importantly they would be living in a wooden hut with a permanent roof over them. This brought a few smiles from the men. When the captain asked "any questions?" They all spoke over each other "what will we have to do? What facilities will we be given? How much time will we be given off? What is the food like at the camp?" and many others. The captain waited for the questioning to subside, sat back and quietly said, "no idea, find out for yourselves."

JOHN AND SAMMY

10

At the end of March 1946, the twelve sergeants were moved into a permanent barracks in Mingaladon, alongside the airfield. There they were joined by other non-commissioned officers from other parts of Burma and India and these men would become army administrators and clerks employed to organise the transition of the country from British control to Burmese control. They were to liaise with Burmese officials and Allied officers in ensuring that the country did not fall into a vacuum with the departure of Allied administrators. They would be expected to organise the transportation of troops and equipment from Burma back to Britain or other bases, and the transference of all aspects of daily life to the control of Burmese personnel. They were told quite clearly that they were still members of the British armed forces and would have to find time to train along with other soldiers. However, this would be done with a degree of sympathy to their office work, at a time when the number of tasks would grow and the number of men designated to carry them out would shrink as more and more men were moved back home.

Each of the men were given an area of responsibility, an office in one of the rows of wood and raffia huts and a team of clerks to help. These might well be Burmese, Indian, Karen, British or possibly other nationalities. They would possess a range of skills at a range of levels and each of the sergeants would manage their team and deal with them with a degree of empathy as at this time of relative confusion they were unlikely to find people with better skills. John moved his kit into the dormitory block along with his mates and was ordered to report to Major Kearns, who introduced him to Captains Elliot and Stevens. John responded to each with a sharp salute while at attention.

Major Kearns said, "first of all I want to inform you that you have been promoted to Staff Sergeant, to comply with the responsibility you will have." John thought to himself, two promotions in six months, this army life is dead easy, more money as well. Major Kearns then asked Captain Elliot to take over and show John where he would be working and who he would be working with.

Captain Elliot then introduced him to his 'bearer', a very subservient Indian dressed in a turban, a grubby loin cloth and not much else, who would be responsible for looking after him, and in particular the washing of his clothes, for a small charge. The hut was equipped with a 'char wallah' who would provide them with refreshments when required and then Captain Elliot pointed out the 'punkawallah' who would operate the air-conditioning which turned out to be a large raffia fan, which the scantily clad gentleman would move up and down creating a draught of air. Captain Eliot then took John to the office he would be working in, where he was introduced to the people who would be working under and alongside him.

These seemed a strange mix of several nationalities and both gender, as well as a range of ages and they, were aligned in front of John. Captain Elliot said that the group had been working together very effectively for the last few months. They stood in line waiting to be introduced, some looking nervous as John moved along the line. John thought this must be how King George VI feels almost every day. First in line was Warrant Officer Pettit, a British Army lady perhaps in her late forties, who technically outranked John. She looked a formidable lady and was certainly not nervous or apprehensive at meeting him. Next, he was introduced to Naik Prem Sukhinder Singh, who stood sharply to attention and saluted John, equally sharply. John returned his salute and asked if he might call him 'Prem', to which Prem answered: "I would be deeply honoured." The captain behind John smiled broadly and John moved along. Next to Prem was Private Gurung Bahadur, a Gurkha soldier who also saluted smartly while at attention. Captain Elliot felt it was important to interject and explain that the Gurkha private had been injured at the end of the war and consequently had been transferred to 'A' Branch. John quickly realised that the captain had explained this in front of the soldier to explain why a fighting soldier was now working as a clerk, so as not to disavow his honour.

Bahadur explained, "excusing me sir, I mean Sergeant but I was shot in the thigh by the extremely cowardly Japanese, as they were running away from me." He quickly added, "but, it will not stop me doing my office work extremely effectively." Both British soldiers were amused but passed on quickly.

At the end of the line were three ladies who were clearly local, or at least Asian. The first, a lady in her late thirties or early forties, introduced herself as Mrs Wilson, who shook hands with John and was clearly in service to the military. She explained that she had been married to a European, a Mr James Wilson, a Scotsman who had been arrested by the Japanese in 1942 and nothing had been heard of him since, though she lived in hope that he had been taken to Japan and some day would be found and returned. John nodded in agreement and said he was sorry to hear of her difficulties. Next, was a very smartly dressed lady, a few years younger than Mrs Wilson. She introduced herself as Mrs Thanda Jervis, the wife of an Australian who had run a local clothing business. Thanda explained that she and her husband had decided at the beginning of the war that he should return to Australia and she should return to her village in Central Burma. Her husband had survived the war and was waiting to be de-mobbed in order that he might return to Burma. She had then moved back to Rangoon to help with any work which needed doing. Finally, at the end of the line was a young attractive girl who was quite light-skinned, just a few years younger than John, and probably Eurasian, Miss Samuels, who said that everybody called her 'Sammy', and she was from Rangoon.

The following day John began work and quickly fell into a routine. The major, or one of the two captains would place documents regarding problems or difficulties that needed solving or dealing with into John's in-tray, and then John personally, by telephone or by letter would deal with each problem as it arose, and after he had solved the problem a report would be put into the out-tray ready to be filed. John's section dealt with the movement of army equipment, wherever it might be down to Rangoon for shipment to

Britain, India or Ceylon, or wherever it was required. Some problems could be dealt with easily, by a phone call, or a dictated letter, whereas some proved more difficult. Some officers involved in using equipment inland did not take kindly to being told what to do by a mere Staff Sergeant. John might have to ensure that there were sufficient drivers to bring the equipment to Rangoon, that there were ships available to take the equipment, or in the case of smaller, perhaps more valuable items that there were aircraft ready to move them to their destination. John would often stop working, look up at those typing, writing or filing and think, a few months ago I was at the bottom of the pile working in an ironmongers shop. People ordering me about and quibbling over a few pennies for this item, or whether there were the correct number of nails in a bag. Now he was ordering the transport of perhaps millions, certainly thousands of pounds worth of equipment from one part of the world to another, Phew, who'd have thought, Dennis where are you? You should see me now, he thought and laughed to himself.

One evening in early April John was relaxing in the Sergeant's Mess with a few of the other sergeants when a dark-haired man in a leather flying jacket appeared. One of the sergeants, Sergeant Tom Hollis, a thick-set Geordie with a 'boxer's nose' recognised him and beckoned to him 'come and have a beer, Clive.' Clive came in and the sergeant joined him at the bar, buying him a beer, and then moving over to sprawl himself over two seats alongside John and the others. Clive turned out to be a commercial pilot who had fought during the war. He had been de-mobbed and had then returned to Asia as a contract pilot to the British armed forces. He looked like a stereotypical American airman with a well-worn leather jacket with an eagle motif on the breast pocket and a pair of sunglasses perched on the top of his head and a scar on his cheek which he insisted was a duelling scar. He had flown into Mingaladon airfield to collect crates of personal possessions for officers who had been reassigned to Ceylon. Tom Hollis said he had met Clive on one of his previous visits. Clive explained that he was to fly to Singapore the following morning to collect the second half of his consignment. After the other sergeants had left the mess he remained talking to John and Tom about their lives at home, and in Burma, interspersed with a few funny and sometimes crude stories to spice up the conversation. At the end of the evening, Clive asked John and Tom if they would like to join him the following day.

Tom said he was on good terms with Captain Stevens and reckoned he could swing it for two days leave for each of them. He scuttled off to ask the captain while John and Clive shared another beer.

An hour later Tom came back and said, "leaves been ok'd by the captain," and then adding "but we'll have to work next weekend to make up time."

John pulled a face but kept quiet as it seemed a fair deal.

The following morning at dawn both soldiers turned up at Mingaladon airfield, John was very nervous as he'd never flown before and turning to Tom said, "I'm shitting myself. It's alright for you worldly wise buggers who've done it all before."

Tom said, "you're not on your own mate. I've never flown before and I think this is going to be a brown trouser job."

John was shocked, as Tom always appeared so confident that he thought nothing would worry him. He couldn't help thinking that appearances were often deceiving and that you had to get to know someone to find out what they were really like. In training, it was often the quiet ones who showed more determination to get a task done. He remembered one private who was continually shooting his mouth off only to cry like a baby when he was on top of a gantry and had to swing down on a rope.

Clive soon appeared and showed the two of them the small set of steps they had to climb to get into the fuselage. He then entered the cockpit and introduced them to his co-pilot Roger Freeman. He told them that the Dakota aircraft they would be flying had only two seats, one for the pilot and one for the co-pilot, and told them to find a secure space and either box themselves in or strap themselves with a piece of rope to the side of the fuselage.

Clive turned to them and offered them a mint from a bag of sweets, saying "this is your stewardess, who was wondering whether you would like any refreshments. We have mints or mints?""

Roger was heard to say, "I haven't heard that before, much." The flight took just over four hours, during which time both John and Tom had been sick several times. On landing, Clive moved back from the cockpit and immediately put his hand over his mouth.

'He said, "what the fuck's that smell?"

Tom sheepishly replied, "Ah, I might have shit myself."

John wanted to laugh and bait Tom but he just didn't have the energy.

Clive opened the fuselage door, and a set of steps was brought, "anyone coming for a beer?"

John turned and vomited all over the steps.

"Ok, perhaps later," said Clive as they moved towards the small terminal which stood as Singapore airfield's central control. The two soldiers agreed to help Clive push a large crate across to the aircraft before they went into town. John immediately asked if there was any way they could get back to Rangoon without having to go by air. Clive said they could probably get a berth on a ship but it would take them four days to get back. Both groaned and accepted they would have to make the return trip by air.

The three of them hitched a ride on a jeep going into the town centre. Clive said they had to start the day with a Singapore Sling in Raffles Hotel. The jeep dropped them off at the hotel and they proceeded to the 'Long Bar'. John bought the round of drinks, which they took to a very colonial looking veranda, equipped with sets of cane chairs, which allowed their bodies to return to earth. John took out his camera from the small kit bag he had brought and proceeded to take photos of them in 'colonial' poses, complete with bush hats.

Clive said, "I'm going to see a friend." He winked at them and said, "make sure you are at the airfield at six sharp in the morning or

I'll be going without you."

John said, "I thought we would be going back this evening."

Clive laughed and said, "and fly in the dark, we couldn't do that, it might make you sick," and with that, he left. The two then wandered off into town, visiting Chinatown, the harbour area, Nathan Road shops and markets, having a few beers along the way and finishing with a curry at a very smart restaurant. John took many photographs as he thought he would probably never come back to Singapore. They then realised they had to find somewhere to sleep. They asked a few drunken soldiers as they walked along the quayside, who pointed them towards the red-light district.

They passed from building to building as girls came out and tried to drag them in repeating "very cheap, very cheap." The two pulled themselves out of the grasp of these females, as they were either old hags or very young girls. Both men had led sheltered lives before being shipped out to Burma though Tom's appearance and demeanour belied this, and persuaded each other, and themselves that they couldn't afford to blow all their money on any of these women. The reality was that the girls frightened them to death and that after having sex they would then have to leave, still without a bed for the night. They turned a corner and noticed a YMCA building, which they approached, explaining to the burly Chinese gentleman on the door their predicament. He said he could get them a bed for a small fee. They both passed over a small amount of change and were shown to a very basic dormitory. After a decent sleep, they were up very early the next morning to catch a rickshaw to the airfield.

Clive was already there and asked with a leer "did you boys have a good night?"

Both remained silent for a few seconds until Tom turned to John and said, "well mine was great, and yours was pretty good as well wasn't she John, and we were obviously up to standard as they let us stay the whole night."

Clive patted them both on the shoulder and said, "well done

boys, you obviously kept up the traditions of the British army, you look as if you've been shagging all night."

The aircraft soon took off, with Clive pointing out the infamous Changi Jail, which the Japanese had used as a prisoner of war camp.

John tried to look out but fell across the aircraft as it made a huge sweep to the left. He quickly tied himself to one of the cross struts. The following four hours were purgatory for the two virgin flyers, who proceeded to throw up much of the previous night's curry and beers.

Clive said his goodbyes on landing, explaining that his aircraft would refuel and then he'd return to Ceylon. He shouted "see you again," as he left.

Both men returned to normal duties the following day feeling as if they had done a day's PT or a day's 'fatigues.'

11

Two weeks later John agreed to go into Rangoon with Rob Charnock. Rob was suffering from toothache but refusing to go to the camp dentist who had a reputation as a bit of a 'butcher.' They both scrounged a lift on a truck going into the city centre and got dropped off on Dalhousie Street where Rob said he had heard about a decent dentist. They asked a few Burmese who were lounging about at the side of the road, but they couldn't speak any English. Through sign language, and Rob opening his mouth and pointing to his teeth and making a face the locals seemed to understand. They pointed to an area further down the street. The dentist turned out to be a small Burmese man of indeterminate age, with a dentist chair on the pavement. John looked down at what looked like a pile of hair on the floor under the chair. He said to the man "are you a dentist?"

The man replied, "very good, very good."

Rob pointed towards where the pain came from and the man tried to look into his mouth while pulling a face. He quickly said, "will do, will do."

John said, "if he pulls teeth like he talks he's likely to pull two teeth out instead of one."

Rob sat in the chair and John, who was more than a little squeamish, said he would be back in an hour.

John wandered off towards the Sule Pagoda. Just as before when he was completely overwhelmed by the sight of the Shwedagon Pagoda the effect of the Sule Pagoda was similar. He sat on some stone steps at the side of an old pillared building and just stared at it. The gold reflected the light so strongly it was difficult to look directly at it. John was mesmerised. He watched people going in and out of the temple, many with bags of offerings to their god. He had brought his camera and took photographs from every angle. In some places the decoration, particularly on the smaller stupas, which surrounded it, was gaudy but if you just looked at the temple as a whole it was breath-taking. John had seen small temples and stupas in many areas of his Asian travels but none with this level of grandeur. For the first time, he felt privileged to see such a wonderful shrine. He thought that he must try to take it in and remember these wonders of the world, as probably when his army career was over he might never see their like again.

His mind began to wander. He thought about the fact that he was halfway around the world from Treafon, his mother, father, brother, Elizabeth and his mates. Twelve months before, he had only just started basic training, now he was a Staff Sergeant in charge of other people with a responsible job to do. He began to appreciate how his confidence had grown. He carried out tasks and spoke to all sorts of people without any further thought. He would now not be afraid to tackle anything. He wondered how this might have changed him when he eventually returned to South Wales. Would he be able to settle back into home life?

Before joining the army, he thought he would be homesick but the reality was that there was always so much to do and to see as well as the social contacts with his mates such that he rarely gave home a second thought. It was only at times like this when he was on his own and had time to relax and reflect that he gave home some thought. His mind wandered to thoughts of Elizabeth. He had written a few letters to her since he had been shipped overseas but not nearly enough. He persuaded himself that he had been very busy with all his responsibilities and had found it difficult to find time to write. The reality was that he couldn't be bothered. He had explained to Elizabeth what the voyage out had been like, what the camps on the way to Burma were like, what Rangoon was like and what his new mates were like. Then he had received a few letters from Elizabeth with little mention of Burma, or the voyage, or the other men he was with. The letters were all about Treafon, and how they'd persuaded Audrey from the shop to go to a dance with them all and how Marjorie had ended up falling out with Audrey. John couldn't believe how boring they were to read when he had made so much effort to make his letters so interesting. He stopped and closed his eyes to try and visualise Elizabeth. It cheered him up that he could see her, her smile, even laughing and the little wrinkles it created at the corners of her eyes. He remembered her hairstyle and the clothes she wore. He thought, wouldn't it be great if they could all be here to see the pagodas. Mam, Dad, David; they would be bowled over by this vision of shining gold. He checked the time and remembered Rob.

When he got back to the dentist's chair Rob was sat on the edge of the pavement, holding a rag against his mouth with lines of blood dripping off it. He tried to speak but made no sense. John quickly pulled him up and hailed a taxi. He spent all the money he had on him on getting Rob back to camp and the clinic, where they sedated him and dressed the wound. John went to see him the following day.

Rob was feeling very sorry for himself. He said, "the bastard took the wrong one out, the dentist had to come and take the one next to it out as well, I had to have fucking stitches inside my mouth."

John tried to stifle a laugh but turned to Rob and said, "very good, very good," in a mock Chinese accent.

Work routine continued throughout April. At one point John looked up from his desk pondering a problem he couldn't seem to solve. He had arranged for a huge consignment of Japanese captured equipment to be brought from Meiktila in Central Burma to Rangoon so that it could be sorted, and the useful and fully functioning could be re-used and the useless and damaged could be simply dumped or sold for scrap. He had the major's consent to bring down the equipment but now he pondered over the railway timetable and what those in charge of the railway could offer him. There was simply too much equipment for the space available. He looked up from his work and suddenly caught the eye of Sammy, the young clerk who was probably two years younger than he was. She smiled and the contrast between her even gleaming white teeth and her darker skin was alarming. John found himself suddenly smiling back, and at the same time feeling embarrassed, which caused him to look away quickly. He immediately stood up and said, probably louder than he intended 'I'm just going out for a fag, eh to collect my thoughts.' No one else took any notice and all continued doing whatever they were doing before.

John stood up and walked over to the other side of one of the huts. He sat on the steps alongside the hut and lit his cigarette. With that Captain Stevens came around the corner and after a moment's hesitation came and sat next to John. John felt slightly uncomfortable. He had never really spoken to Captain Stevens and the word amongst the sergeants was that he was 'a miserable bugger.' Officers didn't socialise with the sergeants or any other ranks and John was unnerved. He offered the captain a cigarette, who accepted it and lit up.

John tried to think of what he might say, without causing any offence, when the captain turned and said, "how long have you been in Burma?"

John answered, "since December."

The captain continued, "Ah, you haven't seen Burma at its best yet then."

John looked for a little more elaboration when the captain offered, "wait till the end of May, early June, won't be long now."

John looked at the captain "and what will be happening then?" and after a moment's hesitation, "sir."

The captain pulled his cap a little further forward, "the monsoon. You see those ditches around the camp and at the sides of the roads, what do you think they are for?"

John shook his head.

The captain continued "well they will be full of water before the end of the first day of the monsoon, and then the rain will just continue every day, perhaps until October."

John didn't know what to say, the thought of it overwhelmed him. He looked at the captain and said, "it's ok sir, I'm Welsh, a bit of rain never hurt anybody."

The captain went quiet for a minute and as he rose to go said, quite cynically, "you've never had so much rain that you want to kill people, anybody, your mates, one of the darkies, your captain, just you wait and see." He walked away a few steps and then turned and came back, he said, "Evans, I like you, you work hard, you treat people with respect, and you respect yourself, do yourself a favour, take my advice and try to book home leave for the monsoon period." With that, he walked away.

John sat for a while and thought, I don't know his first name, I've never had a real conversation with him before. Was that the closest I'll come to a friendly chat with an officer? He's obviously a posh boy, probably went to a good school, why did he want to come and talk to me? He's obviously been in Burma longer than me, probably seen some pretty horrible things during the war. Didn't seem a bad bloke, can't see him squeezing through the fence to watch the dog races back home but I could see me having a beer with him, at a push. My mam would be dead impressed if he came home with me, all posh and that. John thought, it probably took a lot for him to offer me personal advice so I might take him up on that.

With that, John decided he would go to the major the following day and request home leave. He respectfully approached the major in his office the following day, filled out a form as suggested, and four days later his request was granted. He was allowed LIAP leave from the end of July until the end of October. He let it sink in and rushed back to the dormitory to tell the others. That night in the Sergeant's Mess he was inundated with requests to take things back, letters and small items that would save the men postage. John could think only of his return home. He told the office staff the following morning and the news was received in a distinctly underwhelming fashion. John thought, I must keep this under my hat for the next few weeks so as not to bore everyone silly with my excitement.

12

'The Monarch of Bermuda' stood moored at the dockside in Rangoon harbour. She had been repainted white, but it had obviously been done quickly as patches of the beige and brown camouflage paint showed through in places. John was feeling a bit under the weather, as the sergeants had decided to throw a party the night before, to celebrate John's leave. Any excuse for a piss up, he thought. He had put his kit together the day before and had then been forced to repack, leaving clothes behind to make room for items the blokes wanted posting when he got home. His address book was filled with addresses all over Britain. He also had a bag full of photographic film, which he had kept to be developed back home as some of the men had had their films ruined by local pharmacists who didn't really know what they were doing.

The journey home would take about three weeks unless there were unforeseen circumstances, which would cause them further delay. He should be home by about the third week of August. Hopefully, there would still be a little bit of good Summer weather that he could enjoy. He looked up at the sky as the rain continued to teem down. It had got hotter as the month of May progressed, and finally, the monsoon had started on 29th May, only a sharp storm and then it stopped for two days. The 1st June brought very heavy rain. It rained so much you couldn't see more than about twenty feet in front of you. They had to rig up a clothes-line in the office to dry people's coats and shoes and socks as they worked. It was very hot and humid and steam would rise off the clothes as they dried. After the rain had started it didn't stop even for one day until he was ready to board the boat home. As the captain had said the ditches quickly filled with water and stayed that way, the overflow filled all the spaces around the huts. The raffia sprouted holes and the rain poured through, sometimes onto the paper they were working on. They started to rig up systems in the office where they could truss up their coats over their working areas to shelter the typewriters and desks underneath. The constant drumming of the rain and the shear hassle of hiding things to stop them getting wet frustrated everyone. At one point, after about ten days of rain, John stood up, threw down the sodden piece of paper he was trying to read and shouted: "how the fuck do you people put up with this pissing rain all the time?" He was glaring at the Indian and Burmese clerks who all looked down to avoid his stare. John was suddenly aware of someone behind him.

Warrant Officer Pettit made her way around the desk and with her back to the others whispered in a menacing way, "Sergeant Evans, these people live with this inconvenience every day of their lives, their calmness and continued service in adversity is to be applauded, not vilified. You would do well to remember that," and with that, she left.

John felt very embarrassed and quietly, but loud enough for all to hear said, "I'm sorry about that outburst, it was uncalled for, I am the one who needs to get used to the weather, as a visitor in your country. Please go on with your work, I'll not disturb you again." They all looked down and carried on with their work with the exception of Sammy who looked straight at John and gave him a huge beaming smile, which made John feel more embarrassed than he already was.

John hauled his kitbag onto the deck of the 'Monarch of Bermuda', and after being allocated a bunk took his kit to an area where perhaps a hundred men were already berthed. He found his bunk and lay down on it to catch up with his sleep. He certainly had no intention of going on deck in the rain.

The journey home followed a similar pattern to the journey out except that the ship docked in Colombo, Ceylon for two days, to take on supplies, which gave him a chance to take a few more photographs and to experience another country, and he didn't have to travel by rail across India, which he was truly grateful for. He found Ceylon very much like Burma, and by the second day was keen to move on. He heard that a Forces cricket match was being played on the outskirts of the city, to which he made his way. He found a deck chair, caught up with the scores and settled down to watch the game. However, within five minutes the heavens opened and the match was quickly abandoned. John had to make his way back into the city to prepare to catch the boat before it left. However, he now had time for a meal and a few beers. The remainder of the journey passed uneventfully. He played a few games of cards, lost a few pounds but didn't let it get him down. The weather improved dramatically as they came out of the Suez Canal and remained that way for the rest of the voyage. The ship finally docked in Southampton on 18th August and John managed to get a train to Newport within just a few hours, arriving at his doorstep in Treafon before dark.

13

The sun came from behind the clouds and the mountainside was momentarily bathed in afternoon shadow. How different the landscape was from Burma. The air was clear and the sun was warm as it came out from behind the clouds. John's abiding memory of Rangoon was of oppressive heat, woodland and jungle often covered in steam or low cloud as the moisture from the rain evaporated in the heat. He thought both are beautiful in their own way just part of the world's diversity. As he looked across to the other side of the valley a flock of sheep wandered across the grass, their coats regrown after early Summer shearing. All was absolutely quiet. John thought there was nowhere in the world like this. When the preacher gave sermons about 'Peace on earth', this was it. It had little to do with religion, John spiked at his own thought. He could never express that out loud in front of his mother, but even during the war you could come here just above the quarrymen's village of Bont, about two or three miles from Treafon and you could be all alone with your thoughts.

"On my second box now," his dad shouted, breaking the silence and causing John to jump as he came up behind him. John was sitting on a large grey stone.

It interrupted John's thoughts, but he quickly replied, "well done, wonder how many boxes the others have filled?" He could see three figures spread out over about three hundred yards of the extensive grass area. All three were bent over.

"How much have you got?" John's dad asked.

John was embarrassed to show him the meagre few tiny wimberries he had collected in his container. John had let his day-dreaming take over and had eventually given up on collecting the small berries. He looked down at the box his father had collected and relished the idea of the tart his mother would make with these delicious, sweet berries and her thin crusty pastry. His mouth watered and he took a sip of water from the container he had brought with him.

He popped the rubber cork off the top and offered a drink to his dad, who looked up and said, "it's a warm one now." John smiled and thought of India and Burma where the heat was relentless and where he would pray for the breeze they were experiencing at that moment.

It was the last week of August 1946. John had been home a week and a day. He had immediately gone down to Hancock's sweet shop the first morning home and he had arranged to meet Elizabeth after the shop closed to walk her home. They chatted on the way to her house. Well, Elizabeth chatted, relating to John much of what had happened in the town over the last few months. She explained the effects of soldiers returning after being demobbed, where wives welcomed their return, and some, where the homecoming was not so welcome. Two doors up from her house Mrs Morgan had been forced to move out with her two children, one a babe in arms, as her husband had failed to find work. He had come home several times in a drunken stupor, fallen asleep in the chair only to be woken by the baby crying and then taken it out on his wife by beating her quite badly, once when the neighbour, Mr Pascoe had gone in to try to protect her and had been injured himself. The woman was now living with her sister, but the husband kept appearing, threatening her unless she came back.

Elizabeth said, "see John, the end of the war is not good news for everybody."

John remained quiet and related little of his experiences unless prompted. One strange thing was that every morning he got up, and immediately put on his uniform, not so much to show off but because it was a habit. Today, however, up in the mountains he had worn trousers and an open neck short sleeve shirt. Elizabeth said she liked him in it. She said it showed there was another life besides the army.

The whole family had walked up to the mountains above Bont. Elizabeth had walked up to John's house and she, along with John, his mother, father and David had packed a picnic and come out to enjoy the good weather. It was a Saturday and Elizabeth had taken the day off. Mr Hancock was not best pleased as Saturday was their busiest day, but Elizabeth had helped him stock-take for a few evenings a couple of weeks before and was owed time off.

The five of them walked back down the track towards Treafon, the silence momentarily broken by the noise from the crushing machine in the limestone quarry. Elizabeth walked in front with John's mam and dad and David and John walked a little behind.

David was pleased to have John to himself, though he was disappointed that they would walk through town without John wearing his uniform. David had always secretly envied his big brother. Now, since John had joined the army if was more like hero worship. He quickly blurted out "so what guns have you fired?" Quickly followed up before John could answer with, "have you ever shot at anybody?"

John laughed "hey, slow down." He said, "I've passed all four levels of firing a light machine gun and a rifle, and no I've never fired at anyone. Anyway, we're not at war anymore." He suddenly remembered then, "though Ray Walker in our platoon did swing around once and let off a shot which went pretty close to the sergeant major when we at Markeaton." John smiled at the memory.

David asked, "what happened to him?" John replied "the sergeant major knocked him down, and told him the next time he did that he'd rip his ba….., um, head off," suddenly remembering he was speaking to David, his younger brother.

David followed up with, "Do you like being in Burma?"

John thought for a minute and said, "yes, I suppose I do, I've got good mates, good people to work with, though the monsoon was pretty horrible."

"I don't like it when it rains," David replied looking up to the pale blue sky.

John looked at him "it's not quite like the rain you get here, it's quite a bit heavier and it rains every day."

David looked bleakly at John and said, ""all our school cricket was called off in July and August except for two games because of rain."

John laughed, "how awful for you."

David said, "do you think you'll stay in the army after your three years?"

John hadn't given it any thought and suddenly said, "if I did we might both be in the Forces at the same time. If the government keeps it the same you might be in for four years."

David quickly replied, "I can't wait."

With that Elizabeth turned around and told the two of them to speed up and stop dawdling. David ran ahead to catch up with the three in front.

John walked Elizabeth home after they had dropped off the boxes of wimberries at the house. They both stopped to buy an ice cream from Mr Zeraschi, who had pulled up in his horse and cart.

John said to Elizabeth "now this is a business that would go down a treat in Burma. He would have a queue a mile long."

Elizabeth laughed "you'd have to eat the ice cream quickly. I'm sure it would melt if it's as hot there as you say."

John found that on the walk back to his house he was tired after all the walking he had done during the day, and he was glad to be going home to bed.

He was up early the following morning and went and sat at the kitchen table with his dad before the others had got up. He could tell his dad was itching to engage him in conversation.

"What's the Far East like then?" He asked

John smiled at the huge generalisation of the question, "hot," he answered, "and wet."

"Is there still fighting going on?" his dad asked.

"No, all peaceful where we are. I could be working in an office anywhere," John seemed to go into a world of his own. He suddenly remembered that he had gone to the local chemists on Friday and collected his photographs. He went up to his room and brought the bundle of packages of photographs down. He had only looked at them briefly and then his uncle had called to the house to see him and he had completely forgotten about them.

As he put them on the kitchen table his dad said, "better wait for David and your mam to come down, she'll play hell if she thinks I've seen them first, and it will save you explaining each photo three times." John didn't think the photos were such a big deal, they were all photos of places he'd seen in reality, but he would wait. John waited for his parents and brother, and while he waited, he lit a cigarette, forgetting the convention that if you have to smoke, then you smoke outside.

Half an hour later his mam and brother had come downstairs. His mother stood in the doorway of the kitchen "what do you think you are doing? Get that horrible thing outside or even better stub it out and put it in the bin." She brushed past him and opened the back door, making a tutting sound as she went. John threw his head back in frustration and ground the cigarette under his heel, picking up the stub and putting it in the bin. John's mam said, "we've got an hour now before chapel, so make it quick."

John felt like saying "don't bother," but kept his mouth shut. Nothing was more important than chapel. The air was a little tense and the thought went through John's mind that there seemed to be more tension every time he came home. He was about to remind his mother of his age when she sat down and picked up a package of photos, and the moment passed.

Each of them took a package of photos and John exhaustingly tried to explain each photograph to each of them in response to their questions "who's this?" "What's this?" "When did you take this?"

One comment stopped him in his tracks. His mother asked, "who are these people?"

John replied, "they are the people I work with." His mother went quiet, obviously thinking and held the photograph in her hand for longer than any of the others. John wondered what she was thinking when she suddenly furrowed her brow and said, "some of them are black people, you know Indian, or from Burma, or whatever." John smiled at the innocent comment and explained: "that's the work we do, the British troops are pulling out of Burma and we are helping the local people prepare to rule themselves, so they should be involved in these preparations."

John's mother continued to think silently about the photograph and said, "can they read and write? Will you have to help teach them these sorts of things before you come home?"

John pulled a knowing smile and said, "of course they can read and write, the people I work with all went to schools and some to higher education, colleges and universities."

His mother seemed stunned by this, and said quietly, almost under her breath, "but it's in the jungle."

John gave up trying to explain and started to name some of the sergeants he worked with in one of the photographs for his dad, telling him their names and what part of Britain they came from. David was looking at some photos of the Shwedagon Pagoda and John could see that there was no way a black and white photograph could do it justice. He explained that it was covered in gold leaf and when he explained how it shimmered in the sunlight he realised he had lost their attention, and so started to put the photographs back in the packages.

They soon all left for chapel. John was mobbed by distant members of the family, and friends, all trying to ask questions at the same time. Only those men who had been in the services gave him space as they had been through this before. Mrs Evans stood back, almost basking in the glory of showing off her son. John thought, one minute she's telling me off for smoking and the next she's telling people I'm educating all of the Burmese people ready for their independence. However, despite the supposed interest in her son all she wanted to talk about after the service was the chapel. She repeated several times "that was a wonderful sermon, though I don't know who chose the hymns? I can think of a few better choices, and 'I'm concerned for the numbers in chapel. I know there are still lots of people away because of National Service but I am concerned for the future."

John had managed to escape unseen at the end of the service and was first back to the house.

That afternoon, after chapel, he took the photographs down to Elizabeth's to show her and her father. Elizabeth was quite impressed and wanted to know more about some of the photos, but her father quickly lost interest and went back to his chair, with the view that John was an office boy, and a shame that all the fighting was over before he got there.

"Not quite the British army you fought in," John replied. "I have to do what I'm told to do and I'm trying to make the best of it to hand the country over to the Burmese as peacefully and effectively as possible."

Elizabeth's father said, "God help us, I remember standing on the side of the road when troops paraded on their way to South Africa to fight the Boer war, to keep the British Empire, and here we are now giving it away for free."

Elizabeth and John ignored him and continued to look at the photographs. Elizabeth showed the same interest in the photographs of his fellow office workers that his mother had.

John explained who they were and Elizabeth continued to ponder the photos for some time. John wondered what she was thinking and was it along the same lines as his mother.

Eventually, Elizabeth tired of looking at the photos and John had to excuse himself, as he would have to leave to go to evening service with his family.

John would have to content himself with his own company for the next few days as Elizabeth had to work, but in two weeks they had arranged to visit Joan in Bournemouth again. John was hoping that they might have been able to stay with Elizabeth's brother Wesley, who had returned from the R.A.F. and had got a job in the civil service in London, but Elizabeth said he had only been able to afford to rent a bed-sit and that unfortunately there was no room for them to stay. So, Bournemouth it was. John hoped that the good weather would continue into September so they could spend time on the beach and swim in the sea, and he thought of early morning sex when Joan and Bill were at work.

14

John lugged their cases up to the top floor flat and gave Joan a quick hug and shook hands with Bill. They sat down to the ritual of having a cup of tea and a piece of cake after their long journey. The week took a dive when Bill announced that he had lost his job with the council. He said that there was a lot to be done but the council had run out of money and had had to lay workers off. He had applied for jobs as a gardener, a warehouseman and a dockworker in Poole harbour, as well as others and was waiting to hear from them. Elizabeth looked at John who struggled to hide his disappointment, and she quickly guessed what was going through his mind. They hadn't talked about it but John thought Elizabeth was as keen to continue their physical relationship as he was.

The time passed quickly, they caught buses down to the seafront and sat on the beach and the promenade and walked through the gardens, sitting to listen to the military band playing in the bandstand. The weather was warm and dry. The first day Elizabeth was more than a little surprised, as John dressed in his uniform, but she felt proud to be on his arm as they walked along. One unusual moment came when a man walking in the opposite direction suddenly stopped and gave John a very sharp salute. John failed to return the salute as it caught him by surprise, but he turned and gave the man a friendly wave. John promised Elizabeth he would dress in civilian clothes for the rest of the week. The first four days of the week passed with John getting up to see Bill at the small table waiting to have breakfast with them both. However, on the Thursday night, Bill announced that he was sorry but he wouldn't be able to have breakfast with them the next morning as he had a job interview in a local builder's yard. John had to bite his lip to stop himself from giving three cheers. The following morning John woke to find Joan and Bill had left. He quietly pushed open the bedroom door just as Elizabeth grabbed him and pulled him in. They made love tenderly and lay in each other's arms realising what they had missed and feeling a warmth towards each other that had never really gone away. John had wondered what lovemaking would be like after such a long time, would it be like the first time, awkward and difficult or would it be like the end of the previous time in Bournemouth, warm, tender and loving with both of them seeming to be in love. They both seemed to glow in each other's company on that last day before going home, both being reassured of their mutual love for each other.

They left early on the following day for the journey home, thanking Joan and Bill for their hospitality and Elizabeth playfully scolding Joan because she still hadn't been home to see their father. Promises were made, and they left to catch the bus to the railway station.

The following week Elizabeth had gone back to work, and the weather suddenly changed. It got colder and began to rain. The sky looked grey and dark and John thought about Burma in the early part of the year, hot, humid and sometimes sunny, very different from the time of the monsoon, which was more depressing. On the Wednesday morning, he went for a walk across the town centre and promised to pick up a packet of Lipton's tea and some fresh vegetables from the market. After he had completed his shopping he called into the ironmongers for a quick chat with Lionel, who shouted out as he came through the door, "Hail, the conquering hero." John quickly and briefly outlined what he had been doing for the previous months but left as the shop filled up with customers, promising to call in before his leave was up. He went past Hancock's sweet shop and waved to Elizabeth as he passed. He had only gone a few more yards when he thought he recognised a figure shuffling towards him, all wrapped up in a forces greatcoat. He suddenly realised it was Rob, his mate from school.

John stopped in the middle of the pavement, blocking Rob's path. "Hey, how are you, didn't recognise you?"

Rob looked up and smiled "John, I didn't know you were home."

They quickly caught up with what each had been doing for the last few months. Rob was now living with his aunty as his dad had fallen ill. Rob said he thought the drink had finally caught up with him.

John noticed that the greatcoat was a light grey colour and asked, "you doing your bit?"

Rob said he was in the RAF and was now based near Hereford. He followed up with, "ground mechanic, trying my best to learn a trade."

They both parted, promising to meet in the Red Lion back bar on the Thursday night.

John had promised to see Elizabeth on the Thursday night but explained he had bumped into Rob and so would it be all right if they gave it a miss and went out on Friday night. Elizabeth seemed a bit put out and said, "I thought we were going out Friday night anyway." John pulled a face and slowly edged away.

On the Thursday night, John could see Rob arriving at the bar and quickly went to the counter to order two beers. Rob was in good spirits and John could see that he looked better, he had put weight on and his skin looked clearer. Rob explained that he loved it on the base in Hereford, didn't really enjoy coming home and that he had met a girl in Hereford that he thought a lot of, and possibly could see a future with. He explained that she was a few years older than him. She had been married before to a bloke in the Shropshire Light Infantry who'd been killed in France. She had a little girl, two years old, and Rob proceeded to pull out a photograph of the child from his wallet.

John looked at the blurry photo and thought the child looked the same as any other two year old but said, "she's really pretty Rob, well done to you." John then told Rob what Burma was like and how he had been getting on with Elizabeth. Before he could relate any more Rob asked, "and what are your plans for the future?"

John stared into space for a second and simply stated, "don't know, not really thought about it." Rob was a little taken aback and said, "you and Peter were the only ones of us who seemed to know where you were going, the Short Hand and Typing course and all that."

John looked a little blankly at Rob and said, "yea, seems to have gone out of the window a bit since I've been abroad."

The two friends had another two halves of bitter and went their own way home with no plans to meet up again as Rob was going back to Hereford the following day and didn't know when he'd be back in Treafon.

John's life followed a familiar routine in the next few weeks, seeing Elizabeth on Wednesdays and sometimes Thursdays and Fridays, cinema or dancing on Saturdays and a walk on Sundays. They saw each other often, talked about mundane things that had happened to them, or a member of the family or something that had happened in the town. John accepted the routine, which he was a little bored with, but had neither the money nor the inclination to change. As the time for him to return to the Far East came nearer he sensed a change in Elizabeth's conversation. She spoke about what John wanted to do in the future, what job did he see himself doing, and whether he was planning to come back and live in Treafon.

John didn't reply directly to Elizabeth's questions but said when he was on the boat and when he was back in Burma he would have plenty of time to himself, to think and plan. He was speechless when Elizabeth suddenly asked, "and do I figure in those plans?"

John thought for a second and replied, probably too slowly, "of course," and a second later to accentuate his reply he repeated "of course," with a little more conviction.

Elizabeth stopped walking and turned to John "sorry to say it but you don't seem too sure."

John also stopped and turned and said, "sorry, you caught me out a little then". Elizabeth suddenly walked more briskly past John and said, "well tell me perhaps when you are a little more sure, and perhaps I might decide I'm wasting too much of your precious time."

They reached her gate in silence. John gave her a quick peck on the cheek as she turned to go in and shouted after her "see you Saturday."

She stopped and turned and said, "not sure, I think I'm going out with Marjorie and Jennifer, perhaps next week if I've got time." With that, she opened her front door and walked in closing it a little sharper than was required.

John walked home realising that they had just had their first row. There was no sign of Elizabeth outside the cinema on Saturday evening, so John decided to go in anyway. Halfway through the film he got up and walked out, as he couldn't tell what the film was about. His mind had been elsewhere. When he got home only his dad was there, David had gone to a friend and mam had gone to Aunty Maggie's.

His dad said, "you're home early, any reason?"

John replied, "I don't understand women." His dad smiled, put down his newspaper and leaned forward in his chair, "what's happened then?"

John explained the heated conversation, briefly to his dad, who leaned back and said, "well you have been seeing her for eighteen months now, perhaps she's looking for something a bit more permanent. If you want to keep her perhaps you need to tell her you think you two have a future together. You've got to remember she's here in this little town all the time, you are away travelling, seeing the world, and as far as she knows perhaps seeing other girls. You've also got to remember she spends a lot of time with just her dad, and she probably gets lonely." With that John's dad went back to his newspaper. He'd said his bit and the rest was up to John.

John came out of chapel the following morning and wandered into the park. It was a dry but cloudy, cold day. By the afternoon he'd made his mind up. He'd go down to Elizabeth's and apologise. He walked down to the bottom end of town, then realising he was missing Sunday school that afternoon. He thought to himself, I'm nineteen, still going to Sunday school, things have got to change. When he got to Elizabeth's house her dad said she had gone to Jennifer's for the afternoon and that she had seemed a little upset for the last few days.

John didn't elaborate but shouted, "see you" as he closed the gate.

When he got to Jennifer's he knocked, and Jennifer came to the door. Very formally she asked, "and you wanted?" He asked to speak to Elizabeth.

Jennifer was just about to say that Elizabeth didn't want to speak to him, when she brushed past Jennifer and said, "it's ok, I'll see you again in the week."

John and Elizabeth crossed the railway bridge over the multiple railway lines and were suddenly enveloped in smoke as a train pulled into the station below them. They were both used to this and stopped while the train moved slowly on. They entered the park gates and into a totally contrasting environment. While the Summer had passed there was still colour to be seen in the flower beds and the planters placed alongside the gravel path.

John said he had misread the situation, and of course they had a future together. Elizabeth seemed relieved and they agreed not to discuss things any further. John would be leaving on the following Thursday and they promised to sit down and talk frankly on his next leave. Elizabeth pulled a face when John said that could be as far as twelve months away, or even more, but he promised to write, and so did Elizabeth.

John's mother was stood in the kitchen doorway when he got back, "and where were you this afternoon. Too important for Chapel, are you? They did notice you couldn't be bothered to go."

John's father quickly stepped in "now Charlotte, leave the boy alone, he had things to do."

John's mother turned to go into the kitchen. "On his head be it," he could hear her mutter.

Elizabeth and John saw each other every day until he left early on the Thursday morning to travel up to Glasgow, to catch his ship back to Burma. The tension between them relaxed and by the Wednesday evening John began to realise that Elizabeth would genuinely miss him, and he realised he would miss her. He said his goodbyes to his dad and David, and his mother's animosity seemed to vanish as she threw her arms around him.

15

The kit bag flew out of the back of the truck and John quickly followed it. “Cheers mate”, he shouted to the driver, who raised his hand out of the open window and accelerated away. John looked around at the familiar scene, nothing seemed to have changed. He was relieved to be back but he couldn’t work out whether it was a relief to be settled after a long journey or whether he had genuinely missed Burma. He dumped his kit bag on his camp bed and wandered over to ‘Admin’ to look for the major so he could report back. He was told the major was up-country and wouldn’t be back for four or five days.

He asked for Captain Elliot and the corporal who was sat at his desk typing chuckled as he said, “he’s gone mate, after the fuss.”

John asked, “what fuss?”, and the corporal replied, “can’t rightly say, sarge, only Captain Stevens here at the moment.”

As he could see the corporal was not prepared to offer any more information, John left the hut and crossed over to Captain Steven’s office.

John saluted smartly in front of the captain sat at his desk, who replied, “at ease,” followed a second or two later, as he looked up from his desk with “you’re back Evans, enjoy your leave in the coal tips?” and smirked at his own joke.

John replied, “very good sir.”

The captain said, “a few changes since you’ve been away, Captain Elliot has ah.., returned home, oh and Mrs Wilson has gone back to her umm plantation, a few hundred miles north I believe, so you’ll be a few hands short, I’m afraid. They’re not going to replace Mrs Wilson so you’ll all just have to work a bit harder. The work has piled up on your desk a bit I’m afraid. So, best get to it then.”

John had had little to do with Captain Stevens apart from the monsoon conversation up until then, and didn't like his tone, a real smarmy git, if you ask me, he thought. He saluted, turned about and left.

John walked to his office, and on entering, the Gurkha private, Gurung Bahadur jumped up on noticing John. Saluting, he said, "welcome back sergeant."

John replied, "what's all the formality for Gurung, pretend I've never been away." Prem waved from the other side of his desk. Mrs Jervis was nowhere to be seen and Sammy looked up and gave one of her lovely broad smiles. John looked away in embarrassment at Sammy's smile and wondered where Mrs Jervis was. Prem shouted, "Mrs Jervis has gone down to the docks as there's a problem with the loading apparently, oh and Mrs Wilson has gone." This report was met with a stifled giggle from Gurung who attempted to boyishly hide behind his typewriter.

"Come on then you lot, what's been going on?" John asked. This was met with silence. John repeated "well?"

Prem came around from his desk and sat opposite John, ready to explain.

Sammy quickly interrupted with "it's nothing to do with us and you shouldn't be gossiping." Prem waved away her interjection.

He started in an Indian broken English description "it seems that Mrs Wilson and Captain Elliot were how's your fathering."

John failed to understand, and in the meantime, Gurung shouted: "they had been at it."

John was beginning to understand, but then suggested, "Mrs Wilson didn't have a husband, well they hadn't found him anyway."

Prem said, "but Captain Elliot did have a wife."

John asked, "how did anyone find out?"

Prem replied, looking at the others "well, we knew, so I guess it wouldn't take long for others to find out. Obviously the major got to hear about it and now as Sergeant Charnock says 'his arse is back in blighty."

John looked at Prem and said, "thanks for that very vivid description."

Sammy looked up and said, "I still don't think you should be gossiping about it. Mrs Wilson was a very nice and a very lonely lady and she got very upset and embarrassed when the story came out. Anyway, she's gone back to her home now and we will have to do her work as well. It's no laughing matter."

John turned to her "quite right Sammy, well said. Well, we've all got work to do. I'll go and have a shower and change after travelling and come straight back."

That night John went into the Sergeant's Mess for a beer to be welcomed by all his old pals, Rob Charnock asked, "what's the weather like back home?" and Tom Hollis smirking, asked him "did you fly back?", alluding to their Singapore excursion. From the back of the group, another sergeant pushed through.

John had to do a 'double-take' but then recognised 'Chico Marling' who had been transferred to 'A' Branch from Northern Burma while John had been on leave.

"Chico, bloody hell, didn't think I'd see you again."

Chico answered, "hoping were you, Taff?"

They all told their stories about events over the last few months, including the incident with Captain Elliot, the quiet evening turned into a party and John woke the following morning with a 'thick head.'

One morning during the following week Mrs Jervis asked if she could speak to John in private. John followed her out of the office and both walked towards the perimeter fence.

Mrs Jervis explained, "my husband is still in Australia. He had intended to come back to Burma, but I received a letter last week saying that he had found a job in Sydney and because of the tension in Burma at the moment it would be unsafe for either of us to settle here. Also, that the future doesn't look too good with Burma gaining independence. To cut a long story short, he'd like me to join him in Australia."

John turned to her and smiled "I fully understand. Obviously, I'm going to miss you and your work, which was excellent, but you have to do what's best for you."

Thanda Jervis said, "I'm very apprehensive about moving to Australia. I realise I am only going to be able to move there because I'm married to an Australian. Do you think I'll be accepted into white society, it keeps me awake at night, I really fear moving there?"

John replied, "I've never been to Australia and I don't even know any Australians except for those I've met since I've been in Burma, but they seem like good people, perhaps they drink a little too much, but generally they seem to treat everyone including the local population very well."

She seemed a little reassured as she left to go back to the office. Ten days later a little party was held for her in the office.

John asked, "do you want me to ask the major if we can hold it in the sergeant's mess?"

Thanda Jervis became agitated and quickly said, "no, definitely not. I don't want a fuss."

John asked cook to bake a cake and he bought a few bottles of sparkling wine, which was pretty horrible, but no one complained.

Then John had to make a speech for the first time in his life. He stood and banged a spoon against a glass to get order. There were about fifteen people there including Major Kearns and Captain Eliot. It was fair to say that John was in local parlance, 'shitting himself.' "Well, we have gathered here," immediately Tom Hollis interjected, "for the marriage of….."

Everyone laughed and John continued "anyway Mrs Jervis, Thanda, is leaving to start a new life in Australia. She has been a wonderful worker since I arrived in Burma and she will be sadly missed, so Thanda, if it doesn't work out you can always come back and work here." Suddenly realising he had overstretched his authority he blurted out, "as long as Major Kearns says it's ok."

Luckily, Major Kearns nodded his head and said, "anytime."

John then presented Thanda Jervis with a prettily wrapped package. The four workers in the office had contributed to the present, though John had given by far the largest share. John had gone into Rangoon to buy a fountain pen and a bunch of flowers and had been very embarrassed bringing the flowers back into camp, receiving several comments from the camp guards as he entered, related to his sexual orientation. John had told them to "fuck off," in no uncertain terms. Sammy had wrapped the present, very delicately.

John felt he had said enough and turning to Mrs Jervis he raised his glass and said, "good luck for your future." All raised their glasses and this was followed by a few words from the major. John heaved a sigh of relief and started to shuffle away.

Rob Charnock passed him and said quietly "and then there were four." As John moved to one side he felt a touch on his shoulder and as he turned around he noticed Sammy, drawing her arm away. She said quietly "that was really good, I couldn't have done that," with a look of admiration in her eyes.

John felt himself puffing his chest out and saying, "thank you, Sammy," but quickly moved away as he noticed Captain Stevens watching him.

16

The next few weeks were hectic as John tried to differentiate between the work, which was urgent, and needed to be dealt with immediately, and the work which could be left. He often worked weekends, on his own, to help them to catch up and by the end of November, things got easier.

One late Saturday morning a group of about eight of the sergeants decided to go for a swim in Victoria Lakes that afternoon. John had hitched a ride up to Victoria Lakes a few times on his own and thought it was a beautiful place. The lake was still unless rain was expected when the winds would whip up the surface into small waves. The lake was surrounded by palm trees which provided much needed shade. It was a favoured spot for servicemen who would go swimming, particularly during the hottest weather and for locals, many of whom would walk around the edge of the lake in the evening time. At the one end of the lake was the Officer's Club which was based at the local Yacht Club and was out of bounds to all non-commissioned personnel.

They piled into two jeeps and travelled the twenty minutes or so up to the lakeside. It was a beautiful day, the water was cool, and many servicemen had the same idea. One of them had found a ball and for a while, they played volleyball in the water over a net, which someone had rigged up.

It had been great fun, and so the following weekend they decided to repeat the activity. Well, nearly the same. Steve Robinson, one of the sergeants who had arrived in Burma at the same time as John, thought it would be a good idea to invite some of the Karen and Burmese girls who worked in the offices. Three had agreed, with much persuasion, including Sammy. They managed to commandeer jeeps and arranged to meet the girls at the lakes. They found a spot on the grass banking and the girls arrived shortly after. John nodded to Sammy when one sergeant was loudly shouting out their names, to introduce them to everybody, but John steered his way onto the opposite side of the group away from Sammy when they sat down to sunbathe. At one point when most of the group had gone into the water to swim Sammy made her way across to John and said, "if it's embarrassing I will go home? it's no problem, I understand."

John turned and said, "no, no it's not a problem really, you enjoy yourself."

Sammy replied, "I promise I will say nothing to those in the office, and all will be the same on Monday when we are back."

John avoided looking at Sammy as she had this ability to appear to be looking down but would look under her eyelashes, which John found very sexy.

John said, "that's fine, please enjoy your swim," as he tried to think about anything except this exotic young girl who was sat very close to him.'

It got considerably worse when Sammy went back to her place and stood up to remove her sarong. She had a clinging one-piece swimsuit, which had small lemon and lavender coloured flowers on it. The contrast with her dark and wonderfully nubile figure was astonishing. John allowed himself a glance but quickly looked away. He allowed himself a longer look when he could see that Sammy was facing away from him as she moved towards the water. The thought struck him that it looked as if the flowers had been painted onto this beautiful body, so close-fitting was the swimsuit. John became aware of a little discomfort and leaned forward in case it was obvious. He was very glad when Sammy began playing with the group, throwing a ball about, as most of her body was below the waterline and could no longer be seen. Immediately she entered the water John noticed that Steve Robinson was spending a lot of time with her. He playfully came up behind her and ducked her head gently under the water and could be seen chatting to her whenever there was an opportunity. Oh well, good luck to him, John thought, but he couldn't help feeling a little jealous. The remainder of the afternoon saw John going into the water when Sammy came out and vice versa. John wasn't sure whether this was obvious, but no one said anything.

Christmas came and went. The sergeants had decorated the mess and one of them had baked a Christmas cake. They managed to procure by fair means and foul all the trimmings for a proper roast dinner.

Chico commented, "it seems strange to be having a cooked dinner when the temperature outside is in the high eighties." Someone had got hold of a crate of whisky and the whole evening started to get a little silly.

The following weekend six of the Staff Sergeants thought they would do something a little different, under Tom Hollis' instructions. They took two jeeps into the forest west of Victoria Lakes and parked them under the trees. They followed Tom, who seemed to be the only one who knew what was happening. As they came out of the trees Tom told them to drop down to the level of the long grass. In front of them was a large lake and above them the Yacht Club, which was strictly out of bounds to anyone except officers. They crawled past a small guard hut, which was occupied by a local who appeared to be fast asleep. Tom gradually got to the edge of the lake and got into one of the sailing boats at the lakeside. The others got the idea and the six of them got into two of the small yachts, three sergeants in each. Tom immediately got out and unhitched the remaining small boats and tied them to the back of the two occupied boats. They slowly rowed out into the lake, trailing the empty boats behind them and using their hands as paddles to propel them forwards. The two sergeants with sailing experience unfurled the sails on both boats, and the small boats picked up speed with the breeze, moving them towards the opposite shore. After about twenty minutes they could hear shouting from the shoreline. There stood an officer with his army jacket over a t-shirt and shorts, with a young girl, with the obvious intention of taking her out in one of the boats. He was shouting to the occupants of the rows of boats, which were by now in the middle of the lake. The sergeants, being very careful to face away from the shore so as not to be recognised, waved at the officer. The manoeuvring of the boats took no little skill, as they had to constantly move away from the shoreline but still had to take advantage of the wind. This was so that they could not be identified.

When it became clear that they were not going to take the boats back the officer left the young girl and went up to the Officer's Club. A few minutes later he returned with a soldier, who had presumably been standing guard at the club, and was equipped with a rifle. The officer could be heard shouting at the private, and eventually the private was seen to remonstrate with the officer. It became clear that the officer was trying to persuade the soldier to fire at them in an attempt to get them to bring the boats back. Eventually, the soldier raised his rifle and fired into the water, perhaps fifty feet from where they were. The officer began to berate the soldier for his poor accuracy and then the officer grabbed the rifle and fired a shot, this time a little nearer to the boats. Tom started to hurl abuse at the officer and the soldier while still looking away from the shore, and the others began to laugh, a little from humour at the situation and a little from nervousness that they might actually get shot. The breeze picked up and the boats moved further towards the opposite shore.

John noticed that the officer, who appeared to become more irate was now joined by several other officers, who had gone to investigate what all the fuss was about. He further noticed that all the officers were stood holding a drink and that some of them stumbled a little and looked a bit worse for wear. He could hear a few shouting at the officer who had first appeared "come on Spotty old man, shoot the bastards." The noise level from the shore increased.

The officer took one more shot at the boats and fortunately was woefully off target. A huge cheer was raised from the drunken officers. Tom Hollis pulled the tiller around to allow the boat to head for the opposite shore, eventually grounding his boat on the far bank. The other boat did likewise. All six of the sergeants pulled their hats down and their t-shirts up to hide their faces, though they realised they could not be identified at this distance. They pulled the boats onto the bank and hauled the ropes connecting the boats that they had trailing behind them, leaving all six yachts in a neat row. They then crept into the forest on the far side of the lake, all the time making sure they couldn't be seen. They gradually made their way back around the lake under the cover of the trees. When they came around to the back of the officer Tom walked over to him saying "what's the matter, sir, anything I can do?"

By this time all of the other officers had got bored with the entertainment and had gone back into the club.

The original officer said, in quite a posh accent, "those bastards over there have stolen the yachts. I came out for a pleasant afternoon with this young lady," indicating a girl who looked thoroughly fed up with the whole incident, "and some complete arseholes have gone off with them. If I could only catch them I'd give them what for."

The armed private at his side looked carefully at Tom and suddenly realised that he was one of those in the boats, until a few minutes ago. Tom, who was stood behind the officer put his finger to his lips and winked, and the soldier worked hard to stifle a giggle.

The officer said, looking at the soldier, "it's not fucking funny, you know, wasted my day off. I've a good mind to send you around there to get those yachts back."

The private replied "wouldn't be much good me doing that sir, I've no idea how to sail one of those."

Tom suddenly said, "I think I remember some engineers planting a minefield there a few days ago to create a perimeter for the officer's club, to protect them, you know, with all the terrorists and criminals wandering about."

The officer started to walk off, dragging the young girl behind him "I'm really pissed off, I really am."

The private looked at Tom with a huge grin and said, "the owl and the pussy cat went to sea in a beautiful pea-green boat."

Tom interrupted "they took some honey and plenty of money wrapped up in a five-pound note," and with that, they both fell about laughing.

Tom made his way back to the jeeps to tell the others of his conversation with the officer. He jumped into the jeep saying, "always good to have a bit of fun at their expense, they've got all the money, but no sense of humour."

A few days later Major Kearns got the men together to instruct them that under no circumstances were they to go anywhere near the Yacht club as there had been an incident where several boats had been stolen.

Chico looked up and said to the major "big things to pinch, those sir. You need to be looking for someone driving boats on wheels."

The others struggled to keep straight faces and the major left.

John thought that in many ways life in the camp and around HQ Burma Command was much the same as it was before he had left for his leave. However, he had to accept that life outside the camp had visibly become increasingly tense.

When they chatted in the mess Tom mentioned, "I would have expected things to be more stable now than they had been at the end of the war. I would have thought life in the country would have settled into a more peaceful pattern as the country got back to normal, but now there are far less British and Indian troops to keep control." Tom was considered to be the clever one amongst them. He had been to private school and had good qualifications and was ready to go to university after his army service. He didn't know what career he wanted to follow but he thought that studying Economics would be a good bet. He thought economic planners would be needed as countries struggled to make headway after the war.

Rob Charnock said, "nobody'd take you seriously with that broken nose. You need to be looking in the wanted ads under 'gangster."

Chico piped up "I think you should be a banker so when I need a loan I can come to you and you'll be able to offer me very favourable rates."

Tom laughed "if I thought you were a good bet to repay the loan,

Chico, I'd be locked up. You're useless with money, you lose more than you win when you play cards and you still continue to play. Who in their right mind would give you money?"

There seemed to be total agreement in Tom's view of Chico. Tom carried on, "there are only eighty thousand troops left in Burma and over twenty thousand of those are in the Burmese army. I've heard that Aung San is the preferred choice of the British government and that he's agreed to travel to London to meet with the British government to form an agreement for the setting up of the Burmese government."

Aung San had initially supported the Japanese at the beginning of the war but towards the end had switched sides to support the Allies. Some thought this too convenient, to switch sides to the winners at the end of the war. However, Aung San was anti-communist and that was good enough for the post-war British government. There had been a good deal of gossip and information in the press about the handover of control in India and that the British government would be keen to make an agreement with a future government of Burma so that all troops could be pulled out. This would mean a saving to a cash-strapped government in London, but they would want the country to be left to a safe pair of hands.

Tom mentioned, "I've heard rumours of a general strike in Burma to put pressure on the talks in London and that a lot of people including British officers are concerned about what might happen in Burma when Aung San leaves for the talks."

Chico asked, "why is that?"

Tom explained "Aung San leaves behind a very heavily armed militia of about ten thousand men. You know what it's like here, someone who fancies power for themselves might take it upon themselves to try to take control while Aung San is away. I think we all need to be careful."

John left the mess with much to think about. He had escaped the war but perhaps there was more danger to come.

17

Over the next few weeks, information was drip-fed to the soldiers in 'A' Branch, some from the media, some from the officers and some from the office workers who lived in the community. The stories highlighted shootings, robberies and people disappearing, some who might well have been kidnapped and ransomed and some going of their own free will. The results of the talks in London and Aung San's return were reported in the press and suggested that the handover of the country to the Burmese government and the Burmese army would take place on 1st May 1947. Burma was a jigsaw puzzle of different ethnic groups all wanting to have a degree of control, particularly in their homeland areas. Thrown into this mix were the Japanese. There were still thousands of Japanese prisoners who had been used to help administer relatively harmless areas of life, but their plight came to the fore when three Japanese were killed in Maymyo after some items of handicraft had been seized. Japanese prisoners were allowed to make items of handicraft, including paintings, and sell them through an established scheme. It came to light that the prisoners in Maymyo were trying to sell their products outside the scheme, and they were confiscated. The upshot was that the prisoners attacked their Indian Pioneer guards with picks and shovels, three Japanese were killed and nine wounded. It all added to the confusion and the tension.

Earlier in the year, there had been two general strikes and lorry-loads of students drove around Rangoon shouting at anybody who represented the Empire or authority.

John and Chico were sat on the steps of one of the huts after their lunch having a cigarette. John said, "I am more concerned than I have ever been since I arrived in Burma. When I go out of the camp I see more people staring at me as if I'm the next target."

Chico replied "we've just got to see our way to the end of our stint next year and leave this god-forsaken place. Let 'em fight over it when we've gone."

John said, "yea, but I feel we've got to try and leave it in a stable situation, or at least peaceful, if only for the good people we work with, the clerks and secretaries don't deserve us leaving a mess. I don't give a toss for the communists or the dacoits but if we were to just leave this place in a mess l don't want to be reading about a civil war after we get back home."

All of a sudden there was a commotion, which sounded like someone skidding through the dirt, followed by raised voices. John and Chico jumped up and ran around the back of the hut where another hut faced them. The scene they arrived at was to see Sergeant O'Rourke, a burly man with a broad Irish accent, standing over a native bearer in a loincloth. O'Rourke was bawling at the man, but a combination of the broad accent and the words he was shouting running into each other meant that neither Chico nor John could understand much of what was shouted. Chico, though nearly a foot shorter, immediately stood between the sergeant and the native. O'Rourke pushed Chico on top of the bearer and John without thinking grabbed O'Rourke, who turned around and took a swing at him. In turning, he failed to notice Chico who by this time had got back to his feet and taking advantage of O'Rourke being unbalanced pushed him to the floor. John landed on top of the Irishman and held him down until he had calmed down.

O'Rourke got to his feet and muttered "English bastards," under his breath.

John smiled at him in a part menacing way and said, "Welsh bastard, actually."

Chico turned to O'Rourke as the bearer stood and moved to run away. Chico told him to stay where he was.

O'Rourke started to brush the dirt off his uniform and looking at John and Chico said, "the little fucker was taking my money."

The bearer started to interject, speaking quickly "Sarge, he ask me to clean shoes, no take money."

After a few minutes, it was established that the bearer had indeed been asked to clean O'Rourke's boots and that was where he kept his money. The native stated that he had to take the money out of the boots to clean them.

O'Rourke shouted back at the man "you're a thieving black bastard and I don't want you anywhere near my stuff."

John and Chico looked at each other and both could see that they were not getting anywhere. John said that he would try to swap the native bearer with one of the others and after the native had walked away he told O'Rourke to go get himself a drink or go for a walk while he calmed down. Chico and John walked back to the hut to continue their work, assuming the problem was solved.

Two days later O'Rourke, a hard-drinking Irishman, had gone into Rangoon with a group of mates. On their way back to camp O'Rourke had gone down an alleyway for a piss as the others ran to get to the truck that was taking them back to camp. O'Rourke could suddenly feel arms around his neck and a hand in front of him holding a knife. The two men holding him were masked and his wallet, watch, hat and boots were taken from him. For the next few days, he went in search of the native bearer but he was nowhere to be found.

Chico had heard about what had happened, and as he passed O'Rourke said, "be nice to the natives now, or they might cut your balls off next time."

Discussion in the Sergeant's mess revolved around how much safer it was in Rangoon than up country, despite the odd incident that could happen in any other city in the world. Up-country where groups of dacoits, criminal gangs and groups of communists were terrorising the local population and any British or Empire troops that were left there. U Saw and Ba Sein, two other influential politicians, had refused to sign the Burma White Paper, which paved the way for Burmese independence, and this further increased the chances of trouble in the future. Elections were due to be held in April and the communists had already said they were going to try to disrupt the process. In early March Indian army patrols were sent into the delta area as part of 'Operation Flush', which was intended to do just that, to flush out dacoit groups from the area. The dacoit groups, numbering in the hundreds, did not take kindly to the operation and derailed a train, attacking it with rifles and bren guns. Agreement had already been made with the leaders of the frontier states at Panlong, who would now send representatives to the new Constituent Assembly. Aung San was beginning to be seen by the British authorities as a bolster against the communist groups and a worthwhile statesman, and there seemed to be more confidence in the future for Burma.

In the meantime little changed at Burma Command, the work towards the election and Burmese independence continued. John and the other soldiers based there worked hard and enjoyed their leisure time. They went swimming regularly at Victoria Lakes. The group of local girls had increased in number to include friends of friends and John felt that Sammy could be relied upon to keep work and pleasure separate. They would even chat while they were sitting on the grass bank surrounding the lake and nothing would be said or intimated when they returned to work on a Monday. John could admit to himself that he liked to sit and look at Sammy when they were at the lake. She seemed to have a wide range of swimming costumes, one in particular was his favourite, in a plain mid-brown colour, which matched her skin colour and from a distance looked as if she was naked. All of the costumes seemed to enhance her slim and shapely figure. He liked her pleasant innocence and allowed himself the pleasure of looking at her in the office when he thought that nobody else was looking. However, he knew he had to be careful as once or twice she had turned to look at him when he was looking at her, causing him to quickly look away, Once, he was sure that he saw her smile when their eyes had met.

Both at the lakes and in work John would notice Steve Robinson trying to chat with Sammy and while John did not go out of his way to speak to Sammy he felt that Steve viewed him as a competitor for her affections. On a few occasions, Steve would answer John quite brusquely, and tension started to rise between them.

When he was back in the dormitory barracks he read or wrote letters to his parents or to Elizabeth. He had been back in Burma for four months and was finding the routine of writing home a chore, to think of new things to say, to describe things that happened in the camp or Burma in general, that would have some meaning for those back home.

In the Sergeant's Mess one evening in March John was sitting quietly having a beer with Tom Hollis and Rob Charnock. They talked about their girlfriends back home, and they talked about the difficulties they might face when they left the army, with high unemployment in the country, continued rationing and low wages. Sometimes they talked about camp life but rarely did the conversation centre on Burma and its problems. In the corner of the mess sat O'Rourke and a few of his cronies. John noticed that Steve Robinson spent more time in O'Rourke's company in recent days and was with him and his cronies at that point. They had been in the mess when John, Rob and Tom arrived and were drinking heavily. Every so often they would look over at John and the other two, and clearly they were either talking about them or pretending that they were. As time went on the three realised that if they stayed in the mess much longer things could get nasty and so after a long day in the heat they decided to go to bed. As they passed the Irishman and his cronies one of them said, "nigger lover" under his breath. John stopped next to them, glaring at Steve Robinson and saying "you can laugh at that here, and then when you are out at the lakes you can't leave Sammy alone. You fucking hypocrite."

Steve Robinson stood up and squaring up to John said, "I don't think that's any of your fucking business really."

The atmosphere was very tense and the sergeants with John realised that a fight would result in both John and Steve being put on a charge. Tom grabbed John's shoulder and pulled him away, calming him down as they went back to the dormitory. John walked around for a while and had a cigarette while he calmed down.

It was still early and John found it difficult to sleep in the heat and so read for a short while, and then put the book down. He thought about the Burmese people, in general, not anyone in particular. What would happen when the army pulled out? There were too many guns in Burma, as he had noticed when he travelled around the area, ordinary people walking along the roadside with rifles, for apparently no reason. Once you went outside Rangoon the country was lawless and it wasn't just the troops who were under threat, the different factions were threatening, and killing each other. He thought about people like Mrs Wilson, whom he had worked with when he arrived in Burma. She was Eurasian and had moved back to her plantation in Central Burma, would she now be safe? Many of the industries had been set up by Europeans before the war, would they now be safe, or would they have to move back to Europe?

John thought about life back home. The election at the end of the war had brought in a Labour government, which promised to improve life for people like those in his family. He thought Burma could do with a few promises like that, but what a long way they would have to move to give these people a standard of living that was anything like the one he was used to. He said out loud "I'll never complain again."

John's thoughts went back to the incident between O'Rourke and the native bearer, the hatred in O'Rourke's eyes when he was berating the bearer showed genuine hatred. John had never experienced racism at home. There were no black or coloured people in Treafon. The closest was 'Darkie Williams', a tough market trader who people said had moved up to Treafon from Cardiff where his father had been a seaman and had lived in the docks area. John had seen Darkie's wife and she was definitely white. O'Rourke's actions stuck in his mind, he had treated the native unfairly, not giving the man a chance to explain and John didn't know whether O'Rourke's robbery had been due to the native or whether it was just coincidence, but the hatred and the bad treatment had come from O'Rourke first, who he thought should have known better. John felt uneasy about the whole thing. He had made a friend of his own bearer, or at least as near as language would allow it. He had tried to teach him correct

English and the native seemed to appreciate it and respect him. John slipped him a few extra coins every so often. If something had happened between them he wouldn't have attacked the man, he would have tried to find out what had caused the problem. John also thought about Steve Robinson, who could chat up Sammy, a Burmese girl, but could laugh at O'Rourke's racist comments. How could people change like that? How many O'Rourkes and Robinsons were there in the world? It was probably for the best that the British and Indian armies would pull out and then the Burmese could be allowed to sort out their own problems.

John found it hard to believe how different he felt since he had been in Burma. He wouldn't have given politics a second thought back home or worried about people's living conditions or his responsibilities. He tried to treat people fairly and with respect and it seemed to work, as they treated him with respect, but he hoped that despite his rank they thought of him as a friend, or at least someone they could take their troubles to.

John tossed and turned and couldn't get these thoughts out of his mind. His thoughts turned to Sammy in her bathing costume. He smiled to himself and thought how much he liked her company. She was honest. Yes, she was innocent but there was real integrity there. She didn't want to upset anyone, British, Indian or Burmese. He knew nothing of her background or her life outside of the camp and swimming at Victoria Lakes. The best conversations were at the lakes where she probably felt she could speak more openly, where she couldn't in the confines of the camp, where John was technically her boss. With those pleasant thoughts John eventually fell into a not altogether dreamless sleep.

18

Ten sergeants were stood in two rows in front of Captain Stevens. Once they were at ease he explained, "each of you will be in charge of a squad of Indian army troops or Gurkhas, you'll be put in a rota to patrol the streets of Rangoon during the forthcoming election. Each squad will have a signaller with a radio in case of trouble and a further ten to twelve men. You will draw rifles and sten guns from the armoury and return them after each patrol. You are to look out for signs of anyone interfering with the election or causing trouble. If you have any cause to arrest anyone the person or persons causing the trouble are to be held under armed guard. You radio back to HQ and a truck or jeep will be sent. Under no circumstances are you to bring the person or persons back to camp as this will breach security."

John's patrol went out on the following week. This was the first occasion that he could be said to be in combat, or at least the potential to be in combat. John had an Indian army naik, equivalent to a corporal in the British army who patrolled on one side of the street and he patrolled on the other. All the men were very wary, though the civilians seemed used to an army presence and went about their business with little concern for the soldiers. On the previous Friday, a patrol had encountered a demonstration of about fifty to a hundred people with banners, who were communist supporters, who continued marching through the centre of Rangoon. All was fine and the squad stood back and let them shout their slogans until someone picked up a stone and hurled it at a picture of Aung San which had been put up on the outside of one of the shops. Several men came out of the shop and a scuffle took place on the pavement. The squad quickly moved in to separate the two groups and two men were arrested, one from each side. After perhaps thirty minutes a small truck pulled up and the two were loaded into the back under armed guard. When the sergeant radioed in to ask if all had gone well with the arrested men he was told that an armed robbery had taken place at the same time, about a mile away, and that the demonstration had been a cover to draw the troops away from the area where the robbery had taken place. The sergeant, who was now feeling less pleased with himself simply said, "you can't win, can you?"

John's patrols went unhindered through the elections, except for a fight between a husband and wife, which was quickly settled with the threat of arrest. Finally, the result was announced on all radio stations including the one the army listened to, Burma Broadcasting Service, with a resounding victory for Aung San and the socialists. That night the sergeant on patrol had more problems than any other patrol, in dealing with drunken revellers celebrating. Forty arrests were made, but all were released the next morning without charge, and forty dishevelled men left the small compound at the side of the army camp to make their way back home to the city.

The following month passed quietly with preparations for the Burma army to take over in June. The monsoon had started and John felt depressed at the change in the weather. After two weeks of consistent rainfall, he was fed up of getting wet and drying his clothes, and even more fed up that the rain had stopped their weekly excursions to Victoria Lakes to swim. He had to be content with short conversations with Sammy. The group of office workers seemed to come together more closely now that there were only four of them. Gurung and Prem were very sociable and they would often take their breaks in the office as it was too wet to leave the hut. Prem explained that he was from the Punjab in western India and that though he was married he had not been home for nearly four years. He very rarely received any information from home, as his wife would have to pay to get a letter written. He had received his last letter in January and it talked about the increasing tension between Hindus, Sikhs and Muslims in his area. The letter was hopeful that Indian independence would pass peacefully and that there would be no problems between the various groups, though that looked unlikely. Gurung said that he had not been home to Nepal for six years, but he hoped to return soon after Burmese independence and as a soldier, he could expect to marry well and have many children. They playfully teased each other and both Prem and Gurung asked John what he would do after the army, would he go home a hero? Would he have a well-paid job? Would he marry well? All this time Sammy sat quietly at her desk, clearly listening to their conversation but offering nothing of her thoughts, hopes and ambitions.

When Prem asked her she looked up and said, "I will go to university, I will become a teacher and perhaps marry, I haven't decided." She then looked down at her typewriter and without offering any further elaboration got on with her work.

On 10th June it was announced that the Constituent Assembly would meet for the first time. Life seemed to get back to normal, the patrols stopped, which John was a little disappointed about, as for the first time he felt like a real soldier, walking with a gun in his hand, a figure of authority. He never really felt under any threat and relied on the experienced troops around him. The office established their old routines and work progressed as usual.

One afternoon John was passing out of the camp in a jeep, equipped with some documents to pass to an officer based at the dockside. He had been taught to drive while at the camp and had been told that he would be allowed to drive when he returned to Britain after his service was complete. As he left the camp he spotted Sammy walking on the roadside. He stopped and asked, "can I give you a lift somewhere?"

Sammy said that she was going down the road to catch a bus into the city. She said, "it's my mother's birthday tomorrow and I was going to get her something special, some flowers or sweets or whatever I could find that I think she'd like."

John shouted, "that's on my way, hop in."

Sammy got in without any hesitation.

John asked, "are you in a hurry? I was going down to Monkey Point for a walk."

Sammy hesitated, then said, "I have to go into town first, but after perhaps."

John dropped her off alongside a row of shops and carried on to the docks area, promising to pick her up in forty-five minutes time.

When he returned to the shopping area Sammy was stood on the pavement with a small package and a small potted plant. They drove out to Monkey Point, overlooking the riverside. There was a steady breeze and dense cloud making it very humid, but it was not raining. They jumped out of the jeep and stood on the concrete embankment looking out over a busy riverside scene, with barges and small boats going up and down the river. It wasn't exactly a peaceful scene, as some of the boats had noisy diesel engines, which made a high pitched grating sound and poured thick black smoke behind them, but it was certainly interesting.

Sammy seemed to be entranced by the scene. She said very quietly so that John could barely hear it "a river of life."

John said, "pardon?"

Sammy smiled and turned to John, she said, "Kipling, have you not read Kipling?"

John said, "ah no," immediately impressed by this colonial girl and her knowledge of western literature.

Sammy said, "my mother and father used to bring me here before the war. We would bring a picnic and I would play with my sister and brother on the grass bank. It has many good memories for me."

John asked, "are all your family now together?"

Sammy replied "my father and brother were killed in the war when the Japanese bombed Rangoon, but my mother is at home. He was British and worked as a spotter and signaller for the British up-country before the Japanese got to Rangoon. My mother, my sister and myself were not in Rangoon when they died. My brother insisted on staying in Rangoon with my father. The day we left for India and my uncle's house Chris ran away and missed the train, so my father reluctantly let him stay. My uncle is a merchant in Calcutta, importing and exporting goods. Very rich. We moved back to Rangoon just after the end of the war, but my mother finds it very hard. The house was badly damaged and it has many memories for her. She misses my brother and father so much. She cries a lot in the night, I can hear her. My uncle is very good to us, he sends money, but life is still hard, my mother works as a seamstress to help pay the bills. People think we are rich because we have a big house but my father's business paid for everything, and without him we struggle, but we are happy. Well, as happy as we can be." Sammy looked at John and forced a smile.

They stood up to walk back to the jeep.

"We will struggle after independence. I don't know what I will do as Eurasians in Burma are neither Burmese nor European. I still hope to go to university, I enjoyed my school, I worked hard and did well but there is much corruption and many people have to pay to get into university. My father always said, if you are well educated, no-one can take that away from you, and there will always be a place for well-educated people in the world. I thought at first that Burma would need well-educated people after independence but you see the sons and daughters of rich people stepping into good jobs, waiting for the British to leave to have more influence. Money is suddenly very important, corruption is everywhere."

Sammy stopped, walked a little ahead of John and then turned and said, "and what about you?"

They sat back down on the concrete breakwater. John outlined where he came from, what his town was like, the make-up of his family and what he did before the war. Sammy was very curious and wanted to know everything about Britain and how Wales fitted into that pattern. She asked "and is there conflict between the Welsh and the English? Do they attack each other with guns and bombs, and what about the other groups, the Irish and the Scots?"

John laughed at her questions and said,""no, only on the rugby field." She didn't have a clue why he was laughing and she frowned "you are laughing at me?"

John said, "no, not really, but I think your knowledge of society in Britain is as vague as mine is of Burma, but I am trying to learn."

At that point, both seemed to go into their shell, with their own thoughts, of family, of friends of hopes and aspirations for the future, two young people whose lives seemed to be changing before their eyes.

John turned to look at Sammy and noticed that she was looking up at him. Instinctively he leaned towards her and kissed her, she pulled him closer and they held their embrace, neither wanting it to end. Suddenly John pulled away flustered, and said, "I shouldn't have done that."

Sammy said, "I'm very glad you did."

John turned to Sammy and enquired "what about Steve Robinson? He seems to like you."

Sammy thought for a minute and replied "Steve Robinson is a sergeant and I am always polite to him as he is my superior, but I have heard him speak about Burmese and Indian people and it is not nice. He does not know I have heard him but I would find it difficult to like a man who speaks like that. Do you understand me?"

John nodded and thought that she was very perceptive. She doesn't want to be rude to anyone, but she listens and makes her own mind up.

John distractedly stood and moved towards the jeep. He said, "I'd better be getting you home, or your mam will be wondering what's happened to you."

Sammy smiled and clambered into the jeep. Neither of them spoke on the journey to Sammy's house, both conscious of what had just occurred. Sammy asked John to stop at the corner of her street so as not to cause any problems. John thought the houses seemed quite large by Rangoon standards, as he pulled away from the kerbside, giving a slight wave as he left.

He was due to write home that evening but found that he couldn't bring himself to put pen to paper. He lay on his bed thinking of Sammy and what had happened. He had a little more realisation of what normal life was like for the ordinary Burmese. He would not have known anything about Sammy's life if he had not spent time with her. He couldn't stop thinking about the tragedy her family had faced, losing her father and brother. He imagined how he would feel if his father and David had been killed by bombing. Many families in Britain had experienced that, and worse, but he had never before tried to put himself into that scenario. If he had lived in London, Swansea or Coventry it might have been different, where the bombing was really bad. He might have known someone who had lost relatives or family members might have been killed.

He didn't just feel sorry for Sammy, he thought that she was not only a lovely person on the outside, but she was so genuine, friendly and easy to be with, and was a person with plenty of integrity. He found that he was smitten and that he longed for work each day, just to see her, despite trying hard not to let his feelings show in front of the others. He normally longed for rest and relaxation time in the evenings, now he longed for work time, and found the evenings a drag before the next day's work.

19

Then on 19th July 1947, John's world changed.

In the days after, John would often cast his mind back to the events and non-events of that day. They seemed to be firmly implanted into his memory. They seemed to take on a significance paralleled only by the political upheaval in Burma itself. This would quickly find its way home to Britain, the Commonwealth and the world. John would think back and realise that he had been part of something, which would hit the headlines back home and that the part he played in it would have a bearing on how some people in Treafon would view him, and that it would play a part in forming the person he would become.

He remembered sitting and drinking his early morning cup of tea that the tea-wallah had brought to his dormitory. He remembered having some fruit with a sort of sour creamy yoghurt that he favoured in the morning and having a second cup of tea with a piece of toast while he sat on the steps of his hut. He remembered it was a day of cloud with intermittent periods of hot sun. He remembered a brief conversation about bars of chocolate with 'Chico' Marling. He then left for his office and was alone there for a while. He began work on finding out what preparations needed to be made for the possible movement of Indian army personnel, taking into account the likelihood of Indian independence and Burmese independence in the next few months. This involved at least two phone calls to Indian Army H.Q. Admin. He intended to ring them early, as they were often difficult to contact later in the day.

Normally these details would never be remembered much beyond a few hours at most, but the later significance of this day caused his brain to react differently. He remembered every detail, however mundane. He was on the telephone when Sammy came in, quickly followed by Prem. After a quick "morning" from them both, they settled to their tasks, Prem totalling a set of numbers he required and Sammy typing up a report. Gurung came in five minutes or so later but quickly excused himself as he needed to check on truck availability with the transport officer. Gurung returned thirty minutes later and there was little to report of any significance for the next two hours, unless you included the tap of the typewriter or someone trying to compose a letter by reciting its content under their breath, and the offer of a few cups of tea.

Between nine forty five and ten fifteen in the morning, John's life and the future of Burma changed completely.

Captain Stevens sprinted across the yard towards the hut housing John's office. Several other officers, N.C.O.s and other troops could be seen running in different directions. John stopped working and looked up.

Captain Stevens burst into the office "there's been an incident. Some people, we don't know who, have attacked the Burmese cabinet in the Minister's building. There are deaths. Central Rangoon is in uproar." He stopped to breathe and then continued "all troops in Burma Command are to follow procedures as in a state of emergency. Collect arms from the armoury and form up on the parade ground in fifteen minutes, combat-ready."

With that, the captain left. All in the office looked at each other. Quickly Gurung and Prem scurried out to check on what their orders might be, only Sammy was left standing alongside her desk, stunned by the sudden news and activity.

John remembered Sammy was still there and stopped and turned to her, "you had better try and get home. I'll see if someone is going out and can give you a lift home." Before Sammy could answer John disappeared. He rushed back to his dormitory to collect his combat-ready kit and then rushed over to the armoury to sign out a sten gun. Passing one of the privates he asked him if he could find a jeep and take Sammy home. Less than ten minutes later he formed up in order with all the other ranks and N.C.O.s.

Major Kearns came out to address the troops. He said, "from the first reports, some men, possibly gangsters, burst into a cabinet meeting. We think at the moment that possibly seven or eight have been killed and possibly two or three badly wounded. They have been taken to hospital and are being guarded. We have no idea what repercussions this may have. We don't know whether the perpetrators were communists or right-wing terrorists. It is essential at this stage that we protect the local population. Each N.C.O. will be assigned a squad, which must include a radio operator. Each squad will be assigned to a different area of the city and surroundings. As we get information we will radio it out to you. Captain Stevens will come around and give you your orders and the locations you are to patrol and guard." Major Kearns turned to go back into Central HQ.

Captain Stevens called all N.C.O.s to one side and allocated them a location. Rob Charnock was to go into Central Rangoon and guard the Post Office building and the building which housed Burmese Broadcasting. 'Chico' Marling was to go to the docks area and John was told to guard the airport, the nearest site to the Mingaladon offices of Burma Command. Captain Stevens explained that the airport needed to be secured as if this was just the first stage in a general overthrow of the government, and perhaps the beginning of a civil war, the airport was essential, as it would be the means by which the British army would evacuate British and Empire personnel and their families. John was told that alongside his own squad there would be an Indian Army squad about the same size, under the command of an Indian army naik. One squad would be responsible for patrolling one side of the airport, while John's squad would patrol the other in case an attack came from either side.

A truck and a jeep pulled up to collect the two squads. The Indian Army squad were dropped on the far side of the airport and John's squad on the nearside. John ensured the radio operator stayed close to him so that he could receive information as it came in. He split the squad into three small sections and set up a sort of base on a bare patch of ground surrounded by tall grass, and immediately sent each of the smaller groups of soldiers to patrol in different directions, commanding them to move very quietly and to stay as low to the ground as possible. They returned two hours later, and John with a small group of men replaced one of the patrols and moved off to the airport perimeter. He was effectively creating a rota for patrolling the perimeter of the airfield. During the remainder of the day, they noticed activity in the airfield as more troops were brought in. Apart from that, all was quiet. At evening time a few tents and food were brought to them and this helped create a proper base from which they could patrol. Guards were placed at the perimeter of the base and patrols were sent out every few hours. All was quiet throughout the night, except that radio reports came in that British army patrols had been fired on in the delta area. The following day began much as the previous one had ended. John had time to appreciate the sunrise though it was no more than the rays of the sun projecting through the clouds. It produced a strange effect and it reminded John of the Japanese flag with a red sunburst. He assumed the sunrise was much the same as on other days during the monsoon period, but he admitted to himself that he had rarely noticed it. This was very different from the sunrise at other times of year when the sky was often clearer, and John would take his early cup of tea and sit on the steps of his dormitory hut and watch the sun rise slowly across the sky. When the men were ready they once again began regular patrolling. John pointed out to the men under his command that they must not become complacent and that they had to be on their guard at all times, as their lives might depend on it.

During this action, John had little time to think about what they were doing, or its significance, as he was concerned for his men and their safety. He was still a member of the armed forces despite the fact that he had been a 'pen pusher' for almost all his army experience. He was absolutely determined that he would not let his men down, or himself and that he would keep them vigilant and safe. Around about mid-day, a radio call came through which ordered all N.C.O.s back to HQ for a briefing. John left the squad in the hands of an Indian army naik and made his way about half a mile to the roadside where a truck picked him up.

On his return to HQ, Captain Stevens told the N.C.O.s that had gathered there to "get some grub" and meet in the main hall of the barracks at 14.00 hours for the briefing.

After food, the sergeants assembled and Major Kearns addressed them. Present at the front of the main hall was the Major, Captain Stevens and two officers from the Indian Army.

Major Kearns said, "at approximately 09.45 yesterday morning a gang of, we think possibly five or six men, burst into the council chamber in the Minister's Building. British Army N.C.O. guards had been withdrawn at the request of the Burmese government. On entry into the chamber, they proceeded to open fire, killing Aung San, five other members of the assembly and two officials, as well as severely wounding two others. One has since died this morning. Their bodies are in the process of being embalmed and placed at a lying–in state ceremony under guard. We have used every means at our disposal to track down the assassins, so far without success. We think they are probably lying low in safe houses. We were not sure at first which groups might be responsible, however, based on intelligence we don't think the communists were responsible. We have received reports that the politician U Saw might be involved. At the end of last month, a large consignment of guns was issued to a bogus party of police. We think that about a week ago a consignment of ammunition was issued to another bogus party of police. I needn't tell you that this is top-secret information, and you must not relate this to anyone outside this room," Major Kearns thought primarily because it makes us look supremely stupid. He continued, "The day before the assassination there was mounting evidence of a plot against the Aung San government. Yet again I ask you to keep this under your hats." Major Kearns once again thought that at best it makes us look slow to move, and at worst incompetent. "I can tell you that Thakin Nu has been asked to form a government, quickly, to maintain stability and because we need to continue rapidly with our plans to hand over the country to the Burmese early next year, now only six months away. I can't stress enough the urgency with which we need to capture the assassins and bring them to justice. The Burmese are beginning to suspect British involvement in the plot. We have withdrawn patrols from the centre of Rangoon, and the docks and riverside, primarily because of a lack of manpower. These patrols will be taken over by the Burmese army. A contingent of troops is to be brought in from Kalaw for the short term, and they will help with patrolling key sites. For the moment the key area for us is the airport. It is essential that flights are not disrupted, and that the terrorists do not attempt a takeover of the airport. Consequently, the squads that were patrolling Central Rangoon will now help to patrol the airport perimeter and the Mayo Marine Club on the Strand Road where there are many British Army families. Thank you gentlemen, that will be all for now, unless there are any questions?"

There was silence for a short time. No one spoke, either because Major Kearns had covered everything, or because they were afraid that any questions they had would sound silly at this time of crisis.

They vacated the hall and mingled outside while they waited for trucks to take them back to their squads.

John quickly said to Rob, Chico, Tom and a few of the rest of the sergeants "wait here a second, I'll be straight back." With that, he sped off or at least moved as quickly as he could in full kit. Five minutes later he was back with his Box Brownie camera. The men quickly took photos of each other, individually, or in groups and some of the whole group by instructing a passing bearer on how to operate the camera. In all the photos the men held rifles or sten guns and attempted to look suitably menacing. One sergeant even falling onto his stomach in the long grass alongside the huts and attempted to crawl along until the others started to mock his attempts to look mean and nasty. These photos would be part of their 'war albums.' They knew they might never get the chance again and they could embellish their stories back home with elaborate stories of warfare, and produce the photographs as serious evidence.

Eventually, the trucks arrived and accelerated away to return the sergeants to their squads. Throughout that day and the next two days routine patrols continued, the tension subsided a little as it became clear the assassination was not part of a general uprising but there were concerns of danger as the assassins had still not been caught.

20

In the early hours of the 23rd July, John was awoken in his tent by Rob Charnock. He had just returned from his patrol of the airport perimeter and had been stopped by a local man on a bike.

Rob told John that he had left the man at the side of the road. He said, "come and speak to him and see what you think."

When Rob and John got to the man, he was stood with a Burmese soldier who acted as an interpreter. Rob asked, through the interpreter for the man to explain again what he had seen.

The man said, "I saw movement in the bushes over there." He pointed to a place away from the road on the edge of the forest. He continued "when I came back from fishing this morning, I saw several men I haven't seen before, acting suspiciously, they were all armed. I felt I had to report it as I thought they might be terrorists. I believe in Aung San, before he was killed, and that there must be peace for Burma's future. I am also worried for my family with so much killing."

Rob and John both thanked the man and told him that they would investigate. Rob found a few coins in his pocket and tossed them to the man, who looked very pleased with himself, as he peddled off.

Rob and John went quickly and quietly around the tents waking all the members of the squad. They formed separate sections of troops and moved off towards where the possible sightings had taken place, leaving behind three men and one of the radio operators to guard the camp. As they moved away from the airport perimeter the scrub and bushes became denser jungle with a tangle of vines and shrubs. They slowly and quietly worked their way towards where the sightings had been made and settled down to wait and to see if there was any movement. Having heard a rustle in the bushes to their left they all turned in that direction only to realise one of the men had got his kit tangled in the undergrowth and was trying to untangle himself. Rob gave him a stern look and put his finger to his lips indicating that the soldier must remain still, as his life may depend on it.

Nothing happened for nearly an hour when it began to look as if it had all been a waste of time. All of a sudden there was movement in the bushes ahead and several men all armed with rifles and grenades moved across the eye line of the British troops from right to left, towards the airfield. They were not particularly quiet and seemed oblivious of the presence of the British troops. They were all stood upright, and chatted to each other, clearly not expecting any trouble. Rob put up four fingers and made a sign to show that John and three other troops should follow them along their path. He also indicated that his squad would try to get around the other side of them and follow them. John's group followed them for perhaps three or four hundred yards when they stopped. John's group immediately stopped and quietly dropped to the ground. They counted about ten quite heavily armed men. Two of them took up guard facing the direction of John's troops. The others disappeared into what John could now see was what looked like the ruins of a shepherd's hut. He had not noticed this before despite it only being perhaps half a mile from their camp. It was heavily overgrown, and a small, dilapidated wooden door was dragged back. Two of the men pulled a small two-wheeled cart out of the hut, and the others proceeded to carry bundles out of the hut and load them on to the cart. Once that had been done the men sat down and lit up cigarettes and began chatting. This amused John, as he thought they had no idea they were being watched. John assumed Rob and his squad were also watching this from the other side of the hut. He was unsure what to do next and as Rob had the radio operator with his group there was no way he could contact HQ for further orders.

After about ten minutes the men threw away the stubs of the cigarettes they had been smoking. One of them landing on the man lying next to John. John quickly brushed it off him but caught his hand against a twig as he did so. One of the men at the hut turned quickly to look in the direction the noise had come from and said something to the others. They stopped and listened for a few seconds. The one who was clearly in command spoke in a stuttering manner, which John recognised as Burmese and which he could not understand. Four of the men moved off passing John's group. John and one of the soldiers moved slowly to follow them and the other two remained behind. After a few hundred yards John realised that they were headed for a village between the airport and the army camp, and he also realised that if he wanted to capture them he would have to do that before they reached the village, as they could easily hide and then disappear once they were in the village, which contained a few hundred people. John had never been in this position before which demanded an immediate decision. He could let the guerrillas go which would see John and his fellow soldier in complete safety, but that would be the cowardly option, or, he could attempt to tackle these armed men without knowing how they might react. He thought it best not to give the options too much consideration and just to follow his gut-feeling. John whispered to the other trooper with him that he intended to rush the terrorists and hope to surprise them. He moved quickly towards the armed men. He was very conscious of what seemed to be his loud heartbeat and that the men they were pursuing must also be able to hear it. He said to himself, don't think about what you are about to do, just do it. However, he couldn't help but think there are twice as many of them and what the fuck do I do if they start firing. John went to one side of the armed men, and the trooper the other. Once they were alongside John shouted, "put down your weapons."

The terrorists stopped, but did nothing, as they had no idea where the voice had come from or what John's command meant.

John and the trooper stepped out of the undergrowth. The armed men in front of them made no move to do anything, including throwing down their arms. John thought quickly, shit, what do I do now? He lifted his sten gun and fired into the ground. Immediately the armed men threw down their guns. John indicated the grenades. No one moved, so John fired a second burst, at which they placed the grenades carefully onto the ground. John told the trooper to go back to camp and collect some rope, while he guarded the Burmese men. As John stood over the men, who were sat with their hands on their heads, they began to chatter to each other, all the time watching John and the sten gun he held.

John was conscious of time moving slowly and the fact that if these men chose to they could easily rush him and disarm him. John shouted, "for fuck's sake, shut it," and there was immediate silence. The trooper quickly returned and proceeded to tie up each of them and they then marched them back to camp and sat them down with the trooper guarding them. Twenty minutes later Rob returned with the other squad, six prisoners and the wooden cart. John pulled the piece of cloth off one of the items they had put on the cart. Rob whistled between his teeth as he looked at a brand new British army issue bren gun. They totalled ten bren guns on the cart and an assortment of British Army issue rifles, as well as the arms the Burmese men had been carrying which were also British Army issue. John thought, quite a haul. They radioed to HQ and twenty minutes later two trucks appeared with a further squad of troops. Shortly after, Captain Stevens appeared in a jeep, beaming all over his face. He jumped out and went over to pat John and Rob on the back, claiming "heroes, bloody heroes."

As the small convoy moved off Rob turned to John and said, "two-faced bastard."

The patrols along the airfield perimeter continued for a further two days until Rob's and John's squads were relieved by two further squads who would continue the patrolling. The men were collected by truck and on their return to camp, the two sergeants were approached by Captain Stevens who said, "well done, the two of you, Major Kearns wants to see you at 09.00 tomorrow morning. Now, go and get some grub."

The two sergeants appeared outside the major's office just before 09.00 the following morning having been well fed and following a really good night's sleep back in their own beds.

Once they were told to stand easy the major began "well done men, a job very well done. The Burmese you apprehended were brought in and transferred to Army Intelligence. They were interrogated and quickly gave us all the information we needed. They were a pretty sorry bunch. They told us that the arms in the hut were part of an arm's cache that had been hidden by U Saw. The rest we found hidden in a lake alongside his house when we went to arrest him. They said that they were part of the group that had assassinated the Burmese cabinet though they were very quick to point out that they had no actual part in that. When they were asked where the assassins were one of them mentioned a house owned by one of the assassins, which was used as a safe house. This chap had actually stayed in the house when escaping from the Burmese police after a robbery a while ago. This house is in Pegu. Early this morning troops surrounded the house and after a gun battle one of the assassins was killed but four others were captured. Unfortunately, two of our men were wounded but they are in hospital recovering and they'll be fine." The major stopped to let the information sink in. He continued after a second or two "so your part in unravelling the plot to overthrow the government and helping to catch the assassins was vital. How did you capture the ten of them?"

The major indicated a few easy chairs at the other side of his office and they moved over to that side of the room. The major opened a cupboard and said, "drink?" Rob with a broad grin said, "It's a bit early but I'll have a whisky if you don't mind sir." John said, "likewise, sir." After the major had poured the drinks he sat to listen to the tale of 'the capture of the heavily armed terrorists.' With a little embellishment, they both related how the group had been followed, captured and taken back to camp. Rob and John had been talking so much that they hadn't finished their drinks before the major stood to indicate the session was over. As they were dismissed the major stopped them and both turned to hear him say "and a report of your actions will go to Army Command and the War Office and will recommend a gallantry medal." They looked at each other and before they could thank the major he added: "no guarantees mind, depends what frame of mind the top bods are in."

John and Rob walked outside and were speechless. They eventually burst out laughing, neither of them knowing what to make of the events of the last few days. Rob turned to John and said in a mock posh voice, "hey, Staff Sergeant Evans, just pop back in and collect my whisky, there's a good chap." That evening the two men went into the Sergeant's Mess to relate their story and impress the rest of the group with the tale of how they had single-handedly stalled the Burmese Civil War.

On his way out of the mess John was confronted with Steve Robinson who blocked his path "think you're fucking heroes now I suppose?"

John looked him straight in the eye, determined not to show any fear of a man he had come to despise "no mate, just a British Army soldier, same as before. Unlike you who seems to be a bit of a leopard, changing his spots."

John found it difficult to fall asleep that night. He was exhausted after several nights of broken sleep in the tent near the airfield, but the exhilaration of the capture of the terrorists and the possible danger he had been in at the time got the better of him. He had put any thought of danger behind him and he had behaved instinctively. He realised that his life was in peril but somehow getting the job done was more important. It gave him a realisation of how seemingly ordinary men had acted so bravely on the beaches of Normandy and during the Battle of Britain and Elizabeth's father's war in the trenches of France and Belgium. Ah well, he thought it'll soon be back to the monotony of working behind a desk, but at least it's safe.

21

A month later it was almost as if nothing had happened. There were still disturbances and riots in the delta area and up-country, but Rangoon was relatively quiet. The streets were patrolled by the Burmese police and army, and a few of the remainder of the British and Empire forces. Both Prem and Gurung came to John at the beginning of August to say that they would be leaving. Prem was to return to the Punjab along with all Indian forces on 15th August as India was to celebrate independence, and he would then be part of the Home army. Gurung's service was complete in August and he would return to Nepal to farm. The three sat outside the hut chatting for a while. Prem and Gurung were genuinely excited to be going home after a long army service abroad, and letters they had received stated that their families were also expectantly excited.

Prem said, "it will be a difficult time in the Punjab. It is the area of India that has the greatest mix of peoples, Sikhs, Muslims and Hindus and it looks as if the country will have to be divided into at least two parts, if not more. The letters tell me there is already a great deal of trouble between Hindus and Muslims and the Sikhs are caught between the two. Many have been killed. It will not be as happy a time as perhaps it should be."

Gurung said, "Nepal is peaceful and I am looking forward to seeing the high mountains of the Himalayas." He became enraptured in his state of reverie as he described the sun rising at the back of the snow-covered peaks in the morning and bathing the countryside in light. "The air is fresh and clean and we look forward to the Spring blossoming of flowers in the foothills. It is what I miss most when I am in Burma. Here it is all jungle and scrubland, no snow-covered peaks, and it rains too much."

Prem asked, "is it like Burma or Nepal in Britain?"

John laughed and said, "neither, it is often dirty, dusty, wet and cold where I come from, but I love it. It's my home." John's thoughts drifted to home for a moment and he realised during a busy time in Rangoon he had not given much thought to home, and he had sent far fewer letters than he should have. He promised himself he would write that night.

Before Prem left there was a small party where he was presented with a fountain pen. John was beginning to question the validity of giving the predictable present of a pen to everyone who left. He thought I wonder if they have ink?

He honestly could not think of anything that would be useful to them when they got home. Likewise, Gurung was given a pen and John thought, that's going to be really useful to Gurung on the slopes of Everest. Both seemed very pleased with their presents.

By the end of August, only John and Sammy remained in the office. It seemed quiet compared to the busy times of a year or two earlier, but they seemed comfortable in each other's presence. John was completely pre-occupied through the end of July and the whole of August, and Sammy did not once mention the kiss they had shared, as they both carried on quietly with their work. An outsider would have thought they were complete strangers. During the first week of September Sammy mentioned that she would not be in work the following day.

John asked, "is everything ok?" thinking perhaps a member of the family might be ill.

Sammy replied, "yes, it is my eighteenth birthday and my mother and sister are taking me for a picnic."

John looked up at the sky, which looked menacing at that moment. Sammy quickly caught on and said, "it's ok, there is a small shack which has a veranda and a good roof and we have permission from the owners to use it tomorrow. They are friends of my mother."

John smiled and replied, "well, I hope you have a good day and the rain stays away."

Sammy gave her usual winsome smile and carried on with her

work. John couldn't get Sammy's birthday out of his mind and finally decided to drive into Rangoon later and see what he could get for her birthday. After he had finished his work for the day and Sammy had gone home he took a jeep into the city. After wandering around for over half an hour and not being able to think of anything, he noticed an old man with a small shop that had an open front on to the street, with a younger boy working at a bench inside the shop. He appeared to be making jewellery. John was torn between giving Sammy something which you would give to a friend in a platonic relationship or something which might mean something completely different. John noticed a set of gold earrings, with small bright sapphire stones in a really pretty setting. John thought this was a sign from the gods and showed a little more interest in the jewellery. He asked the man "how much?"

The man shook his head and hands at the same time and made it clear they were not for sale. John thought they would be perfect and eventually, the man called the boy out of the shop. The young boy said, "Raj say these are for rich merchant, he already pay, so not for sale." John tried to persuade the craftsman but the man did not budge from his decision. The jeweller then thought, putting one finger in the air and beckoning to the boy said something that John could not understand. The boy said, "we get more sapphire and make a pair for you by tomorrow."

John asked, "how can you do that?"

The boy replied, "We work all night."

John was very pleased with the outcome, and a price was settled. He would have to seriously burrow into his savings but he felt it was worth it, certainly for Sammy.

He left and returned at about the same time the following day. The package lay unwrapped on the work-bench, and John was immediately impressed with the quality of work. He paid the sum agreed and gave the young boy a tip that he seemed more than pleased with and returned to camp. The following morning when Sammy arrived for work John immediately asked if she had enjoyed her picnic.

Sammy said, "it was really good to spend a whole day with my family. My mother doesn't have a lot of money and works as a seamstress for long hours, so when I get home she is often fast asleep. My sister works in Pegu and so I see little of her as she leaves early in the morning and comes home late, so, yes, it was a lovely day, and it didn't rain."

John had written a card he had made himself with a short verse on the front. He had bought a bunch of flowers and she was so excited to receive them. Then he passed her the delicately wrapped package with the ear-rings.

She took the jewellery out of the wrapping paper and looked at them speechless. She said, so quietly you could barely hear her "I have never seen anything so beautiful." She stood looking at them, then, she picked them up to study them more closely. She turned to John and said, "could you put them on for me." John knew that she had her ears pierced as he had seen her wearing small studs. He moved behind her and put both ear-rings carefully on her ears. As he finished she turned and as she was alongside John she reached up behind his neck and pulled him to her, kissing him passionately. After a few seconds, John came back to earth and pulled away from her feeling more than a little embarrassed. Sammy looked down at that moment and realised where she was. She said, "I'm so sorry, I forgot for a moment where…." She failed to complete the sentence.

The last thing John wanted was for Sammy to feel embarrassed about doing what he thought was perfectly natural. The only thing he could think of at that moment to break the embarrassed silence was to move towards her and kiss her back. This he did, and they stayed in the embrace for what seemed like a long time though John thought it was probably only a few seconds. He smiled and turned to her repeating her own words "I have never seen anything so beautiful." He looked at her for a few seconds and said, "I hope it will help you remember the time we spent together." Sammy blushed and sat to continue with her work. John went for a short walk to clear his head.

He realised after a few days that for the first time in Burma he felt a little lonely. Chico had been moved into offices at the docks to help organise the transport of the last few vehicles and pieces of equipment from Rangoon on behalf of what was now called 'Burma Rear Force.' It felt like it. There seemed to be less work to do and fewer people to do it but John suddenly seemed to have more time on his hands.

Purely on a whim John went into the office a few days later and asked Sammy "would you like to come to the Kheung Sin with me on Friday night?"

Sammy hesitated for a few seconds and then replied "that would be lovely, thank you very much. I will check with my mother first and let you know tomorrow."

Sammy immediately looked down, as always when she was embarrassed and continued with her work.

The following morning she said, "I have checked with my mother and she said that it is fine, but I must be home by 10.30."

John smiled and suggested "what if we go straight from work. You bring a change of clothes in, and we can go from here to the Chinese restaurant."

Sammy thought that was a good idea. She arrived for work on Friday equipped with a larger bag than usual. After greeting John she quickly settled down to work. John glanced over at her from time to time as he normally did. He felt a little guilty, as he had missed the deadline he set himself to write letters home to Elizabeth and his family. He tried to conjure up excuses in his mind to show why he had been too busy to write but he knew deep down that his interests lay here in Rangoon for the moment. He had arrived back in Burma after leave nearly a year ago and so much had happened. One other thought that quickly flashed through his mind, and then just as quickly left it, was that his army service would come to an end in just five months time.

When work was over for the day Sammy disappeared to the

toilets to change for the evening. John quickly ran to his dormitory and had a shave. He then changed into jacket and trousers over an open-necked shirt and came back to the office. Sammy came into the office wearing a white full-length cheongsam with a slit on the side so that when she walked her one leg was visible to the thigh. The effect was electrifying. John had never seen anyone looking so stunningly beautiful. Unconsciously, Sammy reached back to push her hair behind her ears and John immediately noticed the sapphire ear-rings, they looked perfect. She pushed her bag under the desk and took her evening bag out of the drawer. John and Sammy walked to the army jeep, which produced a scene observed by anyone else as totally incongruous, a beautiful girl and a smelly diesel-powered jeep, which had seen better days. John had placed his coat on Sammy's seat to protect her dress. As the jeep left the camp John passed O'Rourke who stood looking at the couple with his mouth open.

They were shown to a table in the quirky, thatched covered restaurant. There were tables inside and outside. They sat inside, where cooling fans gently moved the warm air. The restaurant was visited by all; officers and their wives, sergeants and privates, if they could afford it, and the richest of Burmese society, as well as some of the returned European businessmen. John had only been there once before, for Rob Charnock's birthday, but he thought it was a special place. The restaurant created a very romantic atmosphere as it played popular love songs quietly in the background. At that moment 'Prisoner of Love' by Perry Como was playing and this set John thinking, the exotic location and the music and certainly the company can do funny things to your mind. They ordered food and drinks and then chatted, about work, Rangoon and pretty much everything. The main topic of conversation in the camp was Indian independence and the many deaths that were arising from partition. Sammy quickly thought about Prem and said that she hoped he would not be anywhere near the fighting.

The conversation moved on to their plans for the future. Sammy explained, "I hope to go to university next year." The university main building was in what had been Judson College during the time of the

Empire and Sammy said, "I have been there to enquire about the qualifications that are required for entry onto courses. The gentleman I spoke to seemed to be quite hopeful that I would be successful." Sammy then asked John, "and what are you going to do?"

John answered, "I have absolutely no idea."

Sammy asked, "what qualifications have you got from school?"

John said, "none of any use from school, but I did pick up a fair bit of experience in hammer sizes, how to replace handles on spades and the difference between a rawl and a screw."

Sammy could see he was teasing her and so changed the topic of conversation. She looked down at her lap and said quietly "is there anyone at home you will be going back to, uh a girlfriend sort of?"

John said, "There is Elizabeth, she is a girl I was seeing before I joined up, the army that is."

Sammy looking at her lap said, "and will you be getting married when you go back?"

John quickly said, "whoa, let's not live all my life in the next five minutes. I really don't know. I don't want to marry the wrong person. I've been seeing Elizabeth for a few months but we've not talked about marriage or anything to do with our futures."

Sammy suddenly seemed to cheer up and looked up. The conversation came to an end when the waiter brought the food.

After the meal, they went out onto a terrace at the back of the restaurant and sat in the moonlight. It was a beautiful evening and Sammy closed her eyes to listen to the insects and the frogs and other animals in the nearby jungle. She said, "do you do this at home?"

John laughed "yes, all the time, I close my eyes in the evening and listen to the beautiful sounds of the brickworks, the steam train chugging through the town and the pounding of the ingots in the steelworks."

Sammy looked across and said, "you're teasing me again."

John said, "I think you need to realise what Treafon is like. Britain made its money from industry. The trains you see here are probably made in Britain, but to do that there have to be many factories and works in a very small country. There are many beautiful places in Wales and in the rest of Britain but you often have to travel to them, and I don't come from a rich family to be able to travel about whenever I like. I don't have access to a car as I do here. I feel very fortunate to be able to travel to your country and appreciate its beauty, and at a time when war has passed. I know there are troubles in parts of Burma but I think your country has a great future."

Sammy said, "it seems strange that Britain has such a powerful Empire and yet you describe it as a dirty place and that people in Burma think British people are rich because they have an Empire and yet you say you are poor. It is very confusing."

John said, "it's rich because it has such a lot of industry, which makes the air dirty and for many years the wealth of the country was held in just a few people's hands, though that may be changing. The war has cost Britain and it is no longer able to maintain it's Empire."

Sammy looked quizzically at John and said, "why don't the British people get rid of their ruling class if they are not willing to share the wealth as the French did during their revolution."

John laughed and said, "please don't wish another war on Britain. We haven't got over the last one yet."

John suddenly realised the time and the promise Sammy had made to her mother and they hurried from the restaurant after John had paid the bill. They sped off in the jeep, and John realised it would be best if he parked at the end of Sammy's street. He pulled the jeep into the shadow of a tree where it could not be seen easily from the houses in the street. Sammy turned to him and said, "thank you very much for a wonderful evening. I have enjoyed myself very much."

John leaned over to her and kissed her passionately. She stopped and pulled away, but instead of getting out of the jeep, she returned his kiss with even more passion. John looked into her eyes and stroked her cheek gently with his index finger. She smiled up at him and took his hand and placed it on her breast. John slowly slid his hand under the top of her dress where he could feel her nipple rise against his hand. She did not pull away but continued to kiss him. They stopped, conscious of the time. Sammy ran her hands through her hair and checked her make-up in the rear view mirror. John asked if she would like to go swimming on the following Saturday and she said she would. She rushed from the jeep blowing John a kiss and thanking him again.

22

John left to meet Sammy at Victoria Lakes the next Saturday. He continued to feel guilty, as he had still not written home. This was made worse as he had received mail in the previous week from his mother and Elizabeth. He managed to push the thought to the back of his mind. It was a beautiful, hot, sunny day with a little cloud, which offered some relief from the intense heat. A gentle breeze would blow the branches of the palm trees surrounding the lake and if you looked beyond the lake to where the wooded slopes rose up layers of steam would rise from the trees. It was more pleasurable because there was less cloud than normal and so the lower humidity would cause you to sweat less than usual.

John arrived first and lay out on the bank of the lake in his swimming costume. Sammy arrived and caused John's heart to flutter as she kissed him immediately on arriving. She unwrapped her sarong to show her one-piece swimsuit, John's favourite, the white swimsuit with the lemon and lavender flowers. John suddenly became concerned that his pleasure and excitement might show and so he crossed his legs. Sammy suggested a swim and both ran into the water, splashing each other and swimming off together into the middle of the lake. John was a strong swimmer and eventually realised that he had left Sammy behind and so swam back to her. As he got to her she threw her arms around his neck and pulled him towards her. They kissed and then swam back to the bank. John kept thinking that Sammy seemed as eager as he did. They dozed on the riverbank for a while and Sammy suggested they go for a walk. They left their clothes on the bank, as there were several people around who would keep an eye on their belongings. They walked away from the lake for a while and into an area sparsely covered in trees. It was a pleasant, shaded area, which had short grass unlike many grassy areas of Burma. John thought perhaps there had been buildings here at some time. They sat against one of the trees. Sammy immediately began to kiss John and made it obvious that she would be happy for their relationship to develop into something more. She slipped off her sarong and pulled down the top of her swimsuit, after first checking that they could not be seen. She leaned across and pulled John's swimming costume down slowly releasing John from what was becoming a painful entrapment. She slid back onto the grass alongside John and pulled John on top of her. John was more than a little taken aback at how forward Sammy was.

John stopped and said quietly "have you done this before?" She shook her head to indicate this was her first time. John looked at her body in the shadow. Her perfect breasts, with small hard, dark nipples, her flat stomach, and the bush of hair between her thighs. Her skin was amazing, it seemed to shine, and John couldn't work out whether it was because she was sweating a little or that it was a quite natural sheen. It was totally unblemished and John had never felt anything like it. John lay on top of her, stroking her breasts and arms as she quietly moaned. He then entered her slowly. She winced but pulled him towards her. John began rising and falling slowly and seemed to reach a climax quickly, all emotion flooding from him into her. She lay with her eyes closed and John fell back, to lay alongside her. He turned to face her and took time to examine her body as she lay there in her own dreamlike state. The thing that struck him most clearly was the contrast in skin colour. Her perfect brown body, looking almost as if she were a white person who was tanned, with a light sheen and his pale body by comparison. His body looked taut and lightly muscled, without an inch of fat. He pushed his leg against her leg so that the colour contrast was most noticeable. It amused him to do this and by looking at this dark young goddess it made him feel good. He smiled at his contentment.

He thought, if ever there was a perfect moment, this was it. She looked at John and surprised him by saying "was I any good?"

John smiled and replied, "you were perfect," and she gave her usual winsome, innocent and very sexy smile. They walked back to the bank of the lake but after an hour or so Sammy said, "can we do it again?"

John laughed. They collected their belongings and walked back to the glade of trees. Sammy later told him that the second time was better, she said, "I wasn't so scared, I knew what to expect."

They lay on the grass silently for some time and then Sammy leaned over to pick a beautiful bright blue wild flower. She held it up and swirled it around between her fingers. She said, so quietly her voice could barely be heard "If I had a flower for every time I thought of you I could walk in my garden forever." She looked up at John and said, "isn't that beautiful?"

John asked, "the flower or the statement?"

Sammy answered "both."

John then replied, "is that a Sammy quote or is it attributable to someone else?"

Sammy said, "didn't you ever read anything except comics when you were younger?" After a pause "its Alfred Lord Tennison," and more forcefully "an English poet."

John smiled, and said in a very exaggerated Welsh accent, "ah, there you are then, I'm Welsh, don't you know."

They both laughed and with John's arm around her, they walked around the edge of the lake before going back to the jeep. John was a little concerned that he had not used protection but he kept thinking, I couldn't plan for that, I didn't expect it to happen.

It was getting dark when they went back to Sammy's house. John parked the jeep under the same tree and they petted and kissed before Sammy jumped out, blew him a kiss and shouted: "see you Monday."

Before she disappeared John asked, "do you want to go to the restaurant again next weekend?"

Sammy shouted back "I'd rather go swimming," with a very wicked grin.

On Monday morning Sammy acted as if nothing had happened on the weekend. She arrived shouting, "morning" to John and got straight down to her work. John smiled to himself at her unpredictability, her honesty and perhaps her most enduring quality, her innocence.

The next couple of weekends followed the same pattern. Sammy and John would meet at Victoria Lakes, they would swim, make love, eat their picnic and make love again. John insisted on using protection and even though Sammy said it didn't feel the same, he insisted.

In early November Sammy suggested they stay at the thatched hut that she had spent her birthday at, with her mother and sister. She said it was she who had negotiated the use of the hut the last time. She had given her mother's friends a small amount of money and they were happy for her to use it. She explained, "I will tell them we would like to use it again, they won't know it is me and you who are using it this time."

John said, "are you sure you won't get into trouble, you are not really telling the truth."

Sammy replied, "I will think about what I'm going to say so that I don't tell them any lies."

A discussion about the truth followed, and whether truth was something you said or something you thought about.

John asked, "what is deception?" and then felt very guilty when he thought about what he was doing with Sammy.

A few days later Sammy came into work looking very pleased with herself. She said, "it's all ok, our friends said we could use their hut on the weekend, well, they said I could."

John smiled and asked, "does that include me?"

Sammy went to throw her arms around him and then remembered where they were. She replied, "I will only go if you are with me."

Friday night came. John left the office to go to the dormitory to collect his things. He told Sammy to wait for him in the jeep. He picked up the kit bag he had earlier packed and walked out to the jeep.

As he came around the corner he could hear raised voices. Steve Robinson was stood towering over Sammy and holding her arm firmly. John could hear him say "what are you doing with that dope? I could show you a really good time."

Sammy went to pull away, saying "you're hurting my arm."

John arrived behind Steve and grabbed the neck of his shirt, pushing him against the wall. He managed to say between gritted teeth "leave her alone, you fucking bully."

Steve turned to take a swing at John, who ducked the blow. John immediately took the opportunity to grip Steve's collar more firmly. Steve was taller than John but carried more weight and was not as fit.

John said, "what Sammy does is her business. If she chooses to be with you that's fine by me, but let's be clear Steve." He waited a second and then shouted in his face "it's her choice."

Sammy feeling very uneasy at this battle between the two of them tried to prise them apart. Eventually, John let a very ruffled Steve go, pushing him back against the wall.

Before either Steve or John could speak, Sammy said, "Sergeant Robinson, John is right, I choose to be with him. The only way I could be with you is if you force me to and that would not be right, would it? It would make you uncivilised, a brute, an animal even, and I know you are not like that."

Both men were surprised at the effect of her words. Steve Robinson brushed himself off and spluttered a little but said nothing as he thought about what Sammy had said. He turned, and swearing under his breath, he left.

Sammy and John took a moment to get their breath back and then got into the jeep.

As they drove off John turned to her and said, "you ok?"

Sammy said, "yes fine," and then "sometimes it is better to say how you feel rather than resort to violence. It doesn't work with everybody, but I think it did with Sergeant Robinson."

John laughed and shook his head at her calmness and resourcefulness, and how certain she was in her own self. He said, "you are amazing," and they both laughed.

John had packed a change of clothes, as Sammy made it quite clear they would be staying until Sunday. They had both packed some food, blankets, pillows and a mosquito net. Sammy had a bag with some extra clothes but turned to John when she got into the jeep saying "I've brought some clothes, but I don't think I'll be needing them," with a wicked grin.

John smiled to himself, placing his foot on the accelerator and directing the jeep into the road.

The hut was at the end of a long winding track at the edge of the jungle north of Mingaladon. John brushed out the hut to get rid of the insects and debris that covered the floor of the hut. Sammy had brought candles and lit them on the veranda as it got dark, watching the insects above the candlelight. They sat on the edge of the veranda drinking from a bottle of whisky that John had brought. Sammy wrapped herself around John's arm and said, "I don't want this to end, can't we just stay here? We can buy the hut off my friends and live here; it will be perfect."

John laughed, "and what do we do for money and food?"

Sammy closed her eyes in shear bliss and said, "you have to spoil it, talking about things like money and food. We don't need these things."

As it got dark, they went into the hut and pulled the blankets around them underneath the mosquito net that John had rigged up and made love. They lay for a while listening to the sounds of the forest. John was fascinated by these strange sounds, which at times sounded ethereal.

Sammy said, "our house is on the edge of the city and in the evening I can sit in the garden and listen to the sounds coming from the forest. The sounds made me feel safe even though some people would say that some of the animals that made them might be dangerous to me. It taught me that many of the animals would only attack when they felt threatened and that gave me the confidence to go into the forest." She turned to John "silly, isn't it"

John said, "I think you have to have a different relationship with the forest and the animals when you live close to them like this," he continued, "at first when I arrived I was afraid of the snakes, the spiders and some of the bigger animals, but after a time you forget they are there and you get on with your life, just like they probably forget we are here, so they can get on with their lives. You learn to live with them and they learn to live with you."

John woke up in the morning to find Sammy had gone. He got out of bed and then saw her sitting on the veranda, completely naked. He stood for a moment looking at her perfect profile. He could see her back with the outline of one of her breasts, her legs, a light brown, stretching out in front of her, dangling off the veranda. He came up behind her and put his arms around her shoulders, with one of his legs either side of her. She leaned back resting her head on his chest.

They both seemed content with a silence between them for some time. Then Sammy said, "Love is a gift of one's inner most soul to another so both can be whole." Before John could say anything she said, "Lord Buddha and I think it is one of the most beautiful things ever stated." She moaned quietly and asked, "can you make love to me again?" John said, "you are insatiable."

Sammy turned "what does that mean?"

John said, "never satisfied."

Sammy looked into John's eyes and said, "I have to be satisfied as I can't have you all the time and it will all stop sometime in the future, so my brain says make the most of it now."

John realised what she meant and it seemed to change the atmosphere between them. John became a little morose. Sammy realised what she had said and went to him "I'm sorry, I usually think these things but stop myself from saying them."

John held her but realised the idyllic moment had gone. He

suggested they go for a walk. Sammy said, "I know of a lake near here where it's safe to swim." They walked through the woodland for about half a mile and came to a small lake. The woodland was quiet except for a few forest birds. They stripped off and swam naked across the lake. They noticed they could not get out on the opposite bank as it was muddy and so swam back to where their clothes were. They lay on the bank to dry off. Neither of them spoke. They sat and listened to the birds in the trees and the occasional splash as fish in the lake rose to attempt to catch the insects flying above the water. A short while later John noticed a movement in the trees and then an old man appeared, in ragged clothes and a straw hat. When he noticed the naked couple, he stopped and then said something which John did not understand, but assumed was in Burmese. Sammy replied and the man walked off.

John said, "what did he say?"

Sammy laughed, "he said a perfect day for two water creatures."

The two water creatures dressed and walked back to the hut. It was late afternoon by the time they got back. John made a fire and they ate the food they had brought. The following day they were both awake early and walked to the lake which was shrouded in mist. John stood for several minutes, his arm around Sammy watching the birds flying across the surface of the lake and disappearing into the mist. Sammy thought that she could read John's mind and leaned into him while he took in this magical scene. Then they swam and lay on the bank as they had done the day before. Only leaving when the sun rose higher in the sky and they both felt they needed to seek shade. They sat for hours on the veranda in silence, neither of them needing to say anything. When it came time to pack up and go home Sammy seemed to deliberately drag her feet and barely helped at all in packing up the jeep. It was obvious to John that she had enjoyed her time and was reluctant to go back. They made love one more time before they left the hut and headed back towards Rangoon. Sammy seemed to sulk on the way back. She got out of the jeep at the end of her street, kissed John quickly and ran to her house.

John sat for a second realising how young she was. If she couldn't get her own way she sulked. John thought, just like I was a few years ago.

23

The weekend was dreamlike, but as John sat down to work on the Monday morning, he knew he had fallen behind with his work. He immersed himself in his work through the following week and Sammy and he barely spoke. When she asked if she would see him that weekend, he said he would have to work. She asked, "can I help?"

John said carelessly, "no, I'll be fine on my own, you'll only distract me." He meant it to dissuade her gently but she misunderstood, huffed and walked off.

One day in mid-December Sammy came into work and seemed pre-occupied. She briefly said, "hello," and then put her head down on the desk. John came around his desk thinking she might be ill. She looked up and said, "my mother spoke to our friends, the one with the hut, now she knows I spent time there and deceived her and her friends."

John said, "oh," looking concerned, "is that a problem?"

Sammy looked quizzically at John "she got it out of me that I have been seeing you and she wants to meet you."

John said, "is that a problem?"

Sammy suddenly cheered up "you mean you don't mind?"

John said, "not at all unless she is going to employ a group of dacoits to finish me off when I arrive."

They agreed that John would visit on what was Christmas Eve.

John arrived at the agreed time of six-thirty in the evening. Sammy came to the door. She looked at the small packages he had brought, but he said, "I'll give you your Christmas present when I see you next." She nodded.

John was ushered into a living room, which was sparsely

furnished. He noticed a collection of photographs on a sma cupboard and a radio in the corner. Sitting on the sofa along one wa was an attractive lady whose age it would be difficult to defin dressed in a sari. Alongside her was a girl about Sammy's age, perhap a few years older in western dress. John said, "good-day Mr Samuels," and was ushered to a seat opposite. John passed Sammy' mother a bunch of flowers and a box of chocolates that he ha brought and she thanked him. He suddenly remembered that h brought nothing for Sammy's sister and apologised.

She replied, "I did not expect you to bring anything." Joh suddenly remembered that Sammy's name came from Samuels an that he didn't actually know what her real name was. This made hir feel very stupid.

Thankfully, Mrs Samuels said, "it is very nice to eventually me Hla's friend. This is her sister Gawa." Sammy's sister demurel looked down at the mention of her name.

John introduced himself "I am John, and it's very nice to me you both."

Sammy's mother said, "John, you can call me Khine."

John laughed and said, "I am used to calling Hla, Sammy, and did not know her real name before this evening." Khine said he daughter's name in Burmese means "she who is beautiful."

John said, "that is clearly true," but then felt embarrassed an looked down. Sammy's mother said, "her sister is called Gawa whic in Burmese means 'joy and happiness, and my name Khine mean firmness."

John shuddered a little as he wondered whether he detected slightly menacing look from Sammy's mother.

Khine departed the room after a while and John spoke to Samm in quite a detached way as if they had only just met. Gawa said nothin and appeared to John to be very shy. Khine returned with dishes c nuts and fruit on a tray with small bowls of what looked like dal an yoghurt. They all ate the food slowly and carefully until Khine aske

John "how long have you been in Burma and when will you be going back to Britain?"

John thought the question had a little sting in the tail but answered truthfully "I've been here two and a half years, apart from one home leave and my service is up in February." He detected a sigh from Sammy but chose to ignore it.

Khine talked about her husband, Douglas, who had been born in Scotland and was a timber merchant. She asked John "have you ever been to Scotland?"

John replied, "Scotland is a long way from Wales and no I haven't, unfortunately." The conversation revolved around the separate areas of England, Scotland Ireland and Wales and how they were all governed from London and how Ireland was in two parts.

Khine said, "it is like in Burma with the Shan States and the other areas that will all be governed from Rangoon." Khine asked, "are there problems between the areas of Britain?"

John explained, "they have been like that for a very long time."

Khine said, "I think there will be lots of troubles between the peoples of Burma after independence. We have been very happy until the war came, I suppose Hla has told you what happened to Douglas and my son. I miss them both very much, but my girls are very close to me, they help me a lot." She looked very deliberately at John and added: "I could not manage without them." Khine moved towards the photographs on the top of the cupboard and John rose to look more closely. There were photographs of Sammy and her sister and brother when they were younger, playing in the garden alongside a more formal photograph of Khine and a smartly dressed, good looking man smiling into the camera. Khine stated, "that was taken just after we were married, myself and Douglas."

After about two hours John felt exhausted with the formality and what he perceived as awkward conversations and he got up to leave. He said, "well, it has been a very lovely evening. I thank you for your hospitality."

Sammy stood up, but immediately Khine walked past her and said, "it's ok Hla, I will show John out."

As they got to the door Khine turned to John and said, "she is very young, and it would upset us all very much if she were hurt. Goodbye sergeant, it has been very nice to meet you." She quickly closed the door, halting any reply.

John churned the evening and the conversation over in his mind on his way back to camp, and as he sat on the bed after he got back.

On the 4th January 1948, Burma officially became an independent country free of imperial rule. There were huge celebrations on the streets of Rangoon, but John and the few remaining British and Empire troops were told to remain in camp for that day and a few days after so as not to incite the locals who had become distinctly anti-British. Burma had decided not to join the Commonwealth and arrangements were speeded up to remove all remnants of Imperial control.

The following weekend John asked to see Sammy, taking her out for a meal at Kheung Sin's. Both said little that evening, even after John had passed Sammy's Christmas present to her. He apologised for handing over the present so late, but they had not seen each other for nearly a week.

He had framed a picture of them both that they had persuaded one of the bearers to take. John had bought a silver gilt frame and he wrapped it in pretty paper and ribbon. Sammy genuinely loved it, but then went very quiet and John wondered whether it was the right sort of present, as Sammy would have difficulty in sneaking it into the house. She said she would hide it for now and gauge the atmosphere before putting it on display.

John said, "so there is an atmosphere at home? I got the impression your mother did not approve of me?"

Sammy said, "she liked you very much but you can understand she thinks I will miss you so much when you go back."

Neither of them pursued the discussion and when John said,

“there’s definitely an elephant in the room,” Sammy burst out laughing. After John had explained the phrase she said she had never heard the expression and that the room seemed too small for an elephant. They both laughed and it seemed to lighten the mood.

John dropped Sammy outside her house, as there seemed little point in pretending any longer. She kissed him quickly and ran in.

24

John arrived at Victoria Lakes, as usual, a few minutes before Sammy, on a day when the sky was what could be described as 'china blue.' There were some wispy clouds over to the south-east, but otherwise, it was a hot and dry day. John had stripped down to his costume but wore his bush hat to keep the sun off. He lay on the grass thinking of Sammy's anticipated arrival. Their relationship had changed a little since Christmas. Sammy was quieter, not as happy and full of joy as she had been back in October and November. Their love-making had been more intense and Sammy would grab him and cling to him, in what seemed desperation from time to time. John sensed it was all to do with his imminent departure. He had been told he would receive more information regarding his departure, with a date and time, during the following week and did not relish the thought of telling Sammy.

She arrived, wearing a swimsuit he had not seen before. It was a plain black one-piece suit and while it brought out the colour of her skin, John thought the colour ominous and more in-tune with her mood in recent weeks.

Sammy said she didn't want to swim and a while later she also said she didn't want to go for a walk. This meant that she didn't want to have sex either.

John asked, "are you ok?"

Sammy said, "yes, time of the month and all that."

John thought back and remembered she had said two weeks before that it was her time of the month. He replied, "fine, no problem."

Sammy waited a few seconds and said, "it's not all about sex you know."

John replied, "I never said it was, I wasn't complaining."

A half-hour passed in silence and Sammy got up saying "I've got a nasty headache, I think I'd like to go home now."

John got up and collecting their clothes said, "fine, whatever miss wants."

Sammy turned to him and in an aggressive tone said, "what do you mean by that?"

John didn't answer and started to walk back to the jeep.

They both got in and John started the engine. Sammy suddenly burst into tears and put her hand over his on the gearstick, "I'm sorry, I know I'm, well…., the truth is I'm not sleeping, I've had to re-do some of my work when I notice mistakes. I'm just not myself at the moment. I've had a row with my mother and I know it's my fault." Nobody spoke for a few minutes. Sammy turned to John and said, "I don't want you to go back. I love you. I didn't want to feel like this but I thought I could control it. I love being with you and now I know you are going back I know I'm going to miss you so much."

John didn't know what to say. He thought for a few seconds and said, "I think of you all the time, but I couldn't live here and you would hate where I live. It just wouldn't work. In the army, I could only legally take you back if we were married and then we would both end up feeling guilty because you wouldn't see your family. We just have to be sensible."

Sammy started to sob and said, "couldn't you find work here, my father did."

John said, "that was when Burma was part of the British Empire. The country is different now, the Burmese don't want British people here. I don't have any skills in anything this country can offer, even if I was able to find work, it would drive us apart."

Sammy continued to sob and both were silent as they were both sensible enough to know that what John had said was true. After a while John started up the engine and drove back to Sammy's house.

When they arrived Sammy very quickly gave a John a quick kiss and jumped out, still crying.

The following week John was asked to go to the major's office. Major Kearns began "well Staff Sergeant Evans your demob orders have come through. You are to leave Rangoon on 11th February and you will sail on the S.S. Dunera. She is due to dock in Southampton some three weeks later and you have been ordered to attend your de-brief and demob the following week. You'll get paid leave after that probably for a few months to allow you to find employment or decide whatever it is you want to do with the rest of your life. I've been very pleased with the service and work you've put in since you've been here and I've carefully written a reference for you which I hope will help get you work when you return. There is also a short reference in your service record from Lieutenant-Colonel Hayes at Admin. Burma Rear Force. What work did you do before the army?"

John said, "I worked in an ironmonger's shop."

Major Kearns looked at John and said, "and do you want to go back to the ironmonger's shop?"

John said, "no sir, 'I think I've grown up since I've been in the army and the hope is that there might be something a little more rewarding for me back home."

Major Kearns smiled and said, "I thought you were going to say something like that. My very best wishes for your future. I'm sure you will make something of yourself and I hope that the army has contributed in some way to that."

John smiled back "I'm sure it has, sir."

Instead of the usual salute, John shook the outstretched hand of the major and thanked him for all he had done and that he had been proud to serve under him. With that, he left immediately realising he would have to now tell Sammy that his sailing had been announced. He couldn't face going back to the office and found anything to do rather than face Sammy. He wandered around until he knew that Sammy had left for home. He went into the mess for a drink that evening and there seemed to be a party atmosphere as all the remaining sergeants had been given the dates of their departures, most of them on the Dunera, along with John. They planned a party for their last weekend.

John broke the silence the following morning when Sammy had her head down, concentrating on a letter she was asked to write. He told her his date of departure had been agreed and that they had arranged a party in the sergeant's mess the next Saturday evening, but he would be able to go swimming on Saturday morning.

Sammy gave a sullen look and said she was sorry but she had promised to help her mother with the shopping on Saturday and so swimming wouldn't be possible. John accepted what she said and thought perhaps it was for the best.

Sammy left the office on the Friday evening when John had gone to see Captain Stevens. He went to finish some work in an empty office and then walked over to his dormitory. He thought he would have an early night, as the party was the following night. Before turning in he went for a quick drink in the mess.

After about ten minutes Rob Charnock came in and said, "Sammy's outside, she says she's left something important in the office and could you open up for her."

John thought it strange but went outside. Sammy grabbed him as he came out of the mess. She didn't say anything but walked over towards the office hut, pulling John's jacket behind her. It was almost completely dark and she stumbled as she got to the hut. John helped her to her feet and noticed her eyes a little blurred. He said, "have you been drinking?"

Sammy turned to him and pulled him inside the hut and said, "only a little to give me courage to come back." She turned and pushed the papers off the desk, sitting on the desk and pulling down her knickers.

John wanted to tell her not to be so silly but was turned on by the sight of her on the desk. He pulled his trousers and pants down and immediately entered her. She gave a loud moan and only a very short time later John came inside her. She lay back but said nothing. John started to caress her face and she started to kiss him passionately. He pulled up her blouse and started to kiss her breasts. She pulled him towards her and they both fell gently onto the floor. He entered her a second time and came again. They lay back exhausted and both began to laugh. John said, "the number of times I've wanted to do that."

Sammy laughed "I think Prem or Gurung or one of the ladies might have complained."

They dressed and John escorted Sammy to the jeep. He drove to Monkey Point and they walked along the riverside. They talked, and though they could not agree anything that would suit both of them John said he promised he would write if he thought of any solution.

Sammy said, "I feel sad and disappointed, and the fact that I am sad and disappointed sometimes makes me feel angry," and a few silent seconds later she added "and that makes me feel frustrated. Frustrated because I thought all problems were solvable and I can't solve this one."

They were both very aware of their feelings for one another but knew for the moment there was nothing they could do about it and were resigned to the fact they would have to part.

John took Sammy home, and they kissed passionately before Sammy got out of the jeep and crossed the road to her home.

John woke on the Sunday with a very bad headache. The party had been both wild and destructive and a few of them set about repairing damaged furniture.

The Dunera was due to sail on Tuesday morning and Sammy did not turn up for work on the Monday.

Early Tuesday morning the men collected their kit and the presents they had bought to take home, which were boxed and paid for separately. They piled into the back of a truck and said their goodbyes to HQ Burma Command. The truck pulled out of the camp, John was sat at the back of a long bench running the length of the truck and as it turned for the docks John noticed Sammy sat on the pavement. She stood up as the truck passed and raised her hand slowly to shoulder height. John noticed she had her sapphire ear-rings dangling between her fingers. John raised his hand slowly, just showing the palm of his hand, overcome with a deep sadness.

JOHN

25

The ship docked to pick up a few officers in Colombo. John and his mates were allowed a few hours shore leave. They sat outside a bar drinking a cold beer. The others chatted happily, looking forward to going home, while John sat silently. Rob and Chico teased him for a while but getting no response they gave up and left John to his silence. John showed no interest in pub-crawling and remained outside the bar while the others wandered away. He watched the locals pass the bar, some seemingly on business, others shopping and a few looking lonely but out just to pass the time.

John noticed significantly that any Europeans who passed were with other Europeans, sometimes two men, sometimes a man and a woman. Likewise, any Sinhalese were with people of their own race. He persuaded himself that these people were comfortable with people of their own cultures. He suddenly said out loud "it would never have worked." A few people walking past looked in his direction wondering where the voice had come from but quickly moved on. John moped around and walked down to the dockside watching small ships working their way between the bigger ships. It was a day of thick, low cloud, everything seemed to be enveloped, the mountains, even some of the buildings. John thought it matched his mood. He threw a few coins to a beggar sat against the low concrete wall that edged the boundary between sea and shore. He couldn't get Sammy out of his thoughts; would he ever see her again? Would he be able to think of a way they could live together and be happy? Would he miss her so much he would have to return to Burma?

John had never felt so sad. He wondered whether it was just because he might never see Sammy again or did he miss Burma, which despite its problems had a magnetic attraction. The thought that he might never return darkened his mood.

He noticed his mates coming back and joined them to get back on the ship.

As the ship passed through the Suez Canal, the Mediterranean Sea, past Gibraltar and the Bay of Biscay his mates played deck games and generally fooled about. John tried to join in, but his heart wasn't in it. Eventually, in the first week of March, the ship docked in Southampton. John was glad the voyage was over but with each mile, he felt further from Sammy and his despair increased. The group of friends found a bar and booked a hotel for the night. They exchanged addresses over a few beers and promised to meet up within the next twelve months. Two of them expected to be getting married during that time, and all were invited. Firm dates would follow.

John was finally on his own, in a railway carriage. He was on a train heading back up the valley to Treafon, his demob complete. He was told he would be on the army reserve list for several years and would be called back if required. He wore his demob suit, which he thought looked quite smart and carried his kit bag with his army jacket. He would be on leave until the end of May, giving him two months to find a job.

He watched the world go by outside the train's window and thought, nothing changes here, it looks the same as when I left. It was a grey, miserable day with light rain and thick cloud. The drab valley towns passed by, the small patches of grass interspersed with black coal tips and the small villages with rows of terraced houses. Lines of railway trucks carrying coal passed by in the other direction, travelling to the ports of Newport and Cardiff.

He wearily carried the heavy kit bag up from the railway station. He hoped his trunk of presents had arrived ahead of him, he would soon find out. He felt more than a little depressed. He was looking forward to sleeping after a long journey, and the previous night's beers. He walked through the park, his favourite part of Treafon, but even this would not dispel his gloom. Heavier rain darkened his mood. He thought, how my life has changed in the last three years but now it'll go back to normal if I let it. It'll be as if I never went away.

He arrived at his door, took a deep breath and knocked, as he couldn't be bothered to go searching for his key. His mother opened the door, stepped back, and immediately threw her arms around him and kissed him. He brushed away the effects of the kiss with "Mam, stop it." He went into the living room, banging his kit bag against the wall as he tried to get through the doorway. His dad and David both stood up and shook his hand as if he was there for an interview. His dad said, "good to have you back son." David looked as if he had doubled in size. John remembered he was now sixteen.

John turned to his brother "still playing cricket?"

David nodded, smiling "aye."

John carried on "well, it's obviously good for you. You look bigger and stronger than I did at your age."

David puffed out his chest and said, "it's mam's cooking."

Mrs Evans laughed and playfully pushed David away "get on with you, you're eating me out of house and home."

John thought it felt good to be back.

They all went through to the kitchen where Mrs Evans had laid out some food.

John used the next few days to relax and recover from the weeks of travel. He kept thinking he would have to see Elizabeth quite soon or face the consequences, but he felt so guilty.

He had left Sammy standing on the pavement outside the camp in Rangoon four weeks before and that time had helped a little in John trying to balance his life. He made his mind up to go down to Elizabeth's house on the following day, a Saturday.

He gingerly knocked on the door and Elizabeth came to open it. She was so pleased that she threw her arms around him and kissed him. She said, "I've missed you so much."

John suddenly thought that Elizabeth didn't give the impression that she knew he had been home for four days. He said, "I wasn't sure you would be here, been as it's a Saturday an'all."

Elizabeth replied, "I've been popping into your mam's and she said you were coming home last week so I took today off."

John felt a little guilty as Elizabeth confirmed she had known he had been home for a few days. He went in and after saying hello to her father, sat at the kitchen table.

Elizabeth's father said, "too late for the war then, suppose you didn't pick up a gun?" He continued "Elizabeth said you've been doing a bit of pen pushing."

John didn't rise to the bait but replied: "sprayed the terrorists with ink and jabbed them with my ruler."

Elizabeth's father tut-tutted and went back to his paper. Elizabeth said, "shall we go into the front room?"

The two of them went into the room, which was kept especially for guests and consequently rarely used. Elizabeth kissed him again and said, "it's so good to have you home and now for good."

John said, "yea, now all I've got to do is find a job. The army will pay me until the end of May and then when my leave finishes I have to find work or sign on."

Elizabeth said, "what about the ironmonger's?"

John replied "I can go and see if they still have a job for me, but I want to look around and see if there's anything else out there. I think I've changed a bit since I've been in the army."

"Not too much, I hope?," Elizabeth retorted. She said, "don't leave it too long to decide what you are going to do. If they've kept your job open they'll want to see if you want it pretty soon."

John said, "I've brought presents back for you and the family but the package hasn't arrived yet."

Elizabeth said, "I just want you back, I don't care about any present."

John looked down, a little embarrassed but said, "I'll send the diamond ring back then."

Elizabeth was confused and not really sure what he meant, so she didn't comment.

It was quite a bright day and so they agreed to go for a walk in the park. Elizabeth told her father they were going out for a walk. He quickly stated, "don't forget I'll want my dinner at one o'clock."

Elizabeth said, "I'll be back well before that." She left, raising her eyes to the sky as she caught John's glance.

"Happy chap, as ever," John laughed, as they walked down the garden path.

As they crossed the bridge over the level crossing on their way to the park, they were enveloped in smoke from the steam train passing underneath which brought back memories to John of his description of the town to Sammy a few weeks before.

Elizabeth asked, "what were the last few months like in Burma?"

John said, "very busy, we had to arrange for all British personnel and equipment to be brought out after Burma became independent."

Elizabeth asked, "Was there any more trouble from bandits and troublemakers after the problems last Summer?"

John said, "a little, but not really in Rangoon."

Elizabeth asked, "all your mates ok?"

John was getting a little tired of all the questions and he irritably started answering in one-word answers.

Elizabeth asked, "don't you want to talk?"

John answered, "sorry, it's just that I'm still tired after travelling."

Elizabeth said, "of course, I understand, but I wouldn't have to ask so much if you had written more often."

This made John even more irritable, but he decided he wouldn't rise to the bait and said nothing. Elizabeth said, "were you too busy to write more often?"

John said, "I was busy but I really thought you wouldn't be interested in what was happening half way around the world."

"Surely that's for me to judge," Elizabeth answered, a little testily.

They walked through the park gates and John decided silence was probably the best option.

After they had walked around for an hour or so with little being said, Elizabeth finally added: "I'd better be going, dad will want his dinner." John asked to see her the following day and she agreed.

John decided to walk a little before going home as it might lighten his mood. He walked through the centre of town stopping to watch people crowding off the buses that stopped in the small bus station. He considered that things were looking up, people were coming into the town from the surrounding towns and villages to shop. It all looked as if Treafon had a good future.

The following morning John's mam asked if he was going to chapel. John replied that he would go to the morning service but that would be it. She walked off a little huffily. John dressed in his suit and walked with her, David and his father to the chapel. He spoke to friends and other members of the family both before and after the service, all of whom said how pleased they were to see John back safely. John could feel himself nodding off during the sermon and he was thankful that nobody questioned him on its content as he wouldn't be able to offer an opinion.

After dinner, he walked down to Elizabeth's and they walked up the pathway to the east of the town, past the hospital, which had once been the workhouse, up to the mountain behind. They passed the town's reservoir and continued up the track onto the mountain behind. The countryside seemed to raise their mood and John visibly cheered up. They stopped and sat on a grass banking, overlooking the town. While the town was partly under a blanket of smoke it was exactly as he had remembered it and explained it to Sammy when he said, "it's home." Yes, the town was drab and dirty, many of the houses needed painting and the people were poor but if you looked beyond the town, around its edges there was greenery, lots of it, trees, grassland, wildflowers and animals grazing. From this point, you could see the river winding its way through the town and continuing on down the valley. The vision seemed to John a little bit like the people in the town itself, wary of outsiders, sometimes wary of each other, often difficult to befriend but very soft on the edges. The closeness of the houses was synonymous with the closeness of the people, involved in each other's lives and while for some this was interference, for others it was a great help, particularly during difficult times. The war was over but rationing, poverty and despair were still there. It would take time but already things were looking better. These thoughts gave John a warm feeling and a rekindling of his love for the town.

The couple continued to walk, and chat. John said, "it's good to be back home, to see you and the family."

Elizabeth turned to John and leaned over to kiss him. They both held their embrace and John said, "it's strange, one day I'm in Rangoon, the next I'm in Colombo, then I'm home. It does funny things to the mind."

Elizabeth said, "I understand, it's different for me, every day is the same and I did so look forward to you coming home." They walked for a while further, holding hands, both feeling they were getting to know each other again, two lives converging on a single pathway, with a single purpose, after being apart for so long.

They saw each other through the next week and by the following weekend, their relationship seemed to be back on track. John had got into the habit of going to the town's labour exchange and he would regularly buy the local paper. He would circle the jobs that he thought he would like and send letters of application off to a few. He made his mind up that he would prefer to take up a job locally as he could continue to live at home, which would save him money on accommodation. Elizabeth's brother had written to her from London explaining that John would be able to find work there, but he would have to find his own accommodation as he had got married at the end of the previous year and he was living in a one-bedroom flat with his new wife. John asked Elizabeth to thank her brother but he would first look locally. John went to the ironmonger's on the following day and was met by all the people who worked there. He explained to Lionel "I don't think I'll be looking to get my job back."

Lionel smiled and said, "I don't think the owners have kept your job open anyway. We are doing very little trade, there are plenty of people coming into the town but they are poor and are careful with their money. They spend their money on essentials like food, not shovels and spades." John turned to go, shouting "ta-ra," to everyone, and promising to call in regularly now he would be back for good. He felt it was good to leave under pleasant circumstances.

At the beginning of the third week back, John received a reply to one of his letters of application. In the previous year, the government had nationalised the coal industry, bringing under its control all the coal mines, methods of distributing and transporting the coal to private coal merchants and the docks. This organisation became the N.C.B, The National Coal Board. The reply stated that the offices based in Treafon would be extended, to help carry out all the administrative tasks, which were needed to effectively mine and organise the distribution of coal, a very important material needed to power and heat the country. The letter stated that they were impressed with John's application letter, which outlined his administrative experience in the army. They asked him to attend an interview in two weeks at the main offices in Treafon and to bring any references he had from previous employers if he was still interested. It gave a time and date for the interview and asked him to confirm he would be attending.

John told his family who seemed overjoyed at the prospect of an interview and that night he walked down to Elizabeth's to tell her.

However, Elizabeth put a little damper on John's enthusiasm by saying "don't get your hopes up in case you don't get the job, then you'll be disappointed. Just do the best you can. I'll be really hoping you get it." She waited a few seconds and then said, "don't forget there may be other people in for the job as well."

The next week John got another package and letter, which he had to sign for and which was a complete surprise.

John opened the letter carefully and placed the package aside. The envelope that contained the letter was outlined with a gold line. When John opened the envelope he noticed two sheets of paper. The first contained only a few lines but had the address of Buckingham Palace in the top left-hand corner. He quickly read the letter, which stated that the King apologised for not being able to present this medal in person, but it was sent with the King's congratulations and best wishes. It also said that the medal had been well earned. The second sheet of paper explained that the award of the medal, the British Empire Medal, was for gallantry, and the award would be published in the London Gazette. John immediately opened the package that came with the letter. He picked out the medal from the small box. The silver medal felt heavy in his hand and was attached to a grey and lavender band. John was taken aback and for a while couldn't speak. David looked over his shoulder and asked, "what's gallantry?"

John's dad stood with his thumbs in his waistcoat and his chest puffed out and said very proudly "bravery."

John's mother took the medal from his hand and stood looking at it, then, she put her arms around his neck and squeezed him saying quietly into his ear "I'm so proud."

John's dad shook his hand and said, "well done, son."

After a while, John put on his jacket, put the medal into his pocket and put the letter back into the envelope. He walked down to Elizabeth's, house, she was very surprised to see him. She asked him in and he immediately showed her the letters and the medal. She stood silent, in shock at first, then threw her arms around him and said, "I'm so proud of you," and then after a few seconds "you have to take this to your interview, it could make all the difference." John hadn't thought of that but agreed that he would.

Elizabeth's father asked, "what's all the fuss about?"

John said, "I've received the British Empire Medal" and added, "for bravery."

Elizabeth's father said, "well, tell us all about it, what did you do to earn it son?"

John sat down and related to them both the story of the Burmese cabinet's assassination and the aftermath, the patrolling of the airfield and finding the terrorists with their arms cache.

Elizabeth listened silently with a little girl's wide-eyed expression.

Even Elizabeth's father had to say "well done son," but tempered his praise after by adding "course, I had loads of medals in the Great War." John and Elizabeth both laughed and her father looking very peeved said, "well I did," which caused more laughter.

Elizabeth said, "I've never seen the London Gazette, but I'll write to Wesley and ask him to pick up a copy and send it home."

John said, "if I receive the copy in time I'll take it to the interview."

Receiving the medal caused John to cast his mind back to Burma, and eventually to Sammy. He had been so busy settling at home, spending time with Elizabeth and applying for jobs that he hadn't given Burma or Sammy much thought in recent weeks. As he walked home, clutching his medal he thought of her back in Rangoon. He assured himself he was sure a pretty girl like her would find someone to share her life with and would go to university, get a good job, meet someone, and have a family, all the time contributing to the new Burma that she loved. He tried to reassure himself that he had made the right decision in not trying too hard to find a way to stay in Burma or return to Burma.

26

John thought he would search out his mates from school, but he suddenly realised that he had been the first to leave for his army service and they would all still be away doing their service for a few more weeks. He made a mental note to remember to contact them in a few weeks.

Two weeks later John nervously tapped at the door to the office in the main building of the N.C.B., Treafon. The building was large and imposing, it had tall gothic style towers on either end, which made it difficult to identify as a set of offices. It was entered under a high arch similar to those in coaching houses and John pondered whether that might have been its original purpose. He followed a corridor to reception.

Someone called out "come in," and John opened the door to find two typists busily working. One said, "here for the interview? Mr Coles will be with you as soon as possible, please take a seat and what is your name?"

John nervously thought to make sure he gave the right answer to the right question. He said, "John Evans, here for the clerk's job." He drew in a breath as he had nearly said Staff–Sergeant Evans, as that was how he had been introducing himself for the previous three years. He thought, the army is still paying me and I'm technically on leave so perhaps I should have said Staff-Sergeant.

After about fifteen minutes the door to the inner office opened and out came a man about John's age. He turned and shook hands with an older man who was inside the office. The older man said, "thanks anyway Mr Roberts, we'll be in touch by the end of the week. Thank you for your time." The man walked out, thanking the typists as he went and the older man looked at John as he asked: "here for interview?" Before John could answer the typist who had addressed him said, "Mr Evans, here for the clerk's job, Mr Coles."

Mr Coles stood back and ushered John into the office. John carefully moved past the older man and took a seat.

Mr Coles was quite personable and put John at his ease. At least he felt more comfortable as the interview went on. Mr Coles said that he wasn't from Treafon, but he had worked for a coalmine owner for twenty years and was now employed by the N.C.B. He said, after looking at a sheet of paper on his desk, "in your own time, and please don't feel rushed, tell me about your previous job in the ironmongers and then about your army service."

John proceeded to outline his working life so far, and Mr Cole stopped him, from time to time, to ask brief questions and make notes on a pad in front of him, as he went along. Mr Coles seemed particularly interested in the fact that he had served in Burma. He said, "we've had a few ex-servicemen to interview, but you are the first to have served in Burma." When it seemed John had finished Mr Cole started to speak about the nature of the job and it was then that John remembered he hadn't said anything about the medal, the letter from the King and the London Gazette, a copy of which had arrived at Elizabeth's two days before.

John quickly burst into Mr Coles explanation, "I haven't said about the medal," then he realised his rudeness and quickly apologised saying "I'm sorry to interrupt but Elizabeth, ah my girlfriend, thought the medal might be important and I had ...ah forgotten about it until now. I thought I'd better say about it now before I forgot again"

Mr Coles had difficulty stifling a laugh at John's nervousness and lack of experience in being interviewed. The older gentleman could see that if John had burst into the conversation it was for an important purpose. He leaned back in his chair, and smiling said, "well, you'd better tell me about it then."

John had put the letter, the copy of the London Gazette and the medal in a small leather case that he had borrowed from the next-door neighbour. He thought it made him look a little more important. He pulled out all three things and placed them on the desk. Mr Coles said, "very impressive, not everyone gets a letter from the King. Tell me what you did to warrant such a prestigious award?"

John proceeded to explain to Mr Coles what had happened in Burma and his surprise at receiving the medal and the letter.

Mr Coles was fascinated and listened intently to John's description of events. When John had finished he looked at him and said, "well, it's a good job you remembered to tell me all that, you're a brave lad and it looks like this was well deserved. Might make all the difference."

John thought, hmm that's exactly what Elizabeth had said.

Mr Coles then asked him "have you got any references?"

He took out his references from his army service record and a reference from the ironmongers that he had asked for the previous week.

At the end of the interview, John turned to leave, remembering to thank Mr Coles and as he left the office, remembering to thank the typists in the outer office. He noticed three people sat waiting for Mr Coles and suddenly thought, did I speak for too long and will Mr Coles be pissed off with me because he's got to catch up. Mr Coles then said the same as he had said to the previous interviewee "thanks for your time Mr Evans, we'll be in touch by the end of the week."

John felt exhausted with nervous energy, and he decided to walk up through the town on his way home. He popped his head into the sweet shop where Elizabeth worked. Audrey shouted out "morning, soldier boy." John replied with a mumble, not always sure how to take Audrey.

Elizabeth came from behind the counter and said, "how did it go? I've been nervous all morning."

John said that he didn't have a clue as he had nothing to compare it with but, "Mr Coles seemed very nice and said he will let me know by the end of the week."

The following morning the Post Office delivery van brought a large wooden box covered in stickers and stamps. John's presents from Burma had arrived. He brought out a series of wood carvings, a small coffee table, elaborately carved with chinthes, a sort of cross between a lion and a dragon, two table lamps, one an elephant and the other a cobra, and a large Japanese Samurai sword. However, when John took the sword out of its packaging he noticed the pearl handle had crumbled. He lifted it up and said resignedly "Oh well I suppose that'll be my present to myself." He allocated the various items to people and arranged how he could deliver them.

Five days later a letter came through the letter-box offering him the job with the N.C.B. John was ecstatic. He ran around the house with the acceptance letter, his mother wondering what was wrong with him. He explained that he had got the job and once again John's mother gave him a big kiss, which he quickly brushed away. He grabbed his coat and rushed out to go and tell Elizabeth, who was equally ecstatic.

The following day John returned to the N.C.B. offices to see Mr Coles as he had been requested. He explained that there had been eighteen applicants interviewed for the job and thank goodness John had remembered to outline how and why he had received the medal as that said more about his personality and attitude than any CV could.

Mr Coles got up and proceeded to put on his coat, he said, "come with me and I'll show you your office." John was a little surprised as they left the building completely and walked about two hundred yards to the entrance of a disused coal mine which stood alongside the main N.C.B. offices. Mr Coles pointed towards a small red brick building. He said, "you'll be working in there. We've just appointed the man in charge, Mr Ferguson, and you will work under him. He was working until recently in the main office here, but he's been moved out and promoted and he'll be your boss. We are also moving a typist into the small office with you. Come on I'll introduce you."

The two walked across to the small office and Mr Coles knocked on a door opposite the entrance. Someone called "come in," and they were met by Mr Ferguson, who came from behind a large desk. He explained that the typist, Miss Thorpe would be starting the following week. Both men outlined the work that John would be expected to do and explained that he would have to sit examinations from time to time to prove his competence.

John left the two men feeling very pleased with himself, and a lot more relaxed about the job he was about to do.

John began work the week after his army leave finished. He quickly settled into the work. He saw it as a challenge to learn new skills and for the first time appreciated the things he had learnt while in the army. It had helped him organise his time and it had helped with the tasks he had to perform in this job.

By early Summer he had time to reflect. He had attended one of his mates' weddings in Cheshire but couldn't ask for time off to attend Chico's wedding in Leicester. Chico was the last person he expected to get married, so soon after leaving the army. He hadn't mentioned a girlfriend or anybody that he had back home. John wrote to him to apologise for missing the wedding and Chico's reply explained that he had met a girl at a party when he got back and that the rushed wedding was because she was pregnant.

John smiled to himself and thought, that will leave a lot of Chico's acquaintances disappointed.

John felt satisfied with his new job and with his life in general. Living at home wasn't perfect, there was constant tension with his mother who thought he should be attending chapel more often, but his meals were prepared for him and for the first time in his life he had some money. He had enjoyed spending time with Elizabeth and when he pondered on it he had barely given Sammy much thought in the last few weeks. He had been back from Burma for five months and things felt pretty good. He had invested in new clothes for work and when he went to check on his bank account he was pleasantly surprised that his wages when added to his army savings totalled a tidy sum. He began to think that perhaps he should look to his future and think about settling down with Elizabeth. One Summer's evening he went for a walk on his own to give himself time to think. He sat on a large rock high above the town. When he got his breath back he began to plan, sitting and chewing on a reed that he had picked up on his way up the mountain. He thought I don't know, it seems all my serious thinking is done in the quiet of the countryside outside the town. He thought it made sense to walk out to an area where he couldn't be disturbed.

He thought that people's advice was right. When I was a little miserable coming back on the boat from Burma Rob Charnock told me that in time I would forget Sammy, and realise that it would never have worked out. Now I was back with Elizabeth I was happy. If I was honest she was different from Sammy. Sammy was exotic. Yes, she was a beautiful girl, and it was great while it lasted but I had to be realistic. If I didn't begin to plan a future Elizabeth would become impatient, I might lose her and then I would be back at square one. Did I really want to spend the rest of my life with her? Yes, he thought, I do.

After a long period of reflection, the evening started to get dark. John started to make his way back down the mountain. He had made a few firm decisions. He would travel down to Cardiff on the following Saturday and buy a ring.

John caught the bus to Cardiff the following Saturday. He told Elizabeth he was going to meet an army mate. He wandered around the shops in the city centre, checking out the different types of rings and their prices. He eventually settled on rings which contained small diamonds, in a sort of cluster. He had seen three in three different shops and decided on the middle one price-wise. He thought it was the nicest of the three and it would leave him with enough money to organise a small party, all assuming Elizabeth would agree to his request.

The following day he went to see Elizabeth and asked her if she would like to have a meal the next Saturday at a local hotel. She agreed, and John spent the whole of the next week nervously wondering whether Elizabeth would accept his proposal.

That evening when he knew Elizabeth would not be at home John called to her house to ask her father if he had his support in asking Elizabeth to marry him. He felt a little confused as Elizabeth's father bombarded him with questions he didn't have the answers to, such as 'Where will you live? How will you afford a house? Will Elizabeth give up work? However, the evening ended with Elizabeth's father saying that he thought John would make a good husband for her. John thought, praise indeed.

The meal in the local hotel was very pleasant. They both finished their dessert and accepted cups of coffee. John leaned back in his seat and slowly said, "I was wondering, that perhaps if you wanted to.....," and lost his way a little and looked a little flustered.

Elizabeth said, "well, what?"

John cleared his throat and thought, Oh god, I've got to get this over. Quickly he said, "will you marry me?"

Elizabeth obviously didn't see it coming and was speechless for a while. Eventually, she said, "well, yes I will if that's what you want."

John said, "what do you want?"

Elizabeth laughed "well, to marry you."

She immediately rattled off the same questions her father had asked, leaving John wondering if her father had told her and they had compared their views on a forthcoming marriage.

John had to admit he didn't have the answers to her questions and said, "I wasn't thinking right away, I thought perhaps the Summer after next, gives us time to save." The conversation suddenly went quiet as both were considering what had just happened and what options there were for their futures.

Elizabeth told her father that evening and he seemed pleased, but said little beyond the expected "congratulations." John told his mam and dad the same evening. John's mother said she was 'over the moon', and 'it's about time.' Despite being late at night she couldn't stop herself knocking on Aggie' next door, to tell her. It became an impromptu party, until Mrs Evans eventually shooed everybody out, as she was tired and wanted to go to bed.

At the end of August, an engagement party was held in Elizabeth's chapel vestry. It was paid for by John and was helped by contributions of cakes and sandwiches from friends and neighbours. They announced that they had decided they would get married in that very chapel in the Summer of 1950 and after discussions with Elizabeth's father, John would move in with them after the wedding. John added, "if he'll still have me?"

Elizabeth's father added, "it's her you're marrying, not me." Everyone laughed and the evening ended happily. The only point of concern was Mrs Evans constantly badgering John about which chapel he would now attend. John replied, "for God's sake mam."

Mrs Evans retort was "don't blaspheme, and it's for God's sake I'm asking. They are Presbyterian, we are Congregational."

John walked away saying under his breath "I don't know what'll be worse, living with my mother or Elizabeth's dad?"

JOHN AND ELIZABETH

27

The happy couple came out to the front of the chapel for photographs. John and Elizabeth stood in the middle and were flanked by Dennis, the best man, Mr and Mrs Evans, and David who was on three days leave from Hereford and was looking very smart in his R.A.F. uniform after a few months of National Service, on one side and Mr Williams, Elizabeth's dad on the other, alongside Marjorie, the bridesmaid. They moved aside to make way for friends as Audrey, Peter, Jennifer, Jane Thorpe and about five or six neighbours of John and Elizabeth's stood alongside the couple. Elizabeth's brother and his wife and Elizabeth's sister were unable to attend for a range of reasons. Nobody had seen Rob, his school friend, but it was thought that he had moved to Hereford and had moved in with his lady friend. Peter, John's school-friend had travelled down from London where he was still carrying out his medical training. Rob Charnock had managed to come to the wedding and was staying in very cramped conditions in Mrs Evans house. She had said Rob could sleep in John's bed as he would no longer be needing it. Rob thought she had said that with a tear in her eye.

They trooped into the reception in the chapel vestry and all stood and clapped when the newly married couple entered. The food provided caused Elizabeth's father to comment, "it makes a good spread." The meal was followed by speeches, which were fortunately short.

They were all complimentary to John and Elizabeth, except for Dennis' speech which was a little risqué and caused Mrs Evans to raise her eyes and shake her head a few times and following the reception to say to John, "you should have chosen Peter, such a nice well behaved boy, lovely manners."

John walked away without answering. The whole ensemble went quiet as John and Elizabeth moved towards a table in the corner of the vestry on which stood the wedding-cake, a three-layered icing covered cake. This was to be the defining moment of the reception. John had paid for the cake with his savings and along with his suit and Elizabeth's dress were the only things which their meagre savings had to pay for. The hire of the vestry was jointly paid for by John's parents and Elizabeth's father, and friends and family had provided the food. Dennis had provided the bottles of cheap sparkling wine, which allowed them to toast the couple. This caused consternation with Mrs Evans who was dubious about having alcohol in a church vestry, but this had been cleared with the chapel minister who said it was a special occasion and he would take the flak if there was any. Mrs Evans took the smallest of sips at the toast and her husband was highly amused at her religious commitment and the face she pulled. Elizabeth and John jointly held the knife that sliced down through the cake and the audience applauded. This action almost having religious significance in binding John and Elizabeth to the teamwork that would be required from them in facing the tasks that would befall them in the coming weeks, months and years.

John had agreed with Elizabeth that he should move in with her and her dad, as there was more room in that house than in his mother's house. John had spent a great deal of time in Elizabeth's house in the run-up to the wedding. He, along with Dennis, had built a long single-storey building in the yard of the house to incorporate the outside toilet, which was now inside.

Mr Williams was very pleased and said to John when Elizabeth was not about, "good work lad, I won't freeze me bollocks off now going to the lav in the winter." This allowed them to move the cooker and sink into the new building giving them more room in what used to be the old kitchen. John had also helped take down some old sheds in the garden and had painted the new toilet and kitchen and the old kitchen, which effectively became a second living room. He also painted what was to be their bedroom. Mr Williams constantly complained at the inconvenience when the building and the painting was going on but was well pleased with the finished result and complimented John on the work he had done, which he said completely transformed the small house.

John had made progress in work. He had sat two sets of examinations for the Coal Utilisation Council, which he had passed with flying colours and he had firmly embedded himself in the small office. Mr Ferguson was very impressed with him and he had got along very well with Jane Thorpe, the typist. They had formed a really good working relationship and John enjoyed going to work. Mr Ferguson now involved him in negotiations with members of the Coal Miner's Union and all these experiences helped him in his work. Consequently, John had recently had a pay rise, which had helped to pay for the wedding and the building work. The couple would leave on the following Monday for a weekend's honeymoon in London, where Elizabeth hoped to see her brother and his wife.

At the end of the speeches, the formal part of the wedding was over. John sneaked out to go around the corner for a cigarette.

Dennis spotted him and followed him. John gave him a cigarette and Dennis looked up "well, you've done it now, ball and chain forever for you."

John said, "well, it was what I wanted and I'm sure Elizabeth will make a good wife."

Dennis smirked, "they change after marriage mind, you'll see a difference after today, she'll wake up a wild ogre tomorrow and from then on your life will be hell."

John replied, "there speaks a man of experience."

Dennis took another drag on the cigarette "only 'cause they can't catch me."

Dennis asked, "Is she your first, you know, or were there loads of women in Burma."

John had to choke back his reply, and after a few seconds of thought he said, "many dusky maidens, all banging on my door." He hadn't noticed Rob Charnock coming around the corner from the chapel, who had heard the last question and John's answer. He joined the two of them and looking at John said, "well there was one special one John, wasn't there? but that's a while back now."

John looked around to see if anyone else could overhear and turning to Rob and said, "shh, you'll get me into a lot of trouble."

Dennis said, "you old dog, you never told me."

Rob asked, "did you write to her after you got back?"

John shook his head and said, "thought it was best not to, it would never have worked would it."

Rob looked up at the sky and said, "she was a real cracker though."

John recalled a mental picture of Sammy, which had never quite receded and replied: "yes, she really was."

They could see Marjorie bustling out from the chapel in her noisy fashion and coming around the corner to meet them. She burst into their conversation, which immediately came to a halt. She said, "anyone got a fag?"

They stayed for a while discussing the wedding and then gradually filtered back inside the chapel vestry where the older guests were beginning to take back their dishes and collect the rubbish into bins. The men were clearing the tables away and the younger ones were setting up a gramophone in the corner, which Dennis had borrowed.

Elizabeth said that she was going to see her father got home safely and then she would come back to the vestry. John could hear the beating rhythm of 'Slow Boat to China', playing on the gramophone in the vestry and thought, hmm, that's got its attractions.

John said he would see her shortly after he had said goodbye to friends and family who were leaving. However, once Elizabeth was out of sight he went for a walk along a track leading from the back of the chapel. He walked along a few streets and sat for a while on a bench just on the edge of town. The conversation with Rob and Dennis had brought back memories of Sammy. He hadn't thought about her for a long while and now hadn't seen her for nearly two and a half years, but if he closed his eyes he could still picture her in her swimsuit, and then naked outside the hut they stayed in for their picnic, and then sadly waiting at the side of the road as he left the camp for the last time. He thought I could have been with her for good. We could have had a life somewhere. Would we have been happy? or would the effort of trying to make it work have worn us out, destroying anything we had. Well, he thought, he'd made his bed, as they say, and that night he would lie in it. He had to make every effort to make Elizabeth happy. She had worked hard to make a home for her father and she was a sweet and kind person.

John stood up ready to walk back to his new life, confident he'd made the right decision. He was happy in his work and he was happy in his personal relationship and he'd make damn certain it stayed that way.

DOUGLAS KHIAN

28

Charlotte Evans was hanging clothes out at the back of No 2, Union Street when she was sure she heard someone tapping at the front door. All was quiet in the household. She had earlier turned off the radio as William had fallen asleep in the chair and it seemed pointless to leave it on. She walked through the house, glancing at William, quietly snoring in his favourite chair in the living room. She said, almost under her breath in mock annoyance "have I got to do everything in this house?" As she pulled open the door to the very small porch she could see the outline of a man through the glass in the front door.

She opened the front door and waited for the tall dark man to speak. He hadn't immediately turned, as he hadn't noticed the door being opened. On turning around, he said hesitantly, "Ahh, Mr John Evans?" and then thinking seemingly to choose his words carefully "ahh, does he reside at this address?"

Mrs Evans didn't speak at first. She thought, is this a bloke selling something? It can't be the rent man, I've already paid him, it might be a survey or something and I haven't got time to be answering questions all afternoon.

So, she didn't answer immediately. The smartly dressed gentleman followed up with a questioning expression, "Um, Mr John Evans? It's the only address I've got." When Mrs Evans still didn't say anything, he carried on "perhaps I've got the wrong address?"

When it was clear that the conversation was not making any progress she stated "I have a son, John Evans," and then after a few seconds "but he doesn't live here anymore."

The man intent on pushing the conversation forward said, "was he in Burma, during the war?" and then added, "well, to be precise, after the war."

Mrs Evans said, "well yes, he was, why ?"

The young man hesitated and then said, "umm, I may know someone that knew him there."

Mrs Evans, thinking that perhaps she was being impolite, said, "well, you'd better come in."

She ushered the man into the living room when at that moment William Evans woke up and said, "oh sorry, I didn't realise we had visitors."

Mrs Evans scowled at him "just the one William, just the one." William Evans stood, went to shake hands with the young man and introduce himself.

The man stood in the entrance to the living room and said, "Douglas Samuels, I think I might know someone who knew John Evans in Burma. I had this address and decided to pay him a visit."

Mr Evans said, noticing the young man's dark complexion, "you are from Burma then?"

Douglas replied, "no actually, I've never been to Burma."

Mr Evans looking more than a little confused and said, "oh right, there we are then. Well, as you can see John isn't here, in fact, he hasn't been here for twenty-four years." Realising what he had just said he corrected himself "sorry, what I meant to say was John hasn't lived here for twenty-four years. He lives at the other end of the town, but we can give him a message."

Douglas keen not to be drawn into a detailed conversation said, "well I'm staying at the Castle Hotel for the next four days. I've taken a few days holiday and thought I would track John, Mr Evans that is, down. If he's interested in contacting me before the end of the week please ask him, if he's not too busy, to arrange a time and place and leave a message at the Castle, and I'll make sure I'm there." Douglas turned to leave and then turned back "very nice to have met you both, goodbye for now."

Mrs Evans, a little flustered at addressing a good looking, young gentleman, and realising that the man wasn't asking for money ushered Douglas out saying, "John will be up tomorrow, he normally calls on a Wednesday, I'll pass on the message."

Douglas thanked her and walked along the street to where he had parked his car.

The following afternoon there was a further gentle tap on the front door of No 2 Union Street and John Evans followed it up by walking straight in, "hello, only me," he said as he walked in to find his mother and father sitting with a cup of tea and a plate of welsh cakes. Immediately, his mother rose, "I'll put the kettle on, it won't be a minute as it's just boiled. Do you want a welsh cake?" She stopped, glanced down at John's ever expanding stomach and said, "perhaps its less welsh cakes you need to be eating." She continued into the kitchen.

John shouted after her "I'll take just one welsh cake then."

He took his coat off and sat at the only other available chair in the very small living room. He carried on chatting with his dad about the weather, the biased nature of rugby referees on a recently televised rugby match, which was a common obsession of William Evans and the number of cars that would park on the pavement outside No 2 Union Street.

A minute or two later John's mother came in with a cup of tea, which she handed to John.

John's mother was quiet for a while and then she said, "look, I am only repeating what one of the deacons in chapel said to me a few weeks ago, so don't think it's my idea, but...."

John said, "for goodness sake mam, get on with it." His father smiled, as he thought that he would never get away with saying that but John would.

"Well," she repeated and John rolled his eyes. "Mr Oliver Richards, the deacon wondered if your business could sort of sponsor some of the maintenance work needed in the chapel."

John said, "you mean pay for it."

John's mother thought for a second and said, "Ah, yes, I suppose so."

John laughed and replied, "well, the charity known as John Evans Enterprises will think about it and let you know."

John's mother seemed satisfied with that answer and went on to talk about the rising expense of food. She suddenly remembered and said, "there was a young man here yesterday looking for you." John showed little interest and continued biting into his welsh cake, "oh yes, who was that?"

Mrs Evans thought for a second, not being able to remember the man's name, she said, "a tall, smart Asian chap, said he knew somebody you knew in Burma, bit funny really as when we asked him he said he'd never been to Burma, what was his name, William?"

John's father thought and said, "Douglas, I think." Mrs Evans said, "oh well done, that's right, it was Douglas."

John asked, "Douglas what?"

Neither Mr. or Mrs Evans could immediately remember. Both thought and then John's father said, "was it Samuels, Charlotte?"

She replied, "yes, I think it was, you are doing very well this afternoon, William, I probably should have written the name down."

John said, "Douglas Samuels, doesn't sound a very Asian name."

Mrs Evans said, "yes, quite dark he was, probably Indian or from somewhere out there."

He couldn't place the name but assumed it was perhaps the son of one of his mates who were in Burma at the same time as himself. He lost interest in the conversation and after twenty minutes or so he stood up to leave, "well better be getting home. I've got a fair bit of paperwork to do after dinner, I'll be seeing you."

John left and it was only when he was nearly at home he recalled the conversation with his mother and father. He thought, Douglas, no, doesn't ring any bells. Samuels, hmm, I wonder. Then the surname hit John like a bolt out of the blue.

He took a sharp left and at the end of the street another left, followed by a further left to bring him back onto the road he'd just been travelling on but in the opposite direction. He returned to his parent's house walking straight in this time without knocking. He asked both parents who were sat in front of the television, "did this bloke say where he was staying or whether he was going back to wherever he came from straight away?"

Mrs Evans looked a bit taken aback but thought for a second, "he said he was staying at the Castle until the end of the week, but he didn't say where he lived or where he was going back to."

John said, "thanks," and immediately returned to the car.

He couldn't get Douglas Samuels out of his mind and the following morning on his way to work went straight to the Castle Hotel. He asked the receptionist if Mr Samuels was available only to be told that he had just left, but that he had not checked out. John asked if he could leave a message and when told he could, he asked the receptionist to tell Mr Samuels that he would meet him in the lounge bar that evening at seven-thirty.

29

John walked past reception into the lounge bar of the Castle Hotel. There were very few people there as it was mid-week and quite early in the evening. There were just a few couples perched opposite each other on the velvet cushions of the chairs of the lounge bar. John could see the back of a dark-haired man sitting in a corner seat. He noticed the man wore a light coloured suit whereas John had been home after his day's work, washed and changed into a shirt, tie and v-necked jumper. John could see that the man had a small glass of what looked like whisky in front of him, so John went to the bar and ordered a pint of beer.

He came around to face Douglas and introduced himself. Douglas stood, John thought a little unsteadily, shook hands with John and likewise introduced himself as Douglas Khian. John looked quizzical for a moment and said, "I thought my mother said your name was Samuels?"

Douglas said, "apologies, Khian is my middle name, my surname is Samuels."

John noticed Douglas studying him carefully but saying little.

John said, "you have a link with Burma?"

Douglas looked down but replied firmly "yes, I have." He continued, "perhaps I had better tell you the whole of my story."

They both sat and John put down his glass. He didn't answer but indicated with his hand that he would like Douglas to proceed with his story.

Douglas took a breath "this may seem unusual but I would like to tell you my story in reverse, starting with what has happened to me recently and working backwards. I have thought about how it is best told and I think when I finish you will agree with me."

John once again indicated for Douglas to go ahead.

Douglas began "seven months ago I arrived in this country looking for work. As yet I haven't been successful but that does not concern me, as I'm sure I will find work soon. I flew in from Calcutta and I'm staying with an Indian friend in the East End of London. I drove down here primarily to meet you last weekend. Since I've been here I've travelled around the area to get my bearings, as before I arrived I knew very little about Wales. However, I did have your parent's address, the address in which you used to live, but we'll come to that."

John looked intrigued but did not interrupt.

Douglas continued "Before coming here I spent the whole of my early life in Calcutta. I was born there, I went to school there, I went to university there and then medical school. I qualified as a doctor there last Summer. "

John was impressed with the man's educational background and indicated such.

Douglas said, "I was brought up in the home of my uncle." Douglas stopped "apologies, a correction, my great uncle, my grandfather's brother. My grandfather was called Douglas, and I am named after him. He was Scottish. I didn't know my mother, she died when I was five. She became ill with a fever and she died within a few weeks. Unfortunately, it was not a pleasant death as she became delirious, she lost control of her bodily functions and then she went into a coma. She was taken into hospital but when it became obvious that nothing more could be done to save her she was brought home to her uncle's house and died there. That was in 1953. My great uncle William, obviously a Scotsman also had an import-export business and stayed in India after independence. While he did not make as much money after independence as he did before it he was still a member of India's quite prosperous middle class. He visited Britain a few times when he was able and often saw family relatives in Scotland. I never travelled outside India until last year. I owe everything to my great uncle who paid for my education and my livelihood for virtually the whole of my life. Unfortunately, he died five years ago and so never saw me graduate, but my thirst for knowledge and the work I have put into becoming a doctor is to repay him for his sacrifice for my future. He had one son and one daughter. The daughter is married to a lawyer in Calcutta and the son now runs the business my grandfather built up. They are very dear friends to me."

Douglas stopped to draw breath. John was beginning to piece together the jigsaw of Douglas' life and was just beginning to place his jigsaw piece into the whole but would wait for that to be confirmed. He interrupted Douglas by asking "is it ok if we have another drink? Just to give me time to take all this in."

John went to the bar and ordered a beer and another whisky and glanced around at Douglas, curious to watch his mannerisms. He returned with the drinks a little more composed and ready for any revelations, he thought.

Douglas politely thanked him, took a sip of the drink and readied himself to continue "my mother realised she was pregnant when she was in Rangoon, a potential single mother." Did John notice an accusing change to Douglas' voice?

"She very bravely informed her mother that she thought she was pregnant. Her mother, whose name was Khine, and whom I am named after, at least my middle name, sent her to the local doctor who was a friend of the family to confirm it. My mother was determined to keep the baby and asked her mother for advice, her mother said for her to wait for a few days while she thought about it. However, Khine immediately wrote to her brother-in-law in Calcutta and received a reply by return of post. My mother, who you have probably guessed by now, was Hla, or as I think you knew her, Sammy. It was suggested she should travel to Calcutta to give birth. She would be taken care of by her great uncle William and her great aunt Sana, who is still alive in Calcutta. My grandmother said that this would save embarrassment and she would probably get better medical care if she was in Calcutta. There is an irony that she should then die in Calcutta a few years later and medical care could do nothing for her."

Douglas stopped for a second and reached for his wallet which was on the table in front of them. He took out a photograph which had been folded in two. He unfolded it and passed it across the table to John. It was the photograph of the two of them that John had given to Sammy in a frame at Christmas 1947. John picked up the photograph and stared at it speechless. Then he happened to turn over the photograph and he noticed that something had been written on the back. 'Love is a gift of one's innermost soul to another so both can be whole'. John quietly mouthed "Lord Buddha."

Douglas said, "you know your quotations."

John replied, "I wouldn't have if your mother had not told me." After a moment he continued "your mother thought this quotation was one of the most beautiful things she had ever heard," and as he brushed away a tear he said, "and so did I."

Douglas said, "my mother kept this with her until she died, still holding it. She had had to discard the frame to travel to Calcutta, but the photograph of you both was her most treasured possession. It was only this and your previous address that I had to try to find you." John thought that after the sad story and the sight of the photograph he would suddenly burst into tears. The thoughts which crowded into his brain were thoughts of sadness. Sammy did not go on to get married to someone else and live happily ever after. Her short life was one of loneliness, misery and an early death.

Douglas took back the photograph and said, "I would let you have this photograph but it is the only one I have of my mother. However, if you wish I can get it copied."

John replied, "that would be very kind of you, thank you."

John stared into a void alongside Douglas while his description brought back all the pain of leaving Burma. He thought that when he left Rangoon, Sammy had such a short life after he had returned to South Wales. Nothing was said by either of them for some time but then John's thoughts crystallised. He said, "are you telling me that the baby Sammy carried was mine?" He stopped for breath and then continued "and that therefore you are my son."

Douglas realised the significance of his next sentence, "that's exactly what I'm saying," he followed it up with, "can you now see why I told my tale in reverse? You would probably have been overpowered by this knowledge at first and then probably not heard anything else of what I had to say. I've thought for a long time about how I would go about telling you if I managed to find you. There's no easy way to say it without it causing a shock. I do appreciate the significance of what I've just told you."

John felt his whole body shrink in despair. He didn't think that he had felt such sadness. He knew deep down that he had loved Sammy and that it was only because of the impossible circumstances that he had not continued to find a way to live with her and love her. All John could say was "I'm going to the toilet; I'll just be a few minutes."

John went through to the toilets, found a cubicle and simply sat on top of the toilet seat with his head in his hands. He was so confused. He didn't know what to think. After a while he thought, if I had only known that Sammy was ill I would have moved heaven and earth to try to help her. I know it is too late to do anything to help poor Sammy but if I can rectify my guilt by helping this poor boy.

After John returned to the lounge bar Douglas stood up and said, "can I suggest that you go home and think about this. I can see you are shaken by the news. It was not my intention but there was no easy way to tell you. Can I suggest we meet here tomorrow evening? I can't leave it any later as I have to be back in London by the weekend. I have to fill in job applications. I need to earn money, I can't keep relying on other people to support me."

They shook hands and John walked back to his car. His immediate thoughts were that he had just shaken hands with his son. He should be embracing him, not shaking hands. He drove up to a quiet spot just outside Treafon and parked up to think. He didn't get home until after midnight. Elizabeth was fast asleep as he crept into bed, no more resolved in knowing what to do than he had been a few hours before.

30

John had used the excuse of a Rotary Club meeting to go back to the lounge bar of the Castle Hotel the following night. It would provide a good cover story as the Rotary Club always met at the hotel and so if anyone wondered what he was doing there he could easily say he thought there was a meeting but had got the wrong evening.

He walked into the lounge and noticed the figure of Douglas sat in the same seat, this time dressed in a more relaxed fashion. He bought a beer and a whisky at the bar and took them over to the table. Douglas said, "hi, and thanks for the drink."

John asked, "have you had a good day?"

Douglas replied that he had gone for a walk in the town centre, stopped for a lunch at the Queen's Café, which was very good, and then taken a ride out to some of the surrounding mining villages and towns. He added "I phoned my friend in London to see if any mail had arrived for me. Unfortunately, my friend Raj has got the flu or a heavy cold and it was difficult to understand him on the phone. Anyway, I have to return to London tomorrow to peruse the jobs section of the medical journal."

John sat and watched Douglas as he spoke. He was fascinated by the colour of his skin. He thought Douglas' skin colour was lighter than Sammy had been, from what he could remember, but he was clearly Asian. He had Sammy's eyes and his mouth bore a resemblance to Sammy's. John listened to what Douglas said and noticed the use of the word 'peruse' instead of 'look' as most people would say. It merely reflected Douglas' education and how formally he spoke. John thought, probably in Calcutta they think that all British people speak like that.

Douglas turned his gaze on John and asked "so what is it you do. You seem to dress like a successful businessman, so?"

He left the question hanging in the air and waited for John's response.

John said, "well, can I, first of all, say that I have still not fully come to terms with the fact I seem to have another son. Your revelation last evening has knocked me for six, and I still don't really know how to respond to someone of your age who tells me that he is my son. So you will have to forgive me while I adjust to that news." He stopped for a few seconds and then said, "well I suppose you have every right to know what I've been up to for the last twenty odd years, as you told me your story, then….." He took a breath and began "It's not very exciting. I came back from Burma and quickly got a job with the N.C.B., the National Coal Board. They organise all aspects of the coal industry in this country. It was a junior clerk's position and I have to say that my time in Burma helped me get this position and helped me do it effectively, even if I do say it myself." John sat back almost as if waiting for applause. Douglas was listening attentively but a little smirk crossed his expression and John thought, perhaps I need to tell this story with a little more humility.

He continued "I worked for the N.C.B. for sixteen years. I gained a lot of experience and with the help of a Mr Ferguson who was very much my mentor in the job, I applied for a more senior position in the N.C.B. in the Central Offices in Cardiff. That was ten years ago and I worked in Cardiff for four years. I found it hard as I would have to leave home early in the morning before any of the family were up and come back home late at night. It was three hours travelling each day backwards and forwards, and often in heavy traffic. In 1968 I was asked to call in to see an old friend here in Treafon. He had a coal business, the biggest in the town. He was ready to retire and he offered me first refusal in buying up the business. He said the business made a good profit. He had ten lorries and nearly thirty people working for him. I thought that this was something I could do and make it a success. I applied for and got a loan to buy the business. The coal industry was changing. Many people here in the valley's towns used the old domestic fuel but many had modern glass-fronted fires which burned smokeless manufactured coal, anthracite and phurnacite. Many ex-miners still lived in the town and still had their subsidised coal allowance, so business was good. I became a local businessman, joined the local Chamber of Trade, the local Rotary Club and I've been asked to join the Freemasons. These all bring custom, and business is thriving, but you can't stand still, you have to be constantly thinking of ways to expand your business. At the moment I am engaged in buying out a coal merchant's business in a nearby town which will help expand our trade." John noticed Douglas' interest in his story was waning and so fell silent.

Douglas looked up and said, "so you are doing very well?" and a few seconds later "if I may be so bold, what about your private life?"

John sat back in the chair and studied Douglas, wondering what to tell him and whether he should leave anything out. He began "I came back from Burma in 1948 and I married someone in 1950 I had been seeing for a while, Elizabeth. We were unfortunate that Elizabeth had a hard time in her pregnancies and she had several miscarriages. Finally, in 1956 we had Kevin. He's now eighteen." John seemed to drop into deeper thought and carried on "I've not really been fair to Kevin. I've had to work long hours, particularly when I worked in Cardiff and left much of the work of bringing him up to Elizabeth. He's a good lad. He's had his problems. He's a bright lad but he didn't like school. He left school last year but he's found it difficult to find a job that suits him. He's tried one or two but nothing has really grabbed his interest."

Douglas sensed that John was shielding his son and was not being completely honest, but he didn't comment on what really was none of his business. He simply said, "Kevin, hmm, my half brother."

John looked at Douglas and said, "yes," and then with a little more conviction "yes, that's right."

John continued "I thought I would be able to offer Elizabeth more support when I took over the business here but truthfully, it has taken up as much time as my job in Cardiff did. She hates the socialising, but in business it's essential. I've made good friends who have opened doors for my business. Elizabeth still hangs on to her old friends, but personally, I find them a little bit boring, a bit silly, if you know what I mean." He leaned back and said, "well that's about it."

They both fell silent and sipped their drinks. Then John spoke up "I had a long time to think after I left you last night. I have found I can speak to you. I know that we have only just met but I would definitely like to catch up a little more, to get to know each other." John thought before his next statement but decided to proceed "after all you are my son, and nothing can change that, and I'd like to think I take my responsibilities seriously."

Douglas said quietly "I'm not going to need looking after."

This was followed by a longer silence.

Douglas then asked, "what feelings did you have for my mother?"

John considered his answer and decided honesty was best if they were to get along "I loved her. I loved the time I spent with her. She was different, she was innocent. Remember, she was very young, much younger than you are now. She was beautiful and I think if things had been different, the culture difference, the fact I was in the army, paid by the army and I would have to return to Britain and the fact that Burma had just become independent and British people were not really very welcome at that time all played a part." After a few seconds John said, "be quite clear, your mother was a very special person."

Douglas looked carefully at John as he spoke and noticed a dreamlike look in his eyes, as if he was taking his mind back to another age, remembering what he had lost.

John quickly brought himself out of his short period of recollection and reverie. He smiled and asked Douglas "what do you know about Burma?"

Douglas shook his head "less than you probably."

John said, "did you know the cabinet were assassinated when I was in Rangoon? He quickly added, "I didn't have anything to do with it, except, I was suddenly a combat soldier." John took his mind back thirty years and related the story of the capture of the terrorists. He sat back in the chair and said, "I won the British Empire Medal for that, and a letter from the King." When I came back from Burma I joined the Burma Star Association and four years ago they asked me to be key speaker at the 25th Anniversary of the end of the war in Burma. They held the dinner at Treafon House in the park. It was a marvellous honour for me to be key speaker at such an event in my own town." John was getting carried away with his reminiscences and consequently his own self-importance. Douglas brought him back to earth with a bang.

Seemingly unimpressed, he said, "I went to a few political meetings when I was studying in Calcutta and I have to say the concept of Empire was not one that was considered with any affection." John didn't respond and so Douglas continued "if you had told some of my fellow students that you had been given a British Empire Medal they would have said that was not for bravery but was awarded for the continued exploitation of Asian people. The war against Japan was over, you didn't need to be there, other than as a colonial force to keep order by suppressing the local people. I'm afraid to say that it is only Britain that continues to revel in the actions of a people who subjugated millions of Indians, Burmese, Aborigines, Maoris, Masai. Need I go on?"

John said, "we were there to hand over the country in an orderly fashion to the Burmese, in the run-up to independence."

Douglas said, "if you had not built an empire in the first place you would not have needed to give it back."

John knew when he was beaten and though he would enjoy debating this for many hours, he knew he had work in the morning. As he got up he thought, why is it not possible to have discussions and conversations like this with Kevin.

Douglas responded with a smile saying "well, I'd better be going. I have to be up early in the morning. I haven't passed my driving test very long ago and for me, the drive to London needs lots of concentration, even though your roads and these new motorways are far better than any of our roads in Calcutta." He laughed and said, "you would have thought an imperial power would have left us with better roads." They both laughed.

Douglas said, "I hope we can keep in touch. If you would like I can let you know where I get a job, and perhaps come back here in the future to see you."

John stood up "please, don't leave it too long, A few days ago I didn't know I had another son. Now I do, I want us to make up for lost time. I can only do that if we continue to meet up."

Both were hesitant but a handshake seemed the best option in this budding relationship.

John walked out of the hotel feeling that his relationship with his newly found son had made progress and it gave him a warm feeling, despite something in the back of his mind that warned him to be cautious.

Douglas went to his room thinking that for the first time for many years he had met someone who would now become a father figure to him, to help guide his future and be there for him when he needed help. He may be well educated but he still lacked confidence in this new country and culture of his choosing. He had often felt isolated since his arrival in Britain but following the conversation with John, he felt more confident. He thought, how he had worried about meeting his father. He had churned over in his mind many times, how it might happen, whether he would be accepted, where it would take place and what they would talk about. Many times he had considered that his father might reject him and he had prepared himself for that. But John seemed to like him and the evening had gone well. He wondered, was he too outspoken in mentioning an alternative view of the British Empire, then he thought, no, John seemed to enjoy the cut and thrust of debate. This gave him a warm feeling. He thought I'm sure he is genuine. He really does want to see me and to spend time with me.

31

A few weeks later John drove across the main street in Treafon, stopping at the traffic lights. As he waited for the lights to change he cast a glance across the row of shops. It seemed every time he came across town there were more vacant shops. The closure of the steelworks in the next valley, the one his dad had worked at for many years was having a real effect. There were fewer shops and services and the previous owners of the shops were all moving out of town. The town was also losing its middle class. John had noticed that in the Rotary Club, quite a few members had left to join other clubs in other towns as they moved away. John felt that he was a member of the town's middle class and that their position in the town seemed to be under threat. A few factories had opened and the managers of these factories had joined the Rotary Club, but more had left than had joined. Oh well, John thought, at least I've still got a job. He thought back to the time when he was a boy. He had never thought that the town was prosperous, but then he had nothing to compare it with, he had hardly travelled anywhere. People then came into the town to shop and there were no empty shops. As the roads improved, he thought that was a good thing for the town, but it had never occurred to him, that with more cars and better roads people would travel out of town to spend their money and it was then that the local shops suffered. The lights changed and John drove across to his parent's house and parked.

John knocked at the door and then went straight in. It was his usual Wednesday afternoon visit. John's mother immediately passed him a letter. She said, "this came for you a few days ago."

John took it and opened it, curious to see who was writing to him, care of his parent's address. He looked quickly at the name at the end of the letter and the address at the top and put the letter back into the envelope without reading it.

Mrs Evans said, "so, who's it from?"

John didn't answer immediately but had to think of a plausible person. He said, "Ah, it's from an army buddy who only had this address."

Mrs Evans looked at John quizzically, "that's a bit of a coincidence, that chap turning up here, you know, the darkie, and now this letter. What's this chap's name?"

John thought for a minute before answering, "Ah, Chico Hancock," making up a name quickly, as that was all he could think of.

With his mother looking very suspicious John thought it better to beat a retreat, "well, I'd better be off."

His mother replied, "you've only just got here. No cup of tea, and I've baked scones, that's not like you at all," and a second later "are you not feeling well?"

John replied, "I'm fine, just very busy, lots of paperwork to do tonight."

Mrs Evans said, "you always say that when you don't want to do something. Are we going to see you in chapel this Sunday, you've not been for a few weeks?"

John said, mainly to please his mother and to throw her off the scent of the letter enquiries "yes, probably," and then looking up to see her scowling at him "yes, ok, I'll be there."

John collected his coat, said his goodbyes and went back to his car, which was parked outside. Before pulling off he took the letter out to read it, not noticing his mother looking through the front window and watching him suspiciously. The letter was from Douglas and explained that he had been busy applying for several jobs, one in an East Anglian hospital which he did not think he had a chance of getting, one to a doctor's practice in Glasgow, but as it was in a smart area of the city, once again he thought he had little chance. One to a doctor's practice in Yorkshire, a further one to help with research into liver cancer, but he felt he didn't have the necessary experience and finally, an application to a practice in a small town about thirty minutes away, Pontygwyn. John put the letter back into the envelope and thought, I wonder why he kept that one until last?'He decided he would write back to Douglas that evening.

John finished his paperwork that evening and penned a very short note to Douglas which thanked him for sending the list of job applications which sounded interesting and left his office telephone number, asking Douglas to keep him informed of any possible replies he might get. He then had to quickly hurry home for a family summit with Elizabeth and Kevin regarding an incident Kevin was involved in outside a pub in the town.

John arrived home and before he could eat his dinner he promised Elizabeth that he would talk to Kevin. Kevin, a slight and thin teenager came into the lounge. He was pale with a mop of mousy coloured hair, which he continually pushed back out of his eyes. He was dressed in jeans with a Rolling Stones t-shirt he had bought on a trip to Cardiff market. Elizabeth, dressed smartly in an expensive skirt and blouse, followed them into the lounge. Elizabeth had been a housewife for many years and had put on a few pounds in weight but was still not unattractive.

The three sat in the large lounge of John's detached 'villa' style house on the edge of Treafon. John sat forwards on the large settee with his hands clasped together. He looked across at Kevin, "I was very embarrassed by being stopped by a police sergeant who informed me that one of his constables had told him that you had to be restrained outside the Treafon Arms to stop you from attacking a man in his late twenties from a nearby town."

Kevin sat in one of the armchairs sulking. He immediately responded to his father's accusation "it wasn't only me, there were others scrapping, and anyway the bloke deserved it. He was coming on strong to Will, pushed him down on the ground. All I did was help Will, then one of this blokes mates stopped us going in."

John said, "Will is younger than you and so he's not old enough to be drinking in a pub."

Kevin quickly retorted "he was only coming in with us, he wasn't going to drink, well only orange juice."

John said, "the sergeant said you pushed the constable away and he came very close to arresting you."

Kevin replied, "he was just picking on me, he just had a beef about what happened last year."

John thought for a moment and then said, "was he the copper who was involved in the trouble you got into last year?"

Kevin replied in a loud, forceful voice, pulling an angry face, "yea, always staring at me he is, he said something to me last week when I passed him by the library."

John thought back to the previous year when he had to attend the police station after Kevin had been taken in for questioning. That was concerning Kevin being in a car, which was stopped by the police and was searched for drugs. Nothing was found but a police constable said that suspiciously, he had seen a small package being dropped down a drain, which happened to be alongside the car when it was stopped. The police thought the better of raising the drain and searching and decided not to press charges but kept the four boys in custody until they could be collected by their parents.

John stood up and reaching over to Kevin grabbed him by the arm. He pulled him to his feet and pushed him through the hallway and reached for the front door. Elizabeth, who was still in the living room gasped as she wondered what John was about to do. She stood up and quickly followed them to the front door. John pushed Kevin out onto the front path and spun him around. He looked straight at him and said, "see this," pointing at the house. Then "and this," pointing at the large Rover car in the driveway, "and this," pointing at the caravan at the other end of the drive. "These all cost money. I work hard to buy these, to give you a better life. You do nothing to contribute to this household. You are content to swan about, doing nothing and then expect us to give you money. Well, it's got to change. Understand?"

John let go of Kevin's arm and went back into the house with Kevin and Elizabeth following him. Elizabeth now felt less frightened that John might throw Kevin out of the house, which was something she thought might have happened a few minutes before.

John sat back down and Kevin realising that his ticking off was not over, followed suit, looking down at the floor and avoiding eye contact with either of his parents. Elizabeth also sat back down.

John tried to calm himself down and decided to take another tack "are you any nearer finding a job? he asked, and then added in a mock sarcastic tone "that you think you would like to do."

Kevin said, "I'm still looking."

John said, also with quite a sarcastic tone "there's always a job for you on the lorries."

The suggestion of Kevin hauling bags of coal caused him to blow out a gasp of air through his teeth "I don't think so, that's certainly not for me."

John came back with "too good for that sort of job eh?"

Elizabeth stepped in at this point "remember he's got asthma, John."

John decided to give up at that point, as Elizabeth would continue to defend Kevin, as she had done in the past, and it would all be a waste of time. All it would serve to do would be to make John angry and Elizabeth and he would end up arguing about it. It just wasn't worth it.

Kevin asked, "can I go now?"

John quickly retorted "don't forget I said things have to change."

Elizabeth said nothing but indicated with her hand that the discussion was over and that he could now go. John just sat and shook his head.

Kevin passed the living room door with his jacket on and John and Elizabeth could hear the front door close.

John walked into the kitchen to take his dinner out of the oven and sit to eat. Elizabeth walked in behind him and sat opposite "he's still young and he wants to find something that he thinks he would be able to do. Give him time."

At first, John didn't answer, taking a mouthful of food and then he said, "he has everything. He's spoilt. He's eighteen. Jobs are not just going to fall into his lap and he's wasting his time hanging around with a bunch of layabouts."

Elizabeth said, "I think you are being unfair to him. He is looking for work and because he hasn't got a job he can't do the same as his friends who are earning. He's always short of money."

John said, "how can he afford to go drinking in the Treafon Arms if he's got no money?"

Elizabeth was silent. John said, "well?"

Elizabeth very sheepishly said, "I gave him a fiver two days ago, he had no money and his friends were going out, what was I supposed to do?"

John shook his head in disgust and replied in an annoyed tone "we had to work. You worked, before and after you were married. I worked in an ironmonger's shop and then worked as soon as I came out of the army. He's had it too easy."

Elizabeth said, "the town isn't like it was then. There was work to be had, there was a steelworks in the next valley, the shops were all thriving. Now we've got no steelworks, there's only one bank in the town instead of the three that there were, garages have closed, cafes have closed, shops have closed. It's not the same as it was."

John said, "my father was out of work for ten years, I saw him cry when he couldn't get work after walking over the mountain to try to get work."

Elizabeth threw back her head "oh no not that story again."

John followed up with "he was out of work so he couldn't go to the pub or anywhere else. He had no money so he had nothing to spend, unlike our boy who thinks he can swan about, do no work and borrow money when he needs it, well it's got to stop."

John was ready to blame Elizabeth for all of Kevin's failures. He said, "when he was young your father would spoil him and you would say nothing."

Elizabeth said, "it's easy now to blame my dad, he's been dead ten years and not able to defend himself. He loved that boy, he rarely saw his other grandchildren and so gave all his affection to Kevin."

John said, "sometimes you have to be cruel to be kind. It's not the answer to keep on giving him money. He never had to work for any of it and so now he just waits for it to fall into his lap without having to do anything for it."

John stood up and walked out, thinking, the same result as always, that boy will be the death of me.

John sat in the office the following day and the phone began to ring. He picked it up and automatically said, "hello, John Evans, Haulage and Coal Merchants, speaking."

He was surprised to hear Douglas on the line "that was a very well practised line. Sorry, this is only a quick call as I've got to go shopping for Raj. Listen, the jobs in Yorkshire and the research job came to nothing but I got a letter from a Doctor Bevan in Pontygwyn asking me to come down and have a look around. I'm planning to travel down on Friday and then go to Pontygwyn on Monday morning. I wondered if you wanted to meet up for a chat?"

John thought and said, "look, I've got to go to the Weigh Yard at nine o'clock on Saturday but I can meet you for coffee in the Queen's Café at eleven o'clock if that suits?"

Douglas replied, "that would be great, see you then."

John could hear the click as the phone was put down at the other end.

32

John walked into the Queen's Café at the top of the town centre of Treafon. He never ceased to wonder at this veritable palace dedicated to coffee and socialising. He had been in cafes in many of the big cities in Britain and one or two on the continent while on holidays but he was convinced that none of them could hold a candle to this immense space. The café was run by Gino Fratelli, a rotund sixty-year-old, who spoke English with a distinct Italian accent that John loved. He could listen to Gino's sing-song voice and his sometimes unusual phrasing all day long. The café had two rooms, one very large room at the front and a smaller room at the back. The main room had black and white chequerboard ceramic tiles that were spotless. It had a full-length mirror down one wall which gave the impression that the café was bigger than it was. John thought that was pure genius. Facing the mirrored wall on the opposite wall was one long counter with an array of brass and copper fittings, backed by a huge silver-coloured Italian coffee machine. The reflection of the copper and brass gave the whole room the appearance of having a thousand lights which were scrubbed and cleaned to perfection. The combination of the gleaming metalwork and the mirror made it the lightest indoor space John had ever seen. Gino was helped by his son and daughter, who served on tables when they weren't studying. Gino's wife also helped by cooking snacks in a small kitchen at the back. John could see Douglas sat at a table with a large frothy coffee.

John collected his coffee after a brief chat with Gino and took it across to join Douglas, who said, "Hi, good to see you, what a wonderful place this is."

John replied, "pretty good for a small town, isn't it?"

Douglas said, "I can't get over the number of Italian cafes that there are in all the South Wales towns I've been to."

John replied, "They come here for the sun," and they both laughed.

John explained that they all seemed to come from the same area of Italy and that every Summer they would combine to hire a coach that would travel through South Wales collecting the families to take them back to Italy for a holiday and to see their relatives.

Douglas looked at John to see if he was joking.

John could see that Douglas was disbelieving and so added: "honestly, I'm not kidding."

John asked, "Was it a good journey down?"

Douglas replied "it would be fine if I was a more experienced driver but I have to concentrate all the way. By the time I get here I'm worn out, but I had a good night's sleep and now I'm ready for anything."

They finished their coffees and Douglas asked if John would like another and possibly a snack. John said, "that would be great, I missed breakfast this morning and a cheese on toast would go down a treat, but please let me pay?"

Douglas brushed away the suggestion and added: "a cheese on toast would be good for me too." He walked to the counter and gave his order to Gino.

The noise level in the café suddenly rose as a group of youngsters came in laughing and joking quite loudly and with two of them pushing each other. They seemed completely oblivious of their surroundings. All in the café suddenly looked up and John recognised them as Alan Richards, Will Hodges, Stuart Parry, all friends of Kevin's. Also, with them was a girl he didn't recognise. Will Hodges pushed Alan Richards in the back as a response to the push he had received coming through the door. He succeeded only in pushing Alan Richards into Douglas, who dropped his wallet, as he was about to pay. Douglas ignored this and bent to pick up his wallet. As Douglas bent over Alan Richards raised his knee and caught Douglas in the back, sending him sprawling on the floor. This brought hoots of laughter from the group. Douglas got to his feet and brushed himself off. Gino could see what had happened from behind the counter and said, "careful please, you could have injured my customer," and added, "I need my customers healthy to pay their bills so I make money."

Douglas said, "I'm fine."

Will Hodges piped up "oh look an Italian coming to the defence of a paki in Wales, what's the world coming to."

The customers who had heard Will Hodges suddenly went quiet.

Gino turned to Will Hodges and said, "the Italian doesn't have to serve you if he doesn't want to."

Will Hodges glared at Gino Fratelli and said, "look pal, plenty of other cafes in Treafon who do want my trade, and not all of them full of foreigners."

The café was silent. John rose to see if his presence might help at the counter.

Stuart Parry whispered to Will Hodges "that's Kev's old man."

Hodges turned to him "so?"

The stand-off went on for what seemed like a long time but was really only a few seconds.

Hodges turned to the door, "come on, leave these sad fuckers to it." As they left Alan Richards put out his hand and slid a full sugar bowl off the counter sending sugar cubes scattering across the floor. The girl turned and blew a mocking kiss to Douglas as they left.

John asked Gino "you ok? Not the best the town has to offer."

Gino came around from the counter and beckoned John into the back room. He spoke quietly so nobody else could hear "you know that they often come in here, they make a row and sometimes they cause a fuss, like this morning, but I have to tell you that your boy is usually with them."

John looking a bit embarrassed said, "any trouble from him, you tell me, and it won't happen again, I promise."

Douglas and John went back to their table, their snacks arrived and their coffees and the café settled back to its previously quiet state. Ironically, John noticed that someone had put 'Rock the Boat', by the Hues Corporation on the jukebox. John wondered whether that had been deliberate.

John asked Douglas "you sure you want to come and work in South Wales?"

Douglas replied, "nothing worse here than in London."

They both put the incident behind them and chatted about Douglas' forthcoming interview. After a while they left the café and noticed the group of four youngsters sat on a wall opposite the café, watching them both as they left. John and Douglas parted. Douglas visited the chemist just along the main street and the newsagents. When he came back to his rather battered Ford Cortina, the youngsters had left but as he put the key into the lock on the driver's side door he noticed a scratch the length of the door where someone had dragged a sharp object along the paintwork. He smiled wryly and thought, thank goodness I can only afford an old banger. I wouldn't be so unconcerned if this had been a new car.

John wandered along the main street of Treafon and decided he wasn't in the right frame of mind to go home yet. If he saw Kevin he would berate him for the behaviour of his friends and if he saw Elizabeth he would probably end up telling her what had happened in the café and then she would think he was blaming Kevin who wasn't even there. He decided to do something he would not normally do in the middle of the day. He walked into the Castle Hotel bar and ordered a beer. He sat at a table to think. He realised that if he continued to build a relationship with Douglas he would have to tell Elizabeth and probably Kevin, and his mother and father and ….., It was all so overwhelming. How could he do this without causing massive upset? Questions crowded into his mind. Would Elizabeth leave him? Would his mother and father ever speak to him again? and then a few selfish thoughts. He was well respected in Treafon, a member of the Rotary Club and the Chamber of Trade, possible acceptance into the Freemasons and there was talk of him being asked to be a magistrate, but if the story of Douglas got out would that be possible any longer? Douglas had had to grow up without the support of a father. He had done so well to become a doctor under difficult circumstances in Calcutta. He deserved my support now. He decided Elizabeth would have to be told first and he would then decide what to do next. He would have to be brave and 'take the bull by the horns.' He shuddered at the thought of it. Life had been so easy lately, despite the odd problem with Kevin. He decided he would tell Elizabeth that weekend, that would give him time to plan what he was going to say.

John decided he would talk to Elizabeth on Saturday evening, Kevin would probably be out and that would make it easier. By Friday he had persuaded himself that she would understand and would accept what he told her. She was sensible, she never over-reacted and so after a short period of upset, she would come to terms with it and even if she didn't want to meet Douglas she surely wouldn't stop John meeting him.

33

John worked as usual on Saturday morning. He briefly visited his mother and father early in the afternoon and then went home. Elizabeth was baking in the kitchen and John, with his mind clearly on what was in front of him that evening kept going into the kitchen to ask Elizabeth if she was ok? Would she like a cup of tea or a sandwich?

Elizabeth eventually asked, "are you feeling ok?"

John replied, "yes, why?"

Elizabeth said, "you are not usually like this. Asking me if I'm ok and all that."

John said, "it's because I care."

She replied "well, it's not normal. I'm fine, I'm busy and no, I don't want anything to eat or drink while I'm baking but thank you for asking."

John couldn't settle and eventually went out for a walk. He returned a little later, more restless than before. At about six o'clock he decided he couldn't cope with this tension any longer. He went into the kitchen and asked Elizabeth if she could come and sit down, as he had something to tell her.

Elizabeth had finished baking but had not cleared up. John told her to leave it, and that he would clear up later. She followed him into the living-room and sat down.

John sat opposite her and wanted to begin but couldn't remember what he had planned to say. He thought for second and said, "there's something I need to tell you."

Elizabeth replied "this sounds like a confession. You haven't lost your wedding ring as I can see it, and I don't think you've bumped the car so what is it?" She clearly didn't think anything important was about to be said as she sat and smiled.

John looked down at the floor and said, "there's a chap who called at mam's, Douglas, he's come over from India, he's a doctor."

Elizabeth looked a little more serious "is someone ill?"

John said, "no nothing like that, let me finish," and then decided to blurt out "he's my son. He's a son I didn't know I had." He let that sink in before he continued.

Elizabeth suddenly looked a lot more serious. She said, "I don't understand."

John then said, "well when I was in Burma I had what I suppose you could call an affair. I met a girl. She became pregnant and Douglas is her son." He then added "and mine, I suppose."

There was total silence. Elizabeth eventually said in a strained voice "you're serious, aren't you?" Then after a second, she added "this bloke that's turned up, how do you know he's your son. If this girl is a tart, sleeping around, he could be anyone's son."

John said, "I've listened to what he's told me and the times and dates all add up."

Elizabeth said, "what if she's sent him halfway around the world to claim an inheritance, or money or something from you?"

John said, "she's dead. She died a few years after Douglas was born."

Elizabeth was silent for some considerable time and John had nothing more to say. He could see she was becoming more upset and that made him upset. He stood to go to her, but as he got to her, ready to put his arm around her she pulled away "don't touch me, don't come near me. I don't think I ever want you to touch me again." She suddenly burst into tears and stood and left the room.

John sat for several hours but then thought that he didn't want to be up when Kevin came home. He didn't want to have to explain to him as well, that would have to wait for another day.

He got up and went upstairs. Elizabeth had gone into the spare room. He went into the main bedroom. After an hour or two he could hear Kevin coming in and going into his room. By five o'clock in the morning, he was still tossing and turning unable to sleep. Then he must have dozed off. A few hours later he woke and went downstairs to make a cup of tea. He noticed a small note on the work surface in the kitchen. It simply said, "Gone to Joan's, signed Elizabeth." John hadn't heard her leave. He thought, perhaps she hasn't left yet, perhaps she's still here. I can talk to her, persuade her. John went to the spare room but it was empty and the drawers were open where Elizabeth had taken some of her clothes. He could hear Kevin going downstairs and suddenly he thought, Kevin will see the note and then I'll have to explain. Then he realised he had the note crumpled in his hand. He went downstairs and as he went into the kitchen he realised he had to tell Kevin something. He said, "mam's gone to Aunty Joan's for a few days. She rang to say she wasn't well and could mam go down and look after her."

Kevin looked up and said, "that's a bit strange, she was talking to her on the phone a few days ago and she was fine then."

John shrugged and said, "must be a bug or something. I'm not sure."

Kevin walked into the living room and sat down. John went back up to his bedroom. He would have to sort things out with Elizabeth.

John decided he would drive to Bournemouth that weekend, talk to Elizabeth and persuade her to come back. The following morning John's office phone rang. He answered it expecting it to be someone from a coal factor's office to arrange the sale of a large tonnage of anthracite.

Douglas interrupted John's usual response, "hi, just a quick call. I've got this interview in Pontygwyn on Monday and so I'm coming down on Friday night and staying in the Castle. Will you be around at all?"

John was caught a little off balance "no, afraid I've got to go away," there was a moment's hesitation "to Birmingham, business meeting."

Douglas was a little non-plussed "on a weekend?"

John quickly said, "businessmen, obviously got to fit me in when they can."

Douglas said, "what about Monday evening, after my interview, to celebrate or commiserate?"

John said, " I won't be back in time I'm afraid," thinking if I do manage to persuade Elizabeth to come back, she's not going to be very happy if I shoot off on some jolly.

Douglas, feeling that he was being brushed off a little said, "well, I've got to go, give me a ring when you get chance."

John quickly said, "best of luck for the interview."

Douglas said, "thanks," and rang off

John felt bad about not being able to see Douglas but felt that his mission to Bournemouth was of more importance.

Before going home that evening John visited his parents' house. He tapped on the door and walked in. He sat down and said, "I was wondering if you could do me a favour. Joan has been taken ill. Elizabeth has gone down to see her and I have to go down to Bournemouth on the weekend to collect her. I was wondering if I might suggest to Kevin that he comes here for his meals if he wants to."

Mrs Evans hesitated and then said, "we haven't seen Kevin for months. Will he actually turn up?"

John said, "no idea, but I don't want him complaining I've abandoned him."

Mr Evans said, "you know it's no problem."

John passed over a five-pound note but Mr Evans pushed it

back, "if we can't feed our grandson, what can we do."

John didn't argue "thanks dad, well I'd better go."

John arrived at Bill and Joan's house in Bournemouth in darkness on the Friday evening. He sat in the car for a few minutes collecting his thoughts. He was tired and more than a little irritable but he was determined he wouldn't show it.

He tapped at the door, and it was half opened by Bill. He looked around the door and said, "she doesn't want to see you, John," in a somewhat sympathetic tone. Bill came out onto the porch pulling the door behind him. He said, "look, she's still very upset and she's got Joan on her side. I think you'd best leave it for a while."

John said, "what do I do, just get in the car and drive back home? I just want to speak to her for a few minutes."

Bill thought and said, "give me a few minutes, I'll be back."

John waited on the porch and a few minutes later Bill came back to the door and said, "she'll speak to you for ten minutes, no more, but it will be on her own in the bedroom. For God's sake don't kick up rough."

John went into the house and straight into the bedroom where Elizabeth was sat on the bed. It felt strange to John that it was in this room that they had both lost their virginity and now they were talking to try and save their marriage.

John said, "look I can only apologise for what's happened. I didn't know anything about the boy until a few weeks ago." He lied, "look it was only once and we'd both had a lot to drink."

John then proceeded to tell a completely fictional story about a one-night stand, which he had practiced throughout the week. He said, "look, you can't stay down here, you've got Kevin to think about."

After a few more minutes discussion Elizabeth said that John could ring Bill and Joan's house the following morning and she would give him her decision.

John reluctantly left to find a hotel for the night.

Douglas got up on the Saturday morning and after breakfast in the Castle Hotel's dining room, he went for a walk across to the shopping centre. As he passed the entrance to the shopping centre he noticed a group of youths, some sat on a bench and some stood up. As Douglas got nearer, he was spotted by Alan Richards, who shouted: "Hey look, it's the paki who has difficulty standing up."

The group laughed in unison and turned towards Douglas. Stuart Parry got up from the bench and crossed in front of Douglas, blocking his path. He said in a mock Indian accent "well, what are you doing here, my man. It's very, very nice that people come here from far away, but the truth is we don't want them here." He turned to the group and pulled a face. They all rolled about laughing in a very exaggerated fashion. Douglas had faced this attitude before while in London and used his usual tactic, to completely ignore them and walk away. People passing all heard Stuart Parry's and Alan Richards' remarks but chose to ignore them and carried on with their business. Douglas walked on and for a short distance, he was followed step by step by Stuart Parry, goading him to turn around. Kevin was sat on the end of the bench but didn't involve himself with the display as he was too busy talking to Carol Edwards, the girl who had been involved in the Queen's Café incident.

When Stuart came back to the bench Will Hodges turned to Kevin and said, "that was the guy who was with your father in the Queen's a few weeks ago."

Kevin couldn't think why his dad would be talking to an Asian bloke in Treafon but didn't respond. He was much too busy getting to know Carol who was relatively new to the group. He found out that she had got into a bit of trouble in a nearby town where she lived and her parents had packed her off to her grandparents who lived in Treafon. Kevin liked her. She was a pretty girl, a bit wild, but she was fun to be with.

Douglas took a roundabout route back to the hotel to avoid a fracas with the group a second time. He went to sit on a bench to eat a bag of crisps that he had bought. Shortly after he was joined on the bench by an older man. After a few seconds, the man turned to Douglas and said, "hello there, didn't I see you a while back in the Queens café?" Before Douglas could answer the man said, "with John Evans, you were."

Douglas replied "yes, that's right"

The man said, "Tom Price, by the way. You know John Evans do you?"

Douglas answered carefully "yea, a sort of business link."

Price said, "you in the coal trade?"

Douglas lied, "sort of."

Price added "well, you want to watch out for him. Not a nice man. I remember him when he was a youngster, nice kid then, but he's very full of himself now, businessman and all that. Not afraid to step on people to get on, you know the sort."

Douglas thought I need to be careful here, this guy seems a bit of a busy-body. If I say anything it will be around town in a flash. Douglas said, "well better be going. Nice to talk to you, phone calls to make. Sorry I've got to rush."

Price said, "yes, of course, just you be careful with Evans."

Douglas said, "yes, will do, all the best," and walked away.

The phone rang and Joan offered it to Elizabeth "it's him."

Elizabeth told John that she would return with him to South Wales but there would be stipulations. John quickly agreed and began to put his jacket on, but on the way to the car, he wondered what the stipulations would be. Elizabeth said she would discuss them on the return journey. John pulled up outside the house and Elizabeth came out to the car a few seconds later with her suitcase in her hand. John put the case in the boot and got into the driver's side.

The beginning of the journey was spent in silence. Elizabeth made it clear she was not yet ready to talk. After about an hour she said, "how many times have you seen this Asian boy?"

John ignored the disparaging way Elizabeth spoke and said, "two or three times."

Elizabeth said, "do you plan to see him again?"

John answered "well, I'm his father, and he seems to want to see me. He's not been in the country long and he seems very lonely." John thought that whether this was true or not it would serve to gain sympathy for Douglas' position.

Elizabeth said, "I suppose that's understandable. I don't know if I want to see him, I'll have to think about that, but I insist that you tell your parents and Kevin. It's only fair. Your parents are his grandparents and Kevin now seems to have a half brother. So they must know," she followed that up by looking him straight in the eye and saying "Clear?"

John was a little confused, he hadn't thought for one minute about his parent's relationship, even though he had thought about Kevin, but didn't relish the thought of telling him. His relationship with Kevin was at best very tense and this could do irreparable damage.

John sheepishly said, "agreed."

On their return, Elizabeth moved most of her clothes into the spare room and it was clear they would not be sharing a bedroom in the foreseeable future. There was a frosty atmosphere that neither could hide and very little conversation except regarding practical matters such as shopping and the day the bins go out.

As they sat down to a meal a few days later Kevin spoke up "what's going on between you two? It's like living in a house with the American president and the Russian president. Come on what's it all about?"

As Elizabeth was not going to answer John said, "nothing to

worry you. We don't always get along all the time you know. Sometimes things go wrong."

Kevin replied, "so what's gone wrong?"

John realised that he could use this opportunity to tell Kevin but with things still very raw he decided to leave it for another time and got up and left the room. Kevin simply shrugged as no-one seemed ready to give him an answer.

After a difficult few days, John was glad to go to work on the Monday morning. On the Tuesday afternoon, the office phone rang. Douglas spoke before John could say anything "I was offered the job and I accepted it. I start in a month. What do you think about that?"

John tried hard to sound very pleased but deep down he kept thinking that having Douglas living close by could be more trouble than it was worth. How could he juggle seeing Douglas and spending time with his own family. Then he thought, but Douglas is my own family.

Douglas detected a less than enthusiastic response but thought that he didn't know what problems John might have at the moment, in work, at home and phone calls were never the same as face to face conversations.

Douglas said, "look I'll be down on Friday and we can talk then."

John realised he would have to tell Douglas about Elizabeth's stipulations and agreed to see him in the Queen's café on Saturday morning.

Douglas was at the rendezvous early on the Saturday morning. He noticed the girl from the group of youngsters at another table with one of the boys from the group. He seemed to be trying to persuade her for some reason, but she was having none of it. He heard her say "Look Kevin, I'm enjoying myself as things are, and I don't want to get serious with anybody." Douglas registered the name 'Kevin' and thought, I wonder if that's John's boy and after a few seconds, my half-brother. The shock hit him like a double-decker bus. He glanced over to catch the girl looking at him and smiling. He quickly looked away and decided to leave and to stop John before he came in, to avoid an embarrassing scene. However, as he left he was quickly followed by the girl, who brushed past him, with Kevin in her wake. Douglas decided it was now clear to go back in. Shortly after, John arrived and Douglas explained why he had left the café, John explained what had happened with Elizabeth and that she had stipulated that John's parents and Kevin had to know. Douglas said, "I need time to think. How about a drink in the Castle tonight?"

John agreed.

Douglas walked around for a while and decided to go back to his room in the Castle Hotel to think. As he got to the hotel entrance the girl, Carol came from the opposite direction. She came straight up to Douglas and said, "how about buying me a drink?" quickly followed by, "I'm having a terrible day and I just need someone to talk to."

Douglas thought whether an invitation would be wise and then beckoned to the door of the hotel. As he stood by the lounge bar the girl stood very close to him and ran her hands up and down his arm. They took the drinks to a table and sat down.

She said, "I'm Carol, I'm sorry about what happened in the café a few weeks ago and in the town centre. It was silly and childish. They like to show off."

Douglas thought, well, you were with them. He indicated it was of no consequence.

Carol said, "I like the look of you. You're good looking and you look thoughtful, calm, strong. I like that in a man."

Douglas smiled "I think that's probably a line you got from a film. You're what eighteen or nineteen. How many men do you know?"

Carol tried to look as mature and sexy as possible, and said, "enough. I've been around."

Douglas thought enough is enough. I need to find my way out of this. I can't go to my room in case she follows me up. That would be really stupid.

He said, "look I'm very busy this afternoon. I have people to meet so we'd better drink up."

Carol knocked back her drink and stood up.

Douglas followed her out through the entrance of the hotel and as she turned left he turned right.

Before she had gone ten yards she turned to him "thanks for the drink, it was very nice to talk to you, you know where I am if you need a bit of company," and then she walked away.

Neither of them noticed Kevin, who had followed her to the hotel and waited outside. He was close enough to hear everything she said and he turned to kick the pavement edge in a fit of jealousy.

34

Douglas was just getting ready to go down to the lounge bar to meet John when there was a tap at the door. Douglas called out "who is it? Come in."

The receptionist put her head around the door and said, "someone in the lounge bar for you, Dr Samuels."

Douglas said, "thank you, I've been expecting Mr Evans."

The receptionist said, "you mean Mrs Evans?"

Douglas, quickly regaining his composure said, "oh yes, of course."

He closed and locked the door behind him and followed the receptionist down to the lounge bar. He could see the back of a lady where John usually sat, at a corner table.

Douglas walked over and introduced himself "Dr Samuels, Douglas Samuels that is, and you are….?"

Elizabeth turned her head slightly "Mrs Evans, Elizabeth, John's wife."

Douglas was stunned for a moment but then thought, I should have expected this. He decided that she should open the conversation and he should think carefully before saying anything.

Elizabeth said, "I thought I had better introduce myself to my husband's new son."

Douglas pursed his lips and said, "it's very nice to meet you, though perhaps this news has come as rather a shock to the family."

Elizabeth said, "well the family, apart from me, doesn't know yet. I'm sure this news has more shocks in store," and after a second, "perhaps you could fill me in on some of the finer details, as my husband has been reluctant to say too much."

Douglas stayed silent for a few seconds thinking, I have to be careful, as I don't know what John has told her. He decided that his best tactic was to tell the truth as then no blame might be put at his door. He related the story, or rather the parts of the story that had been relayed to him by his uncle in Calcutta. He noticed Elizabeth wince when he said that her husband and his mother had been seeing each other for some time while John was completing his National Service in Burma. He immediately thought I bet John told her it was a bit of a wild fling and didn't last long. Oh well, John has never taken me into his confidence about what he has told Elizabeth, so there we are.

When Douglas had finished his story Elizabeth asked "when John tells his mother and father about you do you want to be there? They are your grandparents?"

Douglas thought for a minute and said, "I think that would be preferable, though I certainly don't want to cause any more upset than has already been caused."

Elizabeth thought, fair play, how thoughtful. She then said, "and what about Kevin, do you want to be there when John tells him?"

Once again Douglas said, "obviously I would like to be part of my half-brother's life, but that would depend upon your and John's advice."

Douglas leaned back in the chair and said, "look, Mrs Evans, I didn't ask to be born. My mother experienced difficult times in Calcutta. She was Burmese, not Indian and she was a single mother living in the house of a British subject and trying to bring up the child of a British soldier and they were not very popular at the time. I had to work hard in school and university and I have had to work hard to get a job in this country. I have thought many times about going back to India to practice my profession there, but I am half British as well, and I feel I have rights in this country. I introduced myself to John and I knew it would be a shock, but he has accepted me and we are trying to get to know each other. Perhaps I should not have tried to get work in South Wales and should have only applied elsewhere, but Indian trained doctors can only get work in this country in areas where it is difficult to attract British trained doctors, in other words in areas where there is great need. I have been given the chance to work in Pontygwyn and I will try my very best to offer that community the benefit of the skills which I have. It is difficult as an Asian or an African or West Indian to fit into your culture but I propose to give it my best shot, as you say. The support of your husband, my father, is extremely helpful to me but……," then there was a lengthy pause "if you think I am trying to draw him away from you and Kevin I promise you I will leave you all alone."

Elizabeth didn't answer. She was thinking how eloquent Douglas was. He was clearly clever and well educated and he seemed kind and unprepossessing.

She stood up and said, "well, I think we have both learnt a little more about each other, Dr Samuels."

It hurt that she did not refer to him by his Christian name, but he liked her. She was forthright and straightforward, perhaps more so than John, where Douglas thought there always seemed to be a hidden agenda.

Elizabeth thanked Douglas for his time and left. She walked out of the hotel and was glad that she had to walk home. It would give her time to think. She thought, what a good looking young man Douglas was. She thought of the nastiness her father used to spout when he talked about the soldiers he had fought with in the First World War, constantly referring to them as 'chinks', who did the work behind the trenches and some of the 'darkies', who manned the trenches alongside him. They were always referred to condescendingly. Yet here was a young man who had come to this country to work in our National Health Service and she thought, I don't know but I wouldn't mind betting he gets stick for it. She walked a while, then thought, so why do I feel so aggressive towards him. Bloody John, why did he have to go and spoil our lives? I suppose I only feel angry because Douglas turned up. If John had had a child who had stayed in India or Burma or wherever then I would be none the wiser. The bastard, why couldn't he keep it in his trousers?

After a few minutes, John arrived at the hotel. Douglas thought "it just goes on and on."

John said, "I saw Elizabeth coming in and so I stayed out of sight until she had left," and then "how did it go?"

Douglas said, "I have absolutely no idea. She asked about my background and I told her the same story I told you a few weeks ago. She seemed satisfied and the only time I thought she was bothered by my explanation was when I said that your affair went on for some time."

John tut-tutted "Oh God, that could be a problem. I told her it was just a drunken one-night stand."

Douglas immediately said, "well, I told her the truth and perhaps you might have done better to have done the same."

John was a little taken aback to be reprimanded by his son, but he said nothing as he knew Douglas was right in his thinking. However, the reprimand didn't stop John thinking about how he could get out of the lie, probably with another lie.

Douglas said, "anyway I'm going back to London for two weeks and then I've hired a van to bring down my possessions to Pontygwyn. I'll have one week to settle in and then I'll begin work. If you are planning for me to be around to meet your parents and, or Kevin I'll have to know now."

John thought and said, "well, what if you can come to Treafon during the week that you are settling into Pontygwyn, the week before you start work."

Both thought that was a good idea and John said he would phone Douglas during the next week to finalise arrangements. They both stood up and walked out to the porchway at the entrance to the hotel.

Douglas stopped and said, "by the way, I forgot to mention that I had a chat with a man here last week, Tom Price, he wasn't very complimentary about you."

John laughed briefly and said, "Tom Price, I'm not surprised. He owns a local builder's merchants. A few years back he failed to pay his bill for coal he had received. This went on for over a year after getting several reminders from me. In the end, I threatened legal action. He came down to see me and said that there were times when he would send out building materials and not get paid for them for years, sometimes never, which was considered goodwill. I told him that was not the way it worked in the coal industry and I couldn't put goodwill on the table to feed my family. I was paid the following week. So I'm not surprised he's not my greatest fan."

Douglas said, "I thought there might be more to the story."

After a brief silence Douglas said, "look, if things are getting too complicated and my presence is causing too much difficulty with your family, we can stop meeting. I don't want to pester you and make your life a misery."

John replied thoughtfully "no, I won't pretend things are going to be easy but I'm glad we've met. I like your company and as long as you are happy I would like to go on meeting up and getting to know each other.'

Douglas said, "ok if you are sure."

Douglas felt he wanted some fresh air and so walked with John for a short while. They chatted as they walked along the street outside the Castle Hotel. Neither of them noticed Kevin walking up to the top of town on the other side of the road. Kevin thought, what the fuck's dad doing talking to that paki again? He immediately remembered Will telling him that they had been together in the Queen's Café. He didn't look like a businessman, but what the fuck, I don't really care what my father is doing with some half-caste bloke. It just niggled at him that it seemed a strange triangle. His dad was spending time with this guy and he'd seen Carol talking to him in a very affectionate way. At least it seemed like that to him.

Kevin caught up with Carol as she walked across to the town centre. The shops were shut and the town was quiet. Kevin came up behind her and said, "what were you doing with Gunga Din?"

Carol turned and said, "I don't know who you are talking about?"

Kevin said, "the Asian bloke. I saw you coming out of the Castle and it sounded like you were offering to see him."

Carol lied "yes, he offered to buy me a drink, so I went in."

Kevin asked, "are you going to see him again?"

Carol answered, "I might," in a coquettish way and followed that up with "you don't own me you know."

They both arrived at the bench outside the shopping centre at the same time and as Stuart, Alan, Will and Nick were already there, no more was said.

Kevin was very sullen throughout the evening and as Carol seemed to be ignoring him he left the group early. As he walked across the top of town he thought, I bet that bloke is staying in the Castle. I'll go and have a word with him, set him straight.

Kevin entered the lounge bar of the hotel. He didn't know the hotel very well, not his sort of place. A bit posh for me, he thought. He looked around and noticed Douglas sat on his own in the corner, reading the paper.

He walked across "mind if I join you," he said as he sat down.

Douglas thought, well that's all the family in one night. He said, "do you want a beer?"

Kevin replied, "don't mind if I do."

Douglas brought two beers back and sat down "what can I do for you?"

Kevin leaned forward in what he thought was a threatening way "well, you can leave my girl alone for one, and then for another, you can fuck off back to where you came from. Yes, I think that would make me very happy."

Douglas smiled at the threat "I haven't got any reason to leave your girl alone as I only met her this afternoon when she asked me to buy her a drink, which I did out of politeness. She drank it and left. I think that was pretty kind actually after the way she and your friends treated me in the café a few weeks ago."

Kevin was a little taken aback but continued "I was outside when the two of you left the hotel and I heard her say 'you know where I am if you need company. What did she mean by that?"

Douglas said, "I have absolutely no idea. You will have to ask her. I spent perhaps five or six minutes in her company. That was the only time I have spoken to her and I can assure you that by anyone's standards that is a very short time for intimacy to take place."

Kevin was more than a little confused by the way Douglas spoke and was becoming more and more frustrated.

He said, "and what are you doing talking to my old man all the time?"

Douglas didn't know how to respond to that, so he kept quiet, but when it was obvious that Kevin was waiting for an answer, he said, "you'll have to ask your dad."

Kevin was getting no answers, and so said, "haven't you got an answer for anything. You can't keep saying you'll have to ask her, you'll have to ask him.' For fuck's sake, take some responsibility."

Douglas refused to say any more. Kevin had a short temper and he could feel it getting the better of him. He stood up and shouted at Douglas "well you can fucking leave her alone. If I see you anywhere near her again I'll fucking paste you, I promise," and with that, he hurled the remains of his drink in Douglas' face.

Kevin walked out, Douglas took out a handkerchief and attempted to dry himself off, desperately trying to avoid the stares of some of the other customers.

35

Ten days went by before John got a phone call from Douglas while in work telling him that he had just arrived in Treafon having driven down in a van, which he had borrowed, loaded with his possessions. He had booked into the Castle Hotel for just one night and would be driving on to Pontygwyn the following day. He said, "I realise I'm not going to have time to come back to Treafon for a while after I start work as I can see I'm going to be too busy."

John thought that Douglas was quite forceful in effectively giving him an ultimatum. John realised that if he wished Douglas to visit his parent's house with him, and possibly with Elizabeth it would have to be that evening. John said, "ok, let's do it then," in a very decisive way. He said, "you know where they live, you've already been there, I'll meet you outside the house at seven-thirty, I'll be wearing a suit of armour."

Douglas smiled at John's ironic joke but felt quite relaxed as he felt he had done nothing wrong and so could sort of view proceedings from the outside.

John left the garage where his lorries were stored early, after asking the foreman to supervise the locking up and seeing the men safely off the premises. When he got home he went looking for Elizabeth who was in the garden planting some bulbs. John said, "Douglas has just phoned and we have agreed to go and speak to mam and dad this evening. Do you want to be there?"

Elizabeth finished what she was doing and stood up, brushing the dirt off her fingers "no, you two are quite capable of doing that on your own. It's nothing to do with me really, so I don't want to go and give any indication that I am complicit in what you are going to tell them."

John said, "is there anything you want me to say about how you feel about the whole situation?"

Elizabeth looked up from under her eyebrows, with quite a stern look, "no, if I have anything to say I will say it on my own when I go to see them tomorrow."

John took a deep breath, seemingly to ward off Elizabeth's frosty reaction, but, he thought, all her reactions were frosty at the moment, that hadn't changed in the last few weeks.

John arrived at his parent's house just as Douglas was pulling up in his borrowed van. John turned and said, "you ok?" but could find nothing else to say as the prospect awaiting him filled him with dread. He tapped the door and walked in, with Douglas just behind him. His father sat in the armchair but there was no sign of his mother. John said, "hi."

Mr Evans replied, "hello there," but as he was about to rise to put the kettle on, the normal procedure when John arrived, he noticed Douglas behind him.

John said, "I've got something to tell you, and I've brought Douglas along."

John's dad gave a quizzical look at Douglas but did not forget his politeness and said, "Hello son, didn't think we'd be seeing you again."

Douglas nodded, but before he could respond John said, "mam about?"

His dad said, "just upstairs, changing the beds, do you want me to give her a call?"

John nodded and his dad went to the bottom of the small staircase and called, "Charlotte, John's here."

Mrs Evans shouted down "I'll be down in a while."

Mr Evans shouted back up the stairs "I think you'd better come down, he's got a visitor with him."

Douglas smiled at the careful way Mr Evans had put it.

Mrs Evans came down the stairs into the living room and said, "Oh John, don't normally see you on a Tuesday," and then on noticing Douglas, "Oh sorry, I didn't see you there." She looked a little nonplussed at the unexpected visitors but on regaining her composure she asked her usual first question "do you want a cup of tea?"

John said, "not for me," and Douglas also shook his head.

Immediately John's mother became more concerned, thinking, John arriving on a Tuesday, with someone else and not wanting a cup of tea, something must be up.

John spoke into the silence "I uhh, we've got something to tell you." The silence persisted. John looked at his mother who had not moved "mam, I think you'd better sit down."

All four of them found somewhere to sit and suddenly the four people filled the small living room.

As John was thinking how to start his mother said, "well, don't keep us in suspense."

John said, "you've met Douglas before when he came to Treafon to look for me," he drew breath a second, "well, he was looking for me to tell me that he was my son. He is a qualified doctor and he has just got a job in this country and his mother had told him that I was his father." John let that sink in.

There was a stunned silence and both parents were staring at John and then at Douglas as the realisation sunk in. John watched his mother's jaw visibly drop, but neither of them could find anything to say.

Eventually, Mrs Evans said, "how did that happen?"

John said, "well, I won't go into details but basically I had….." He couldn't find a word that his mother would find acceptable, "an affair, I suppose you would call it," then he thought for a second, can you have an affair if you are not already married or promised to anyone else?

John then continued with the background story of Sammy leaving for India when she discovered she was pregnant and Douglas being born in Calcutta. When he felt that there was nothing relevant that he could add he turned to Douglas and said, "is there anything I've missed out?"

Douglas shook his head and was suddenly aware that he had not said anything since entering the house, and so he said, "no, I don't think so."

After a further period of protracted silence, Mrs Evans got up and said, "well. I definitely want that cup of tea." She stood up and quickly went into the kitchen. After a few seconds, John who was sat closest to the kitchen could hear her sobbing from the other room.

After a minute or two, she came back into the living room carrying a cup of tea, her eyes red where she had dabbed them dry.

She immediately sat down. In this time Mr Evans had said nothing. Suddenly he said, "does Elizabeth know?" and then thinking out loud said,""of course, she must do."

John confirmed that she did in fact know. Mrs Evans said, "what does she think?"

John didn't know what to say to that question and so answered "I don't really know, she doesn't say much. She is going to come up to see you tomorrow, so you can ask her."

Mrs Evans then asked, "what about Kevin, does he know?"

John said, "no, not yet, we thought we'd tell you first."

Mrs Evans then thought and said, "but Douglas will be Kevin's half brother."

Douglas inwardly smiled as he thought of Kevin throwing a pint of beer over him. He thought he's got a hell of a shock coming.

Mrs Evans then thought out loud "what do I tell people? What do I tell people in chapel?"

John thought, trust mam to worry most about what the self-righteous people in chapel would think. He said, "you'll have to decide what you want to tell them. What's done is done, I can't change that, I now have two sons and I have to try to form a relationship with Douglas as well as Kevin."

Mr Evans suddenly shuffled in his chair and said, "good luck with that. Kevin is a handful without this knowledge. Saw him and his buddies knocking old men's caps off in the street last week, for a bit of fun, you know. Well, the people they did it to didn't find it funny. One man was walking with a walking stick and nearly fell over trying to pick his cap up off the floor after they had knocked it off. All they could do was run off laughing. Mr Owens was a war hero and to be treated like that. The boy needs a firm hand."

John thought I can't be side-tracked to talk about how I should be dealing with Kevin, just at the moment.

John stood up and said, "well, I've told you now. I'll let you think about it and I'll pop up tomorrow evening for a chat."

Mrs Evans, who looked stunned by the news and was clearly hurting said, "don't bother coming up tomorrow, we'll be out. This will take time to think about and make decisions."

John said, "as you wish." He turned to the door and then turned back and said, "I take it you won't now be needing my help with the building work in the chapel?"

Mrs Evans said, "I don't think any financial help coming from you to aid a place of worship would be appropriate, under these circumstances."

John felt stung by that comment but thought that he couldn't add anything to what had already been said and so stood up to leave along with Douglas. As they were going out of the door Mr Evans said, "lad, Douglas I mean, please don't think badly of us, it's been a bit of a shock and we know none of it is your fault."

Douglas stopped and turned "thank you, Mr Evans." He thought, I wanted to call him granddad, but it certainly wasn't the time for that.

The two left, closing the door behind them. John exhaled deeply on reaching the street, said his goodbyes to Douglas, saying that he would contact him in a few days. Douglas said that he would be driving to Pontygwyn the next day and he quickly ripped out a sheet of paper from a notebook he kept in his pocket, writing down on it the telephone number of the doctor's practice he would be working at.

36

John relaxed in the camping chair he had brought in the boot of his car. It was a dry day but there was a cool breeze and both the spectators and the players were wearing sweaters and in some cases windproof jackets as protection against the cool breezes. John was sitting on the edge of the boundary rope of Pontygwyn cricket club, watching their game against Black Rock Cricket club, who had travelled about fifteen miles to play. He suggested meeting Douglas as they had not seen each other for nearly a month. Douglas said that meeting up was a little more difficult and that he was not being obstructive but between work commitments and his attempts to involve himself in the local community there was little time left. They agreed to meet at the cricket match and go for a drink afterwards.

Douglas explained that he had wandered out to the cricket field a few times after work, in the evenings, he had watched the local cricketers practising and after this had occurred a few times one of them had wandered over to speak to him. Iestyn, the club captain asked him if he enjoyed cricket and when he said he did Iestyn asked him over to meet the other lads in the pavilion at the end of the practice. When he got into the pavilion one of the lads recognised him saying "hey, you are the new doctor I saw last week, I told the boys we've probably got a new spin bowler in the village."

Douglas laughed at the assumption that because he was Asian he would firstly be a cricketer and secondly a spin bowler. The truth was that apart from playing cricket in the street outside his house in Calcutta he had only ever played competitive cricket once before, and that was while he was at medical school. He played for the first-year medical students, he didn't bowl, he batted number eleven and he was out for nought. They never asked him again. However, he went to the Pontygwyn's practice sessions a few times and he was beginning to get the hang of it, at least fielding, even though he thought he was still useless with the bat and was never asked to bowl. A few of the players had helped him with his technique and he was enjoying learning a new skill and being part of a team. The game had just started and Pontygwyn were fielding. John was enjoying the match, though so far Douglas had only touched the ball twice. At the end of the Black Rock innings, they had scored one hundred and eighty-four and the players trooped in for tea in the pavilion. Only a few people were watching and so John began to amble around the edge of the boundary, leaving his chair alongside his parked car. As he came near to the pavilion Douglas came out with a cup of tea in a plastic container and a paper plate with a sausage roll and a few sandwiches. He offered these to John explaining that he had had his tea already. John took them willingly, thanking Douglas.

John asked, "I'm assuming you've found somewhere to stay?"

Douglas laughingly said, "no, I've been sleeping on the street," but then said, "yes, I'm sharing a flat with a local primary school teacher. I saw the advert where Chris was looking for someone to share with and we've gone halves in a rented house in the village, it's perfect."

Douglas walked on with John. He asked, "did you go back to your parent's?"

John said he did once in the week after their visit but the response was so frosty that he left quickly.

Douglas said, "what about Elizabeth, did she go to see them and did she say anything?"

John said, "yes, she went up the day after. She only said that they were very upset and that my mother was still fretting over what she would tell the people in chapel," he continued, "Elizabeth still barely speaks to me, she finds any excuse to be out of the house."

Douglas asked, "does Kevin know?"

John said, "I had to reprimand him for his behaviour in town, after what dad said. That didn't help. Kevin sulked for a few days and again partly because of the atmosphere he keeps out of the house, so no I haven't told him. I can't make my mind up which is the best way to tell him." John thought for a second and said, "I'll have to bite the bullet this week and tell him." He then asked, "anyway, enough about me, how has work been?"

Douglas said, "yea, ok, A few problems, but generally alright."

John said, "a few problems?"

Douglas said, "well, I started two weeks ago, seeing patients that is, and in my first surgery a Mr Watson was called in. He opened the door, looked at me, turned to the receptionist and said, 'Doctor Samuels, that's an English name but he's black.' The receptionist didn't answer and he turned around, closed my door and walked out. At the end of the surgery, the receptionist came in and closed the door behind her. She said, 'sorry Doctor, about Mr Watson, but when he went back through reception he announced to everyone waiting that you were…..', she stopped 'well, he said black.' He walked out and another four people walked out with him. So, I had to say to the receptionist, we can't make them come in, they have to make their own minds up.' Douglas then said, "Doctor Bevan was complaining that his list was getting longer because people were refusing to see me and were insisting upon seeing him. I told him there wasn't anything I could do about it, but I could hear him say under his breath, what's the point of taking somebody on if I still have the same workload. I felt guilty and so I've offered to clear up the rooms every day after surgery."

John asked, "what are the blokes in the cricket team like?"

Douglas said, "they are a good bunch of blokes. They've helped me to settle in. One of them came up to me last week and said, 'my missus refused to come and see you because you are…….., well coloured, you know, but I told her 'he's alright, he's a good bloke and I said I wouldn't have any problem coming to see you doc.' That cheered me up, so hopefully things will get better in time. It's a big step for these people to accept me into a small community." Douglas remembered one thing that had happened and laughed.

John said, "what?"

Douglas said, "well, one old bloke came in and before I could speak he said, 'you are not one of those witch doctors are you?' I jokingly said yes, I've got a box of dolls under the desk and anyone I don't like I stick pins in them. The thing was, he didn't laugh."

The two smiled at the story and continued their walk, Douglas nodding to a few people they passed who were sat in deck chairs waiting for the Pontygwyn innings to start.

John said, "how do you manage to cope with the...." He couldn't think what word to use, "you know, the anger, the animosity, the aggression of people who don't know you at all but treat you in a particular way because of the colour of your skin? I don't know how you do it."

Douglas said, "the term is racism. I suppose you get used to it. The strange thing is that some of the people I met in London would refer to me in a particular way, calling me a nigger, or blackie or paki and not think anything of it. These people would be, well not friends exactly, but acquaintances shall we say. They would be saying it in a matter of fact way as if it meant nothing. They wouldn't mean to harm, but their words would sting, each time they said them. When I mention this sort of casual racism to friends in London they would try to differentiate between actions and words. They would say 'if someone refused to interact with me much as Mr Watson in Pontygwyn, by refusing to be treated by me, then that was a serious act but if someone said something, perhaps using the word nigger or paki then that was not so serious as it was only a word."

John said, "you don't agree with them?"

Douglas replied "It is my belief that you must view these things from the point of view of the person receiving the words or the actions. If they hurt, they are wrong, whether they are words or actions. It is the thoughtlessness I cannot cope with when the people see no wrong in what they say or do. I just ask that people respect me for who I am, not the colour of my skin."

John said, “well, I can’t fault any of that and you give me food for thought. There are issues I’ve never thought about, despite having been in Asia.”

Douglas stopped and looked at John, he said, “you loved my mother, she was a person of colour, a half-caste, but you loved her for who she was, skin colour didn’t enter your head.”

John cast his mind back and said, “there’s no doubt about that, she was a lovely person with a wonderful disposition and I did love her and given different circumstances we might have been together longer.”

Douglas smiled and said, “well, I’d better be getting back to the pavilion after that deep discussion, although there’s no rush unless our batting collapses, as I’m batting number nine.”

John said, “not eleven?”

Douglas said jokingly, “a boy of six is batting ten and a man with two wooden legs is eleven.”

They both laughed and Douglas ran off across the field to the pavilion. Pontygwyn were one hundred and sixty for seven when Douglas came in to bat. John could hear a cheer of support from the pavilion when he came out, padded up, “come on doc, you can do it,” and “give ‘em hell, Dougy.”

John was buoyed by the local support for Douglas and glad there seemed to be no racist innuendo or inappropriate comments. Pontygwyn lost their next wicket on one hundred and seventy-five for eight. Two wickets standing, and ten runs to get. Douglas was still there on nine. There was a gasp as Douglas’ partner was caught on the next ball, one hundred and seventy-five for nine. Out came the last man, well, boy of about fourteen. Douglas went down the wicket to speak to him. He nodded at whatever advice Douglas had given him. He had two balls to face. The quick bowler almost took the young boy’s head off with the next delivery and Douglas turned to the bowler and said, “he’s only a young boy, you don’t have to kill him.”

The bowler stopped and turned to Douglas, "he's a fucking player, not a young boy, and who are you, his father?" He went to walk back and then turned back to Douglas and said, "of course you can't be, he's white and you're a black bastard." The umpire stepped between them and said, "that's enough of that."

Douglas could feel his hackles rise but chose, as he did at other times, to walk away. The young boy survived the next ball. Towards the end of the next over Douglas caught the ball a glancing blow to third man and they ran three. Seven to win. Douglas now faced the bowler who had just abused him. He galloped in with a look of intent in his eyes. The intent to take Douglas' head off. He bowled a short ball, which rose to head height. Douglas stepped back and swung wildly at it, partly in temper. It sped out to cover point, passing a fielder and going on for four. Three to win. A huge cheer came from the pavilion, who sensed there was animosity between batsman and bowler. The bowler, now even more incensed ran in even quicker and let loose a full toss aimed at chest height. Douglas stepped back and lashed out with a shot he didn't know he was capable of playing, which sped to the boundary and produced the winning runs. Douglas, twenty not out and the third highest scorer in the team. He turned to shake hands with the umpire and then could see the incensed bowler coming down the wicket very hot and bothered. Douglas held out his hand, but the bowler refused to shake it, and as he passed the bowler said, "you can fuck off with that, fucking arsehole, you should have stayed in India. We don't want you here."

The Black Rock captain heard the altercation and immediately went over to the bowler "Neil, calm down, you'll get us all into trouble." The captain then walked across to Douglas "well played lad. I haven't seen you before, very impressive. Sorry about Neil, he's a bit quick-tempered, but his hearts in the right place. He'll probably buy you a drink later."

Douglas nodded and walked back to the pavilion to a huge cheer, lots of pats on the back and the captain saying "you'll be playing up the order from now on. We've never beaten Black Rock since I've been playing, you've just become a legend."

Douglas showered and then went out to meet John who was standing alongside his car. John congratulated him on his performance and the team's win.

Douglas said, "thanks, we normally go to the 'Red Cow' for a drink. Come on up and meet some of the boys." They both got into John's car and drove to the pub. Douglas introduced John to a few of the players who were very impressed with their new star. However, when Douglas would say to any of the other players "this is my dad," they would look very suspicious, thinking, hang on this white guy has got a coloured son. What's going on here? Douglas would not satisfy them with any explanations. Douglas could see the hot-tempered bowler slouched over the far side of the bar, scowling at him. He thought, there's no way that bloke is ever going to offer to buy me a drink.

Before John left Douglas passed him an envelope which John opened up to find a copy of the photograph of himself and Sammy, taken in Rangoon in 1947. He said, after a moment's silence as he took in the image of the two of them once again "thank you for this, you know I will treasure it."

Douglas replied, "no problem."

Eventually, John drove back to Treafon, promising to meet up with Douglas the next weekend and Douglas went back into the pub to say his goodbyes.

On the Monday morning, Douglas went into the surgery to meet his first patients of the week. The first was a little boy with a sprained wrist that his mother thought might be broken. Douglas arranged for the boy to have an x-ray and they left after Douglas had given him a sticky lollipop for being brave. Mother and son left very happy. Then, the receptionist called in Mrs Stewart, a lady in her eighties by the look of her, Douglas thought. She stepped through the door and stopped, turning to the receptionist she scowled "he's a man, and he's black. There's no way I'm seeing him and taking my clothes off. I might consider it if he was a white man but a black man, no chance." She left, slamming the door behind her. The receptionist came in to apologise. Douglas told her it wasn't her fault, but he thought, I started the day on a high and now this again.

The following day Douglas was doing his rounds. He had to visit a small girl called Laura. Her mother was very concerned and agitated. Douglas asked what symptoms the little girl had. The mother said she had been sick, she had a high temperature, a headache and she had a rash.

Douglas said, "hm, could just be the start of flu." Before he could say any more the mother said, "oh, and she keeps saying the light in the room is hurting her eyes and can I turn it off." Douglas thought, well, that confirms it. He asked if he could use the telephone and the mother showed him where the phone was. Before he picked up the phone Douglas said to the mother "I'm almost a hundred per cent sure its meningitis, don't be alarmed, she'll be fine, I'm sure, but she does need to go to hospital. I'm just about to phone for an ambulance."

The ambulance came and took away Laura and a very distraught mother. A few days later Douglas decided to look into the hospital to see how Laura was getting along. When he went into the children's ward Laura was lying down but she looked better than she had a few days previously. Her mother and father were sat at her bedside. When Douglas was assured that she was on the mend he excused himself. As he left the ward Laura's father followed him out, he said, "doctor, can I just thank you so much. Your quick thinking possibly saved her life, at least that's what the doctor here said. We are so grateful, we cannot thank you enough." He then turned and went back into the ward to sit with his daughter.

For the first time for a while, Douglas felt good about himself. It cheered him up and he thought, perhaps I am contributing to the community and doing some good.

37

John decided to go for a walk in the park, as he did when he was younger. He parked his car, a large Rover with plush leather seats at the top of town. He had persuaded himself that you had to flaunt the trappings of success as with this people would have more confidence in you if you appeared to be successful and consequently that would bring in more business. John's father would often ask him if he needed to be quite so ostentatious with all he owned, but John believed that his father enjoyed the fact that his son was a successful businessman. The reality was that John's attitude to people in the town had changed as he had moved from the relative poverty of his youth to a position of affluence. He no longer socialised with the friends of his youth, some had moved away but some still lived in the town. John now spent his spare time with other successful businessmen. Deep down John's father believed that his son had betrayed his socialist principles and that possessions had become more important than people. He got the impression that people didn't like to mention his son in conversation because his father would be embarrassed by some of the things he heard.

John started to walk across to the park. He remembered that when he needed to clear his head he would head for the park, find a bench away from everyone, or failing that he would walk up to the top of the mountain. He glanced down at his ever-expanding waist and thought a walk to the park might be a better option, he didn't want to give himself a heart attack. He wandered around the flower beds and the ponds where the swans still swam as they did when he was younger. He stood alongside the war memorial and read the inscription for perhaps the first time. He realised he hadn't come into the park for perhaps five years. He was now a busy man with little spare time to amble through the park as he did when he was a teenager. That would have been at least thirty years ago. Time just went faster as you got older.

He sat on a bench and lit up a cigarette, despite admitting to himself that he should really have made a better effort at stopping smoking, having tried several times unsuccessfully. He began to feel sorry for himself. He felt his life was passing him by. He had no money worries as the business was doing well. He had a large house on the edge of town and because of the area house prices were lower allowing him a larger property. He had a happy marriage, until this last few months, but he hoped that could be repaired in time. Kevin was causing him problems, with no job and no prospects, and with a bunch of friends that he would never have chosen for him, but he hoped that as he got older he would settle down and become more mature. He had started to build a relationship with Douglas and even though he saw less of him because he was spending time settling into his new job, he hoped he would see more of him in the future. His mam and dad were getting older and even though his relationship with them was going through a sticky patch in recent months because of the arrival of Douglas the hope was that they would come around and things could get back to where they were. John decided that he needed to try to introduce Douglas into Elizabeth's life and to his mam and dad. In time they would be able to see that he was a very respectable person. He was a doctor, well-educated and well-spoken. They would be bound to like him, but that would all take time and effort on his part.

People called them 'hopes and dreams.' John's hopes and dreams all seemed at present to revolve around relationships. He thought, my head has been so full of developing my business and improving my standard of living that I had forgotten about people. Mam and dad have always put people first. Mam with her interests in chapel and dad with his workmates, who he continued to meet up with. He thought, I really enjoy Douglas' company. He speaks to me more like a friend than a son. If only I could get to that point with Kevin. It's a paradox that Douglas is one of the positives in my life at the moment but it's his arrival that has caused all my other important relationships to suffer.

John failed to resolve any of the problems that were playing on his mind but he did feel more relaxed for giving these issues some thought. He decided 'time' and 'the mending of relationships with the people he loved' would be important factors in helping to correct the wrongs he had inflicted on those close to him.

As he left the park to walk back to his car he recognised a figure walking towards him. As she got nearer he said, "Hi, how are you Aunty Maggie?"

John's Aunty Maggie didn't answer immediately, screwing her eyes up. John thought she hasn't recognised me.

Maggie speaking in quite a dismissive way said, "hmm, didn't expect to see you walking around, freely."

John looked at her quizzically, "what do you mean?"

Maggie answered, "well, under the circumstances."

John didn't say anything but waited for her to elaborate.

Maggie said, "been speaking to your mother, she said things weren't good between you. She's getting older mind you, not going to be around forever. You only have one mam. Not sensible to be wasting time falling out."

John thought, Maggie always had this strange way of speaking. Short sentences which don't always have an ending and often left you wondering what she really meant, like crossword clues you had to work out.

John said, "well, I've tried, but she doesn't want anything to do with me at the moment."

Maggie said, "well, should have thought of that before... well, can't stand gassing to you all day, things to do. Don't suppose we'll be seeing you in chapel…' and then she walked off. John could just hear her mutter 'for a while."

John walked on and thought about what she said and how she said it. He thought to himself, it sounds as if mam has told her about Douglas and that's why she's being so obtuse. John began to think of the consequences of his mother telling Maggie and perhaps others. He suddenly became very depressed, thinking it's bad enough trying to sort out a problem when the family members know. If people in the town know, it didn't bear thinking about.

John was sat watching television when Kevin came into the living room and asked, "the news, why are you watching this rubbish, it's bloody boring?"

John said, "perhaps if you took a bit more notice of what was happening in the world you might learn something."

Kevin asked, "can I turn it over and see what's on the other side?"

John said, "no, I said I'm watching it."

Kevin was just about to get up when he sat back down as if he'd just remembered something, "who is that black bloke you keep talking to?"

John was more than a little taken aback. He thought about his answer "his name is Douglas. He's a doctor. He lives in Pontygwyn." He suddenly realised he should have left it at his name and occupation.

Kevin said, "if he lives in Pontygwyn, what's he doing in Treafon all the time and why did he need to stay in the Castle if he only lives a few miles away?"

John said, "he was only staying in the Castle before he moved to Pontygwyn. He lived in London before that."

Kevin waited a few seconds and said, "you seem to know a lot about him and spend quite a bit of time with him."

John thought again before he answered and then said, "I met him a few weeks ago and he's good company."

Kevin obviously in an antagonistic mood said, "I think the Asians should bugger off back to their own country, taking our jobs. Enoch Powell's got it right."

John looked up "how would you know about Enoch Powell?"

Kevin didn't know very much about Enoch Powell other than he had made speeches about immigrants coming into the country so he quickly said: "Will told me."

John said, "Anyway he's a doctor so he's not taking your job. You don't want a job so nobody's taking your job."

Kevin replied, "well Will said in London and Birmingham it's crawling with blackies like him and the sooner they bugger off back to where they came from, the better."

John was starting to get visibly riled by Kevin's ignorance and Kevin was achieving what he set out to do. Kevin started to laugh and stood up saying "you could give 'em a job on the coal round. They wouldn't need to wash after work," and walked out laughing at his own joke.

The phone rang and John went to pick it up. On the other end of the line was David, his brother. John quickly closed the Hall door so that his conversation could not be heard in the rest of the house. David said, "hello, haven't heard from you for a while, so I thought I would give you a ring."

John asked after David's family, his wife and three boys.

David said, "went to mam's yesterday. She said things weren't very good between you, so I thought I'd give you a ring and find out what was wrong."

John explained the whole situation and David went quiet at the other end of the line. He finally said, "oh, I see, she sort of hinted at something like that but obviously I didn't know the full story."

John was a little frustrated by everybody's attitude and said, "so, you have a new nephew."

David said, "yes, as you can imagine it's a bit of a shock to be faced with the fully grown variety."

John said, "look David, we both know this situation is not ideal.

I knew nothing of Douglas' existence until a few months ago, but I would welcome your support in trying to patch things up with mam and dad."

David said, "I'll see what I can do. Any more skeletons in the cupboard I should know about?"

John said, "very funny," and rang off.

38

John had gone into work early and had been working for three or four hours, completing some invoices when there was a gentle tap at the door. He shouted, "come in."

The door opened and Douglas looked around the door, saying "fancy a break?"

John replied, 'you know the right time to turn up, most unexpectedly, but most welcome."

Douglas sat down on the worn, dirty leather armchair in the corner "well, I had a day off as Doc Bevan feels things are beginning to work out and he offered to take my surgery today so I thought I'd see if you were around."

John collected his jacket from the back of the chair and said, "come on, I'll treat you to lunch."

They left the office and both got into John's car for the journey up to the Castle Hotel.

Douglas went to the bar to get two halves of bitter, as John was paying for lunch.

Douglas said, "well, how are things in sunny Treafon?"

John replied with a cynical sneer "never better, my parents are still not speaking to me, Elizabeth tries to find anything to do not to be in my company. Ironically only Kevin is speaking to me and I cringe with every conversation I have with him. So not so good really, I suppose."

Douglas said, "do you think it will improve with time?"

John related the conversation he had with Aunt Maggie and his thoughts that perhaps more people in the town might now know. John remained silent for a minute or so and then said, "anyway, enough of my problems, how are things with you?"

Douglas smiled and said, "well, pretty good actually. Doctor Bevan and I seem to have sorted out a rota and it seems a better working partnership. He is certainly more chatty now. He discusses cases and we talk about where he thinks the practice is going. So big strides really."

John said, "I'm really pleased things are working out."

Douglas said, "yes, one of the blokes at the cricket club asked me to go for a beer with him and his mates. He's an electrician and it did me good to spend time with people with different interests. Yes, I feel I'm beginning to settle in."

John explained to Douglas that he had spoken to his brother David and then realised that he had said very little to Douglas about his brother's family and the work he did, and so he outlined his brother's background.

Conversation dried up for a while as both were immersed in their thoughts. Suddenly John said, "I have to tell Kevin. He's asking who you are and why does he and his friends see us together so often."

Douglas said, "yes, I agree, the sooner the better."

John began to think out loud and said, "it's Wednesday today, I'll make sure I tell him as soon as possible. Elizabeth has started going back to the chapel she attended as a child, so Sunday would be a good time. Kevin will probably be at home and there will be no one else there and the phone is less likely to go on a Sunday." He suddenly stood up "yes Sunday, it's settled. Well, I'd better get back to work."

Douglas said, "I may pop in to Treafon on my way to the cricket on Saturday morning. Ok if we meet up in the café?"

John said, "yes fine, and I'll give you a ring on Sunday night to let you know how it went with Kevin. Come on, I'll give you a lift back to your car."

Douglas replied "yes, let me know how it goes with Kevin. I won't have a lift back, I'll walk. I want to pick up a paper on the way."

They both stood up and left, walking in different directions. Both saying their goodbyes and hoping to meet Saturday morning.

As John turned to where the car was parked he could hear someone behind him saying "well, fancy seeing you here."

John turned around to face Tom Price, "Oh hello."

Price said, "haven't seen you around for a while, well since we had a few words that is."

John said, "no, that's right," thinking, I have seen you but I often cross the road to avoid you.

John was just about to make his excuses and rush off to the car when Price said, "you haven't been to the last few Chamber of Trade meetings. Your absence was noted by a few of the committee." He drew breath and carried on "we wondered was it because of a rumour you might be having a bit of trouble."

John pursed his lips and asked, "and what trouble might that be?"

Price thought for a second and said, "well at the end of the last meeting Rhys Davies, Rob Sellars and Peter Wright, you know the butcher, well, they were having a bit of a gossip about something and as I joined them, I could hear your name mentioned. All I caught was that they thought you might be having a bit of difficulty. Well, when I realised that they were gossiping about someone and a member of the Chamber of Trade, I moved away immediately. You won't catch me gossiping about other people. All rubbish I expect. Not in any trouble are you? You know where I am if you need any help."

John thought, yes, I bet.

He began to move away but heard Price say, "nothing to do with the dark chap you were just talking to is it?"

John moved further away shouting over his shoulder "no. got to go, loads of work to do." He thought as he got into his car, nosy bastard. If he knows anything you might as well put it in the newspaper. It'll travel faster than the speed of light now.

John arrived home a little flustered after his encounter with Tom Price. He could hear Elizabeth in the kitchen. He walked into the kitchen, though she failed to acknowledge him as usually happened now. He said, "hello, listen I've decided to tell Kevin about Douglas this weekend." There was no response from Elizabeth so John said, "did you hear?"

Elizabeth turned and said, "I did, but it's of no concern to me as long as you do it sensibly and sympathetically. Kevin probably won't take it well, so you have to be prepared for that."

John nodded as Elizabeth passed him to go into the lounge.

39

A few days later John was at a Rotary Club meeting. He was glad to be there, amongst friends and not having to think about his family problems. They met upstairs in the Castle Hotel and when the formal business was over, they moved downstairs to the lounge bar. This brought a few recent memories back for John but he quickly pushed them aside and sat with the club president and three other Rotarians having a quiet beer. John was anticipating being asked to stand as Vice President for the next year. He had been in the Rotary Club for nearly ten years and should be the next to be anointed into the prestigious position. The vice president would automatically become the president the following year. At the end of the evening, a few of the members drifted away. As John got up to leave the club president, Steve Harris, also got up and said, "have you got time for a quick chat?"

John said he had and they moved back into the small room where they held their meetings.

They sat opposite each other at the large table in the centre of the room, Steve said, "you probably think it's about your turn to be asked to be vice president next year?"

John looked up but didn't say anything.

Steve continued, "well, Roger, Dave, Jack and myself and a few others have had a chat and we think you've got a lot on your plate at the moment," he hesitated and then continued "so taking on the role of vice president wouldn't be a good idea at the moment. Sort out your problems and we'll have another look at the situation next year."

Steve rose out of his seat as if the conversation was over.

John was dumbfounded and quickly said, "whoa, sort your problems out. What problems?"

Steve said, "just rumours but I think one person has spoken to another and I heard that you have a bit of family trouble. Anyway, none of my business eh?"

Steve started to walk away and John called back before Steve reached the door, "these so-called problems, if they are personal they have nothing to do with you or the Rotary Club."

Steve stopped, thought for a second and said, "if you were vice president you would be representing Treafon Rotary Club to other clubs and possibly to functions abroad. We couldn't have that. We would be ridiculed and the members wouldn't stand for it." He stopped, raised his hand and said, "that's all I've got to say, nothing is going to change our minds," and walked out.

John was upset by the discussion at the Rotary Club meeting and was sat in the lounge at his house relating to Elizabeth the conversation with Tom Price earlier in the week. He said, "people should mind their own business. It's like living your life through a microscope. This town drives me up the wall."

Elizabeth said, 'it was only a few years ago you were saying what a wonderful place to live it was, everybody looking out for everybody else, a real community."

John snapped back "yes, well I've changed my mind."

John was beginning to feel more despair at the intrusive nature of people's interest in his affairs. He smiled as he thought of the double meaning of the word 'affair' and how relevant it was to his present situation. He felt he was becoming increasingly isolated with fewer people he could rely on to discuss his problems. The only one he could speak to seemed to be Douglas and that probably wouldn't be good if other people found out. He gave a deep sigh. Elizabeth continued to freeze him out at home. They slept in separate beds and their only conversations involved practical details of the running of the house. He had started to go back to his parent's house, but while his father normally said little, he now rarely spoke at all. John's mother, who previously you often couldn't shut up, now rarely said anything at all. John would stay for a cup of tea but could see little point in just staying there and sitting in silence. He had had little contact with Douglas as, even though there was no problem between them, Douglas was fully immersed in his job and in involving himself in local activities in Pontygwyn. John spent all of his spare time on his work, which seemed to be a great deal, as he was now no longer in the local Rotary Club or seemingly the Chamber of Trade.

The phone rang in the office and John picked it up. His accountant, Roy Harding, went through the usual pleasantries and then said, "any chance we can have a meeting in the next few days?"

John asked, "sure, what's the problem?"

Roy replied, "not sure, but if you could find time to pop in, we can have a chat."

John said, "yes, tomorrow at about two o'clock ok?"

Roy said, "great, see you then."

Roy's secretary showed John into his office the next day.

Roy said, "how are things?"

John said, "sorry Roy, a few problems have cropped up with one of the lorries, can we do this quickly?"

Roy, a little taken aback by John's urgency, said, "the question I asked yesterday, how are things, was also a business related question."

John looked a little confused.

Roy said, "look, to get to the point, you asked me to check over your books before the end of year audit, ready to send to the taxman." He hesitated, waiting for John to agree. John then nodded. He continued, "I checked the books and I then had to check them again. I then went back to last year's figures. To cut a long story short, your profits are down by nearly twenty per cent compared to last year, just in the last couple of months. That is huge. What's been going on?"

John didn't have an answer. Eventually, he said, "I knew things were quieter than usual but I put that down to people switching to oil or gas."

Roy said, "I know people are doing that, but twenty per cent?" After a pause, he said, "There would be a small drop in profits, but never that much, something else is happening. If this continues then you will have to lay people off or you take a much lower salary out of the business."

John guessed what must have happened but didn't feel he wanted to share that with Roy. Well, not just at the moment. John stood up and said, "let me have a think about it, and I'll get back to you."

John left the office, a worried man.

He got back to the office and poured himself a cup of tea and sat down to think, feeling even more depressed. The one thing that kept coming back to his mind was that he felt he knew the local community and he knew the way they thought and lived. It was their sanctimonious attitude that forced him out of the Rotary Club and the Chamber of Trade and now was destroying his business. He could forget about the Freemasons and possibly any chance of becoming a magistrate. It's the "Chapel squad". Mam had started the ball rolling by gossiping details about his personal life and now the whole town thinks it knows the sort of person I am. Not the war hero who came back from the Far East with a letter from the King and a medal for valour, but a dirty pervert who sired a child and left a pregnant girl to give birth on her own. It would have been just the same if I had murdered nuns while I was in Burma or robbed the government treasury. They are making me pay and they see me as a target. I've become successful, more successful than them, so this indiscretion allows them to knock me off my perch.

40

Douglas picked up the phone, "Hello, Doctor Samuels here, what can I do for you?"

The receptionist had just left for the day and had put all calls through to Douglas.

John was on the other end of the line, "just checking that we are still able to meet up on Saturday morning. Don't tell me you can't, you are the only person speaking to me at the moment. Well, except for Kevin and that could all change after Sunday."

Douglas thought John sounded very fed up and said, "I've got a cricket match on Saturday afternoon in Abertallin, so I've got to pass through Treafon. What about a coffee in Gino's at about ten o'clock?"

John said, "that would be great, see you then." John began to visibly relax.

The following morning was Saturday, so John allowed himself a brief lie-in in bed and then left to call in at the office. Once he'd checked everything was in order he got into the car and made his way up to the Queen's Café.

Douglas was first to arrive. He ordered his coffee and a bacon sandwich and went to sit down. He glanced into the back room as he went to his seat and noticed Kevin and the girl, Carol sat at a table. He could hear Kevin raising his voice but Carol seemed to be silent. As Douglas sat down, Alan Richards, Will Hodges, Stuart Parry and Nick Pritchard came in and sat at a table near the front window. Alan and Will went to the counter to order their drinks and Stuart and Nick passed their money over to them and sat back down. Moments later Kevin and Carol came through from the backroom as they had noticed Alan and Will at the counter. They pushed two tables together and arranged themselves around the tables. As Will walked back from the counter he noticed and recognised Douglas at his table. He said nothing but on getting back to the table he said loud enough for everybody to hear "hey look, Carol, there's your paki buddy."

Carol quickly glanced back but tried to ignore Douglas' presence.

Kevin seemed agitated from the minute he had arrived in the main room of the café. He said, loudly "it's just that black bastard, thought he would have fucked off back to Bongoland."

Douglas was in two minds whether to walk out but didn't want to miss John, but then he thought John isn't going to want to come into this. It sounded as if he had enough problems at the moment.

Carol turned sideways in her seat, acting as if she was uncomfortable in her present company.

Douglas collected his coat and was just about to leave when he realised he hadn't paid for his coffee or received his bacon sandwich. He went to the counter and said to Gino "I need to pay for my coffee."

Gino said, "that's fine, your bacon sandwich is on its way"

Douglas said, "sorry Gino, I just remembered something I have to do, I'll pay for the coffee and the sandwich, but I have to go."

Carol glanced at Kevin and thought, I'm sick of him hanging around me like a little puppy dog, I'll show him. She stood up and walked to the counter, brushing up against Douglas' shoulder, provocatively, as she had done once before. She looked up at him and said, "you never got back to me about having that drink. What about tonight?" She glanced back to see if Kevin was watching. She noticed he had moved to the edge of his seat and had his hands clamped together to make one large fist. The others in the group had noticed Carol get up and glanced to watch Kevin's reaction.

Will leaned over to Kevin "you want to fucking get him, look what he's doing to your girlfriend, the bastard."

Alan and Nick smirked when they could see Kevin's reaction. Kevin didn't move,

Carol moved nearer to Douglas saying, "I think we could be good together."

Douglas attempted to brush off her advances and turned to leave. Carol blocked his path and with an attempt at a sexy pout said, "you know you can have me anytime, don't you?"

Kevin heard this and without any thought for what might happen next, he leapt out of his seat, brushing aside a man coming into the café. The man was John, who slipped sideways into the edge of the counter, and then tried to regain his balance. He could see the back of the person who had knocked him over but didn't recognise him as Kevin.

Kevin pushed Carol out of the way. She stumbled into a table with two customers, who had watched what had happened and quickly got up and moved out of the way.

Kevin stopped directly in front of Douglas, looking up at the figure who was perhaps four or five inches taller, and between pursed lips said, "what the fuck do you think you are doing?"

Douglas didn't answer initially but simply drew his eyebrows together. He then looked at Kevin and said, "what?"

Kevin had lost all sense of reason and said, "you heard me you piece of shit."

Douglas went to pass Kevin and caught a glance of John, who had now got back to his feet and was moving towards them. When Douglas was just about to pass Kevin and would then make it easily to the door, Kevin barged sideways catching Douglas on the hip and propelling him into the counter. The drama of the confrontation caused the whole café to go silent. Gino came around from behind the counter saying "I don't want any trouble. If there is, I'll call the cops."

If the situation had not been so tense the customers would probably have burst out laughing at Gino's American movie dialogue.

Catching Douglas off-balance Kevin reached across him to the café's cutlery tray while still staring up at Douglas. He picked up the first piece of cutlery he could feel which happened to be a sharp steak knife. Before anyone could move or speak, he pulled back his arm and had thrust the knife up and into Douglas' chest. A few gasps were heard from the people who realised what had happened. The effect was impossible to identify immediately, as Douglas was bent forward but in silence, his body began to unravel and he came up straight. Those near enough could now see a huge red bloom on the front of his shirt. He gasped and slid to the floor on his back. John and Carol were the first to get to him. Kevin suddenly realising what he had done dropped the knife and scuttled past the figure on the floor and out through the door, quickly followed by Will, Nick, Alan and Stuart. Gino ran to get towels to stem the bleeding as the dark red pool got larger. Douglas was able to whisper through his pain but neither John nor Carol could understand what he was saying. Carol asked, to no one in particular "what did he say?"

John put his head nearer to Douglas as he gave a last gasp and his life slipped away. John's head came up from Douglas' inert body and said, "he said, Love is a gift of one's innermost soul," and after a few seconds of silence he looked up and beginning to understand what had just happened, turned to those standing around the inert body and said, "to another so both can be whole."

Lightning Source UK Ltd.
Milton Keynes UK
UKHW021909040321
379804UK00005B/219